MURDER HAS NINE LIVE

"Enjoyable . . . This outing will keep cozy readers amused and wondering what absurdity will happen next."—*Publishers Weekly*

"Jaine pursues justice and sanity in her usual hilarious yet smart way, with Levine infusing wit into her heroine's every thought. A thoroughly fun read that will interest Evanovich fans."
—*Booklist*

"Another expertly conceived whodunit."
—*Fresh Fiction*

KILLING CUPID

"Jaine is absolutely hysterical . . . this author continues to write the best cozies."
—*Suspense Magazine*

DEATH OF A NEIGHBORHOOD WITCH

"Levine's latest finds her at her witty and wacky best."—*Kirkus Reviews*

DEATH BY PANTYHOSE

"Fun . . . Ja...
antics wi...

05165642

THE PMS MURDER

"Jaine can really dish it out."
—*The New York Times Book Review*

THIS PEN FOR HIRE

"Laura Levine's hilarious debut mystery, *This Pen for Hire*, is a laugh a page (or two or three) as well as a crafty puzzle. Sleuth Jaine Austen's amused take on life, love, sex and LA will delight readers. Sheer fun!"—Carolyn Hart

Books by Laura Levine

THIS PEN FOR HIRE

LAST WRITES

KILLER BLONDE

SHOES TO DIE FOR

THE PMS MURDER

DEATH BY PANTYHOSE

CANDY CANE MURDER

KILLING BRIDEZILLA

KILLER CRUISE

DEATH OF A TROPHY WIFE

GINGERBREAD COOKIE MURDER

PAMPERED TO DEATH

DEATH OF A NEIGHBORHOOD WITCH

KILLING CUPID

DEATH BY TIARA

MURDER HAS NINE LIVES

DEATH OF A BACHELORETTE

Published by Kensington Publishing Corporation

A Jaine Austen Mystery

MURDER HAS NINE LIVES

LAURA LEVINE

KENSINGTON BOOKS
www.kensingtonbooks.com

KENSINGTON BOOKS are published by

Kensington Publishing Corp.
119 West 40th Street
New York, NY 10018

All Kensington titles, imprints, and distributed lines are available at special quantity discounts for bulk purchases for sales promotion, premiums, fund-raising, educational, or institutional use. Special book excerpts or customized printings can also be created to fit specific needs. For details, write or phone the office of the Kensington Special Sales Manager: Attn. Special Sales Department. Kensington Publishing Corp., 119 West 40th Street, New York, NY 10018. Phone: 1-800-221-2647.

Kensington and the K logo Reg. U.S. Pat. & TM Off.

ISBN-13: 978-0-7582-8510-2
ISBN-10: 0-7582-8510-8
First Kensington Hardcover Edition: July 2016
First Kensington Mass Market Edition: May 2017

eISBN-13: 978-0-7582-8511-9
eISBN-10: 0-7582-8511-6
Kensington Electronic Edition: July 2016

10 9 8 7 6 5 4 3 2 1

Printed in the United States of America

DEDICATION

In loving memory of the best brother a girl
could ever hope for
Michael Paul Levine
1935-2015

ACKNOWLEDGMENTS

As always, a big thank you to my editor extraordinaire, John Scognamiglio, for his unwavering faith in Jaine—and for coming up with both the title and the premise of the story you are about to read. Merci beaucoup, John. You're the best!

And kudos to my rock of an agent, Evan Marshall, for always being there for me with his guidance and support.

Thanks to Hiro Kimura, who so brilliantly brings Prozac to life on my book covers. To Lou Malcangi for another fantastic dust jacket design. And to the rest of the gang at Kensington who keep Jaine and Prozac coming back for murder and minced mackerel guts each year.

Special thanks to Frank Mula, man of a thousand jokes. To Mara and Lisa Lideks, authors of the very funny Forrest Sisters mysteries, for telling me exactly what to do with Prozac. To Peter Serchuk, acclaimed poet and cat commercial guru (whose facts I'm afraid I fudged quite a bit). And to Shelly Garcia, for sharing her hilarious shoe-shopping story.

Hugs to Joanne Fluke, who takes time out from writing her own bestselling Hannah Swensen mysteries to grace me with her insights and friendship—not to mention a cover blurb to die for.

Thanks to John Fluke at Placed for Success. To Mark Baker, who's been there from the beginning. And to Jamie Wallace (aka Sidney's mom), the genial webmeister at LauraLevineMysteries.com.

XOXO to my friends and family for your much-appreciated love and encouragement.

And finally, a heartfelt thank you to all my readers and Facebook friends. I wouldn't be here without you.

Chapter 1

I sat in the doctor's waiting room, my cat Prozac in my lap, praying the poor thing wouldn't suffer, that the procedure would be over quickly, with no need for extra painkillers. I had to remind myself that she'd had a good life and that if the worst happened, she wouldn't even know what hit her.

Wait a minute. Is somebody out there wiping away a tear? Did you actually think Prozac was about to bite the dust?

Heavens, no. It wasn't Prozac I was worried about. (That cat makes Vin Diesel look like Tinker Bell.) It was our darling veterinarian, Dr. Madeline Graham. Last year she wound up getting seven stitches after simply trying to clean Prozac's teeth.

Now I sat in Dr. Madeline's waiting room, Prozac baring her soon-to-be-cleaned teeth at me from her perch in my lap, and prayed that no blood would be shed in the course of her annual checkup.

Dr. Madeline practiced out of a converted bungalow near the beach in Santa Monica, her waiting room a former parlor with lace curtains on the windows and a fireplace filled with a carton of well-worn pet toys.

Behind a faux antique desk sat Trudi, Dr. Madeline's receptionist, a no-nonsense woman with a steel-gray ponytail and a faint scar on her arm—the latter, compliments of Prozac.

Between answering phone calls, Trudi chatted with the waiting clients—a middle-aged man with a hulking rottweiler, and a young gal with a gorgeous white kitty.

The rottweiler, who just a few minutes ago had come sniffing over to make friends with Prozac, now sat cowering at his owner's feet, still shaken by the wrath of Prozac's fiery hiss.

I smiled apologetically at his owner, but the guy just glowered at me.

"It's never the animal's fault," I heard Trudi say to him in a booming stage whisper. "It's always the owner."

I certainly wasn't winning any popularity contests in this waiting room, was I?

"You're going to be a good girl, aren't you?" I cooed in Prozac's ear. "All we're going to do is check your heart, look in your ears, and give your teeth a teeny little scraping, okay?"

She gazed at me through slitted green eyes.

Go ahead. Make my day.

I could practically see the EMTs wheeling Dr. Madeline off on a gurney.

Ignoring the angry thump of Prozac's tail on my thigh, I forced myself to think about all the good things in my life. Like the two-for-one special on

Double Stuf Oreos at my local supermarket. And the Starbucks gift card I'd discovered in a pile of unpaid bills. And, most important, my upcoming vacation in Hawaii.

Yes, in less than a month, I, Jaine Austen, a gal who usually watches her ocean sunsets on *Beach-front Bargain Hunt*, was about to take off for ten glorious days in Maui. True, I'd be spending those ten glorious days with my parents, not anyone's idea of a romantic getaway. But still, ten days in the sun, with nothing to do but sit back, sipping mai tais, and have my parents fuss over me, sounded quite heavenly.

Who needs romance, I always say, when you've got parents with an unending supply of love and fudge?

I was thinking about how I really needed to get myself a cute pair of strappy sandals for the trip when the door to the waiting room whooshed open and in breezed a hefty gal swathed in layers of crinkly gauze, a mass of bangle bracelets jangling on her arms. Her hair was swept up in a sloppy bun, anchored in place by two bright red enamel chopsticks.

She swept over to Trudi in a cloud of patchouli.

"Trudi, love," she said, bending down to give her an air kiss. "Where's that darling kitty you told me about?"

Trudi pointed to the other cat in the room, the snow-white beauty sitting demurely on her owner's lap.

"Oh, she's precious," Ms. Chopsticks crooned. "But not exactly what I was looking for."

And then she caught sight of Prozac.

"My God!" she cried, her eyes lighting up. "That one's perfect!"

And like a shot, she was jangling across the waiting room.

"What a darling kitty!" Ms. Chopsticks said, plopping down in the chair next to me. "What's her name?"

"Prozac."

"Prozac? Just what the doctor ordered! At least mine did. Three times a day," she confided with a jolly wink. "Mind if I pet her?"

"I wouldn't if I were you. She scratches."

"And I've got the scars to prove it," Trudi said, eyeing her arm ruefully.

"Oh, the precious angel would never scratch me!"

And before I could stop her, she was swooping Prozac up in her arms.

Visions of lawsuits danced in my head, but much to my relief, Prozac had suddenly switched to Adorable Mode, all big eyes and loving purrs.

I was soon to discover the reason why.

"Would Prozac like a yum-yum?" Ms. Chopsticks asked, taking a Baggie full of cat treats from her purse.

Was she kidding? When it comes to treats, Prozac's a gal who can't say no. (She takes after me that way.)

Soon Prozac was inhaling kitty treats at the speed of light, making disgusting snorting noises as she sucked up her chow.

"She has quite an appetite, doesn't she?" My companion stared down at Prozac in awe.

"If it's not nailed down, she generally eats it."

"That's wonderful!" Ms. Chopsticks said. "She's

going to be perfect for the Skinny Kitty commercial."

"Skinny Kitty?"

"It's a new diet cat food. She's eating it now. They're shooting a commercial for it next week, and we've been looking all over for a cat to star in it."

In her lap, Prozac inhaled the last of the cat food and belched in content.

"I'm Deedee Walker," Ms. Chopsticks said, handing me a business card. "Agent to the Animal Stars. I know star quality when I see it, and I see it in your darling kitty."

We both looked down to where Prozac was now sniffing her privates.

"We're holding auditions tomorrow at ten a.m. The address is on my business card. Please bring Prozac. I'm sure she'll be wonderful."

Really? The cat who, for as long as we've been together, has refused to sit still for a single Christmas photo?

But before I could voice any objections, Deedee had plopped Prozac back in my lap and was sailing out the door, bangles jangling in her wake.

I sat there, stunned. Was it possible my fractious furball had what it took to be a star?

I gazed down at her now and watched as she plucked an ancient Cheerio from the depths of her tail.

She lobbed me a look of sheer pride.

I think there's a gummy bear in there, too!

So much for stardom.

Chapter 2

I'm happy to report that no blood was shed in the course of Prozac's exam. Perhaps Prozac was feeling mellow after her recent snack. Or perhaps it was the Kevlar vest Dr. Madeline had chosen to wear for the occasion.

Back home, Prozac resumed her usual perch on my living room sofa, licking herself free of the evil smells of Dr. Madeline's office.

I checked my phone and saw I had a message from Phil Angelides, proud owner and prop. of Toiletmasters Plumbers, serving the greater Los Angeles area since 1988. And one of my biggest clients. I've been writing ads for Phil ever since I first came up with the slogan *In a Rush to Flush? Call Toiletmasters!* (Winner of the Los Angeles Plumbers' Association Golden Plunger Award, in case you're interested.)

I pushed the PLAY button and heard Phil saying words that always bring joy to me and my checking account:

"Give me a call, Jaine. I've got an assignment for you."

When I called him back, he was bubbling with excitement about a breakthrough product in the world of commodes, the Touch-Me-Not toilet.

"All you have to do is wave your hand in front of an infrared light, and the toilet flushes itself!"

Phil's one of the few people on the planet who can wax euphoric over a toilet bowl.

"I need you to write a brochure for the Touch-Me-Not," he said. "Stop by the office tomorrow afternoon, so you can see it in person. It's a work of art, Jaine! A work of art!"

I assured him I'd be over the next day to see his miracle commode and hung up, delighted at the prospect of an incoming paycheck. I was just about to head to the kitchen for a celebratory Oreo (or three) when there was a knock on my door.

I opened it to find my neighbor, Lance Venable.

Lance and I share a duplex on a jacaranda-lined street in the slums of Beverly Hills, far from the mega mansions north of Sunset.

"Hey, Jaine." He breezed into my apartment in a designer suit and bow tie, his tight blond curls moussed to perfection.

Accompanying him on a leash was his adorable pooch, Mamie.

"Doesn't Mamie look fab?" Lance said. "I just picked her up on my way home from Neiman's."

For those of you not in the Venable loop, Lance spends his working hours fondling ladies' bunions in the shoe department at Neiman Marcus.

"Lucky Mamie had a luxurious Day of Beauty at the Chow Bella Pet Spa," Lance said, "where she was treated to a 'pawdicure,' a detoxifying thermal wrap, and a soothing lavender/aloe shampoo!"

Prozac looked up from her privates and shot me a baleful glare.

And all I got was a crummy teeth scraping.

Indeed, Mamie looked quite fetching, her white coat gleaming, a dainty pink bow in her hair.

Prozac gazed at her in disdain.

What a weenie.

"You really should bring Prozac in for some grooming," Lance said as my little angel began clawing a throw pillow.

"Are you kidding? I'm happy I made it out alive from her annual checkup. By the way, you'll never guess what happened at the vet's office today. Some gal who reps show biz animals stopped by and fell in love with Prozac. She wants her to star in a commercial."

Lance's eyes widened in disbelief.

"Prozac? Take direction? The cat who can't sit still for a simple Christmas photo?"

"Crazy, right? But the gal swears she can make Prozac a star."

"That's the silliest thing I ever heard," Lance scoffed. "I love Prozac dearly, but we all know she's a whacked-out little maniac."

Prozac glared up from her attack on the throw pillow.

Hey! Who're you calling "little"?

"The very idea of Prozac in a TV commercial is ludicrous," Lance went on, bursting out in a most annoying peal of laughter.

By now I was starting to get ticked off. It's one

thing when I doubt my pampered princess's capabilities. But hearing Lance dis her was a whole other story. Frankly, my hackles were more than a tad raised.

"I don't know," I said. "She might do okay."

A derisive snort from Lance.

"If that cat can act, I'll eat my bow tie."

At his feet, Mamie gave a happy yap, thrilled at the prospect of either Prozac acting or Lance eating his own tie.

With dogs, it's hard to tell.

"Well, gotta run," Lance said. "Time to show off Mamie's new look to the neighbors. Everyone loves her so!"

And off he sailed, Mamie trotting in tow.

Up until that moment I hadn't really planned on showing up at the audition. But now I was steamed. I took Deedee's business card out of my purse. On the back she'd written the address where the audition was to take place.

I made up my mind to be there.

"We'll show Uncle Lance just how clever you are. Won't we, Pro?"

But my kitty prodigy was too busy chasing a dust bunny to hear me.

I woke up the next morning to the sweet sounds of Prozac yowling at the top of her lungs, clawing me for her breakfast. Through bleary eyes, I watched her ricochet around the bed in full-throttle Feed Me mode. And suddenly my dreams of showbiz stardom went poof. No way was Prozac ever going to behave herself long enough to land a part in a TV commercial. Why even bother showing up at the audition?

But then I remembered the insufferably smug look on Lance's face when he said Prozac would never make it in advertising.

And just like that, I was angry all over again. So what if Prozac didn't have a snowball's chance in hell of getting that part? We were going to the audition!

And so at exactly 9:30 a.m. Prozac and I were in my Corolla, heading over to the Mid-Wilshire office building where the audition was scheduled to take place.

Unwilling to risk one of her hissy fits, I left Prozac's cat carrier at home. True, I had to drive with my little darling scampering around the gas pedal, playing havoc with my blood pressure, but that was a small price to pay for her goodwill.

Now with Prozac nestled safely in my arms, I took the elevator up to the third-floor offices of Skinny Kitty, Inc., and headed into a waiting room filled with adorable cats and their fiercely proud owners.

I signed in at a reception desk, where a harried receptionist in dangly cat earrings told me to take a seat until my name was called.

Prozac and I plunked ourselves down next to one of the show biz kitties, a pro by the name of Mr. Jingles. I knew this was his name because it was embroidered on the sash he wore, Miss America–style, across his furry torso.

Mr. Jingles' trainer, a big-boned redhead in a

MR. JINGLES FOR PRESIDENT T-shirt, was giving her charge a pep talk.

"Who's the smartest cat ever? Who's gonna beat out all the other cats and get this part? Mr. Jingles, that's who! Now, gimme five!"

She held out her palm, and I watched in awe as Mr. Jingles stood on his hind legs and brushed his owner's palm with his paw.

"Wow!" I said to the redhead. "He's amazing."

"He is, isn't he?" she beamed. "He can roll over, jump through a hoop, and play the piano."

Prozac yawned, clearly unimpressed.

Yeah, but can he cough up a hairball the size of a S'more?

And Mr. Jingles wasn't the only talent in the room. All around me, perfectly groomed cats were doing clever tricks and heeding their owners' every word.

Meanwhile, in my lap, Prozac was busy hissing at a nearby philodendron.

Once again, I felt hope ebbing away. Compared to her competition, Prozac didn't stand a chance.

I was just about to pack it in and go home when Deedee came sailing into the waiting room, bangles jangling and chopsticks poking out from her bun.

Her eyes lit up at the sight of Prozac.

"Jaine, dear! I'm so happy you made it!" she cried, sitting down next to me in a cloud of patchouli. "I just know Prozac's going to run away with this part."

"But, Deedee. All these other cats are trained professionals. Prozac's never performed before in her life."

"Yes, but I doubt any of these other cats can eat like Prozac. Never have I seen a cat suck up food with such gusto. And that's just what they're looking for."

"You really think she stands a chance?"

"Absolutely!" Deedee assured me.

"That cat over there," I said, pointing to Mr. Jingles, "can give his owner a high five."

"Really?" Deedee eyed Mr. Jingles as he struck a few chords on his toy piano.

"Not to worry, hon. I'll take care of him."

"What a darling kitty!" she exclaimed, jumping up and making a beeline for the piano-playing prodigy. "Mind if I pet him?"

"Not at all," Mr. Jingles' trainer replied. "He loves attention."

Deedee crouched down, her back to the red-headed trainer, blocking her view of Mr. Jingles. Then, in a move so fast I almost missed it, I saw her slipping Mr. Jingles a kitty treat. Which he gobbled up eagerly.

Her job done, Deedee got back on her feet.

"Such an angel!" she cooed to the redhead. "Best of luck to you, hon!"

Then she trotted back to me, a sly grin on her face.

"What on earth did you give him?" I whispered

"The teensiest dose of kitty Valium," she whispered back. "He'll be out like a light in minutes."

Indeed, as I looked over at Mr. Jingles, he was curling up into a ball, his eyes narrowed into sleepy slits.

"Mr. Jingles!" the redhead chided. "What's got

into you? This is no time to be napping. We need to rehearse your piano routine!"

Next to me, Deedee was smiling smugly.

"See? I told you I'd take care of him."

"But, Deedee—"

"No need to thank me, hon. That's what agents are for!"

I was still reeling over Deedee's duplicity when a door at the far end of the waiting room opened and a pale woman in jeans and a T-shirt consulted a clipboard and called my name.

Gathering Prozac, I hurried to her side.

"Knock 'em dead, hon!" Deedee shouted out after me.

I just prayed she wouldn't be doing the same out in the waiting room.

"Hi," said the clipboard gal as she led me down a short hallway. "I'm Linda Oliver. I'll be producing the commercial."

Wow. She sure had me fooled. With no makeup, unflattering harlequin glasses, and her hair scraped back in a headband, she looked like a secretary on a really tight budget, not an advertising bigwig.

Now she opened the door to a conference room and ushered me inside. A large mahogany table dominated the room, a handful of people sitting at the far side.

"I'd like you to meet my husband, Dean," Linda said, "the inventor of Skinny Kitty."

A handsome guy with jet-black hair and what looked like a freshly sprayed tan, Dean sat at the head of the table, rifling through kitty head shots. He looked up and nodded at me curtly, and I couldn't help wondering what a slick dude like him was doing with a mouse like Linda.

"And this is our director, Ian Kendrick." Next to Dean sat a sixty-something man clad in a black turtleneck and jeans jacket, his thinning silver hair in a scrawny ponytail.

"Hello, love," he said, in a plummy British accent. Then he reached for a Starbucks thermos and took a swig.

"And finally," Linda said, "this is Zeke, our writer." She pointed to a lanky young guy in horn-rimmed glasses.

Zeke managed a faint smile, but his eyes were riveted on Linda.

"Everybody," Linda announced, "this is Jaine Austen and her cat, Prozac."

Dean looked up from the kitty head shots.

"Prozac, eh? Unusual name. Guess she's a real calming influence, huh?"

I figured it was wise not to mention that Prozac was about as calming as a ride through downtown Beirut, so I just stood there and nodded weakly.

"Let's get started, shall we?" Linda said.

"All your cat needs to do for this commercial," said the director, "is eat and sleep."

Bingo! Two of her specialties.

"Put your cat down here, please." Linda pointed to the foot of the conference table. "I'll just give her some Skinny Kitty to see how she likes it."

Over on a sideboard were a couple of packages of the dry kitty treats Deedee had fed Prozac in Dr.

Madeline's office, as well as several cans of wet cat food. Now Linda popped open a can of wet food, plunked the contents into a bowl, and set it down before Prozac.

I prayed the little rascal liked the wet food as much as the dry snacks.

And I'm happy to say my prayers were answered. Prozac plunged into the stuff like an Olympic diver going for the gold.

Dean put down his kitty head shots and sat up, interested.

"My God, I've never seen a cat inhale food like that."

Indeed, everyone around the table was gazing at my chow hound, impressed.

"She's like a four-legged vacuum cleaner!" Zeke cried.

"Very good, Prozac!" Linda said.

"Wonderful!" added the director. "Now it's time for her to take a nap."

"Right now?" I asked.

"Yes. In the commercial she's going to have to nap on command."

Oh, hell. Prozac never did anything on command. It's one of her major principles in life.

Once again, I saw her show biz career going up in smoke.

But then, in a moment of what I'll always think of as divine inspiration, I got an idea.

"Oh, Prozac!" I whispered in her ear. "I've had the most horrible day. Let me tell you all about it!"

And sure enough, my ever-empathetic kitty did what she's done countless times in my moments of need. The minute she heard my plea for a shoulder to cry on, she was out like a light. Snoring like a buzz saw.

"Very impressive," said Dean, his head shots now totally forgotten.

The others nodded in assent.

"We have several other cats to interview," Linda said, "but you're definitely a front runner. We'll call your agent by the end of the day."

With a song in my heart, and a few gobs of Skinny Kitty on my sweater, I made my way across the corridor to the waiting room.

Deedee pounced the minute I entered.

"So? How did it go?"

"They seemed to like her. Linda said I'm a front-runner."

"See?" Deedee said. "I told you everything would work out just fine."

And it had. For me and Prozac, anyway.

The last thing I heard as I walked out the door was the redhead crying plaintively, "Wake up, Mr. Jingles! Wake up!"

Deedee and I rode down in the elevator together, Deedee kitchy-kooing over Prozac, babbling about how she was going to be a superstar.

"Bigger than Garfield, bigger than Marmaduke, bigger than King Kong!"

I refrained from pointing out that none of these stars were actual animals, afraid to burst her bubble of enthusiasm.

"Au revoir, mes enfants!" she cried, getting off

at the lobby and waving good-bye with wrists ajangle.

Prozac and I proceeded down to the lower parking level, where Prozac had a joyous reunion with her good buddy Mr. Gas Pedal. So grateful was I for her bravura performance at the audition that I hardly even minded when she began bouncing around my feet like an errant pinball.

Yes, I was pulling out of the parking lot in the rosiest of moods, wondering exactly how much star kitties got paid, when I happened to look across the street and saw Deedee getting on a bus.

I blinked in surprise. She'd told me she was getting off at the lobby because she'd found a parking space on the street. Obviously, she'd been fibbing.

"That's odd, Pro," I mused aloud. "Why isn't an agent to the animal stars driving a fancy foreign car with vanity plates? Why on earth is she taking the bus?"

But my frantic feline was too busy shredding the floor mats to give the matter much thought.

Chapter 3

My heart always swells with pride when I show up at the headquarters of Toiletmasters Plumbers.

There, painted on the front wall of the building, next to a caricature of a plumber brandishing two plungers like six-shooters, is my slogan *In a Rush to Flush? Call Toiletmasters!*

True, the building is located in one of the San Fernando Valley's seedier enclaves, and my slogan is now festooned with several X-rated works of graffiti, but I still get a kick out of seeing my words splashed across the wall.

And that afternoon was no exception as I pulled into the lot to meet up with Phil Angelides and his Touch-Me-Not commode.

I found Phil in his back office, his battered desk drowning in a sea of papers and assorted wrenches. Sitting amid the clutter was a supersized jar of hand sanitizer.

"Great to see you, Jaine!" Phil said, leaping up to greet me as I walked in the door.

A mountain of a guy with hair everywhere on his body except his head, Phil's got the personality of a Labradoodle, happy and slurpy and bursting with enthusiasm.

He gave my hands an eager squeeze, almost breaking a knuckle or two in the process. Then, the minute he let go, he proceeded to douse his hands with sanitizer.

It never ceases to amaze me that Phil, who still goes out in the field and sticks his hands in God knows what, is worried about catching *my* germs.

"Wait'll you see the Touch-Me-Not!" he gushed, leading me out to his showroom. "You're gonna flip over it! But first, you gotta see what I just bought for my collection."

The collection to which Phil referred was his stockpile of celebrity commodes.

Yes, you read that right. The guy collects toilet bowls of the rich and famous.

Whenever he learns of a celebrity home demolition, he's the first on the scene to pick up the commodes. Apparently, there's a market for this stuff. He's even been known to bid on toilets from overseas. The crown in his collection is a nondescript white porcelain number that used to belong to Johnny Carson, which he has proudly dubbed Johnny's Johnny. He claims to own commodes used by Winston Churchill, Cary Grant, and J. K. Rowling (Potter's Potty).

"Look!" he said, pointing to an old-fashioned toilet with a wooden seat and a pull chain. "Queen Elizabeth's toilet from Windsor Castle! Just think!" he beamed. "I own the queen's *other* throne!"

After several minutes of oohing and aahing over the royal toilet, Phil finally got down to business.

"Time to see the Touch-Me-Not," he said, heading over to his display of toilets for us mere mortals.

"Here she is," he said, pointing with a flourish to a sleek white toilet.

The guy was so darn proud, I almost expected to hear a fanfare of trumpets blaring in the background.

"I just hold my hand over the tank," he said, placing his hammy palm over a small round sensor atop the tank, "and like magic, the toilet flushes."

Of course, the sample we were looking at did not flush, since it wasn't hooked up to any actual plumbing, but Phil assured me it worked like a charm.

"Isn't it great?" he said, waxing euphoric. "Fewer germs to pick up or leave behind!"

He grinned at me expectantly, waiting for me to be amazed.

"It's a miracle!" I cried, fearing I might be overdoing it just a tad.

But if I was overdoing it, Phil didn't seem to notice.

"You're going to have so much fun writing the brochure," he said. "C'mon back to my office and I'll give you the specs."

Back in his office, Phil started rooting around the papers on his desk, looking for the info on the Touch-Me-Not.

"By the way," he said, tossing aside a stray Danish, "I hope you can make it to the Fiesta Bowl."

No, Phil was not inviting me to a football game.

The Fiesta Bowl to which he referred was Toilet-masters' annual employees bash, held at Phil's house out in Tarzana.

It's usually a rather raucous affair, featuring lots of beer, hot dogs, and plumbing jokes. Not exactly Noel Coward territory, but who was I to turn down a free hot dog?

"Wouldn't miss it for the world," I assured him.

"Aw, honey, you're the best!"

By now Phil had dug up the Touch-Me-Not info and handed it to me in a manila folder dusted with Danish crumbs.

"I can always count on my Jainie, can't I?" he said, giving me a loving pinch on my cheek and then immediately splorting his hands with sanitizer. "One more thing," he added. "I almost forgot. My nephew Jim just moved to town and started working for me. He's a great guy, and I thought maybe you might want to go out with him."

He shot me his Labradoodle smile, eager and hopeful.

A blind date? Wasn't gonna happen.

Blind dates are God's way of telling you that nuns don't have it so bad, after all.

No way was I subjecting myself to a torturous evening with some goofball with whom I was certain to have nothing in common and who would at the end of the night no doubt whip out a calculator to figure out my share of the bill. Don't shake your head like that. If I had a calculator for every time that happened to me, I'd own IBM.

And Phil's nephew? I could just imagine what he'd look like. Phil's a darling man, but he's got enough hair in his ears to stuff a throw pillow. And his nephew was a plumber, to boot. Call me shallow, but I didn't want to date a guy who spent his days elbow deep in poo. I wanted someone creative—a writer, a musician, an artist! Someone intelligent and sensitive, with impeccably clean fingernails.

"So, Jaine? How about it?" Phil asked. "Are you up for a date with my nephew?"

Not if he were the last plumber on earth and I needed my shower snaked.

Time to haul out my imaginary boyfriend.

"Thanks so much for thinking of me, Phil, but actually, I'm seeing someone."

"You are??"

He needn't have sounded so surprised. I mean, it's not that impossible, is it?

"Yes, Collier and I have been dating for a couple of months."

I've always wanted to date a guy named Collier.

"Aw, that's too bad. I was hoping you and Jim might hit it off."

"Sorry, Phil," I shrugged, trying to look disappointed.

I gathered my purse and was just getting up to leave when the door to Phil's office opened and in walked the Collier of my dreams, a studmuffin of the highest order—tall and rangy, with a fab bod, streaky surfer-blond hair, and blue eyes no doubt reincarnated from the late Paul Newman.

"Speak of the devil," Phil said. "Jaine, meet my nephew Jim."

This hunkalicious piece of hubba hubba was Phil's nephew? I simply could not believe that these two guys swam in the same gene pool.

"Jim, I wanted to set you up with Jaine."

"That would have been really nice," said Mr. Incredible, revealing another weapon in his arsenal of good looks—a megawatt grin.

Suddenly dating a plumber seemed like a Must Do on my bucket list.

"But, unfortunately," Phil said, "Jaine has a boyfriend."

"That's too bad," Mr. Incredible said, with what looked like genuine regret.

Why on earth had I told that ridiculous lie? Why couldn't I be one of those people who always say Yes to life? Why did I have to be the eternal pessimist, certain that any blind date of mine would inevitably turn out to be a loser and/or serial killer? If only I hadn't invented that stupid imaginary boyfriend!

"Actually," I said, "my boyfriend and I aren't all that close. In fact, last night Curtis and I had a bit of a spat."

"I thought his name was Collier," Phil said.

"It is. It's Collier-Curtis. Hyphenated. He's a Brit."

By now Phil was looking at me like I was nuts, but I plowed ahead.

"So maybe we could meet up," I said to Jim, "just to see how things work out."

"Oh, no. I couldn't possibly intrude on a relationship. I'd feel funny about seeing you when I know you're involved with someone else."

"But we're not involved. Not really. Collier-Curtis and I have always been more friends than boyfriend and girlfriend. Really, we're just friends. Honest. I'd love to go out with you."

My God, have you ever seen such a disgusting display of groveling?

"Well, if you're sure you're not in a relationship . . . ," Jim said.

"I'm positive."

"How about dinner?"

"Sounds fab!"

"I'll give you a call, and we'll set something up."

"Yes! Absolutely!"

And with that, I waved good-bye and headed out the door, a new assignment in my hands, and not a shred of dignity to my name.

Chapter 4

That night I left my future star of stage, screen, and cat food commercials waging her unending war against my throw pillows and drove off to meet my good buddy and longtime dining companion, Kandi Tobolowski, for an early dinner.

Kandi and I have been friends ever since we met at a screenwriting class at UCLA and bonded over bad vending machine coffee. Kandi has since clawed her way to the middle in the ranks of show biz, with a lucrative career writing for the Saturday morning cartoon, *Beanie & the Cockroach* (while I, alas, still toiled in the fields of Touch-Me-Not commodes).

We were meeting, as we often do, at our favorite restaurant, Paco's Tacos, a lively Mexican joint with margaritas to die for and burritos the size of a VW bus.

Kandi was waiting for me when I got there, blithely ignoring the bowl of golden corn chips right under her nose. Which is one of the reasons

Kandi can slip into her size six jeans without emergency liposuction.

"Hey, sweetheart!" she cried, jumping up and wrapping me in a bony hug. "I already ordered us margaritas."

"Bless you!" I said, my eyes lighting up at the sight of two frosty margs on the table.

I wasted no time taking a healthy slug of mine.

"So, what's up?" I asked when I came up for air.

"Big news." A dramatic pause as she pulled my hand out of the chip bowl and held it in hers. "There's something wrong with me. Something very wrong."

"Oh, no!" I moaned, picturing Kandi hooked up to an IV in intensive care. "What is it?"

Gathering her courage, she took a deep breath and intoned:

"I, Kandi Tobolowski, am a shopaholic."

"Is that all?"

Tell me something I didn't already know. Kandi has always been a world-class shopper, a Kung Fu master of the credit card. Luckily, with her salary from *Beanie & the Cockroach*, it's a pastime she can well afford.

"It's gone too far, Jaine. Last week I came home with a pair of the most glorious knee-high boots I bought on sale at Nordstrom, only to discover I had the exact same pair in the back of my closet. In two other colors.

"I finally faced up to the fact that I've been using shopping as a way to drown my sorrows and ease the frustration of still being single after all these years."

It's true. Kandi has kissed about a zillion frogs

in her unending search for Mr. Right and has reaped nothing for her efforts but a bunch of emotional warts. It's hard to understand why she's had such poor luck. With her glossy chestnut hair and slim figure, one would think she'd have landed her Mr. Right ages ago.

But one would be wrong.

My theory is that Kandi keeps going after the wrong kind of guy—the egomaniacs, the no-goodniks, the self-centered jerks—in other words, your typical Los Angeles available man.

"But my spending days are behind me," Kandi was saying. "I've cut up all my credit cards. From now on, I'm going to learn how to drown my sorrows in chocolate and chardonnay like you, Jaine. Only not quite so much chocolate, I hope."

At which point, our waiter, a slim Hispanic guy with the sad eyes of a medieval saint, came whisking to our side.

"What will it be, senoritas?"

Kandi ordered the red snapper. And even though I was yearning for the crunchily delicious deep-fried chimichangas, I made up my mind to order the low-calorie snapper, too. The last thing I needed was a bunch of chimichanga carbs clinging to my hips if Jim Angelides decided to call.

"And for you?" The waiter turned to me, pen poised above his pad.

"The chimichanga combo plate," I blurted out before I could stop myself. "With extra sour cream on my refried beans," I had the temerity to add.

I swear, any day now my picture's going to be on Weight Watchers' Most Wanted list.

Meanwhile, Kandi was still lost in the saga of her brave new life.

"I've enrolled in a money management class, and I've taken up the most fantastic new hobby to keep my mind occupied when I feel the urge to shop: Knitting! In fact, I made something for you, hon!"

With that, she reached for a shopping bag under her seat and pulled out a ginormous mass of lumpy wool, filled with dropped stitches and gaping holes.

"How nice," I said with a feeble smile. "An area rug."

"It's not a rug. It's a scarf. Somehow the stitches got stretched out. I'm still working on my technique."

"It looks great," I lied, wondering if I could use it as a bath mat.

"So what's new with you, hon?" she asked.

I wanted to tell her all about Jim, my dashing surfer boy plumber, to rave about his streaky blond hair and Paul Newman eyes, but I couldn't. Not when Kandi was at such a low point in her love life. I'd have to keep my Prince Charming under wraps for now.

So I swallowed my excitement, along with a handful of chips, and told her about Prozac's Skinny Kitty audition instead.

"That's fantastic!" she cried. "Maybe I can knit her a tutu!"

After I convinced Kandi that Prozac wasn't a tutu kind of cat, our entrées showed up, and we spent the rest of the night gabbing—discussing the joys of knitting, the paucity of decent men in

L.A., and the pros and cons of ordering margaritas with or without salt.

At the end of the meal Kandi paid for her half of the bill with cash, her wallet empty of all credit cards, but sheathed in a lumpy hand-knit "wallet cozy."

We hugged each other good-bye outside the restaurant, and I drove off with my new scarf wrapped around my neck at least seven times.

Kandi may not have mastered the art of knitting, but I was proud of her for recognizing she had an addiction and showing some discipline.

There was a lesson to be learned there. It was about time I showed a little impulse control of my own.

And so I'm proud to report that instead of making a pit stop at the supermarket for an après-chimichanga pint of Chunky Monkey ice cream like I usually do, I drove straight home and got in my jammies.

Then, and only then, did I throw on a raincoat and drive over for my Chunky Monkey.

Hard to believe, but true: By the time I got home from my Chunky Monkey run, I was feeling so guilty, all I ate was a couple of spoonfuls, and then I shoved the rest in the back of my freezer, behind some frozen peas and a Lean Cuisine dinner I'd been avoiding for months.

I really had to cool it on the calories if I expected to look halfway decent for my date with Jim.

Now as I lay in bed, watching *House Hunters* and

trying to get Prozac to stop hogging my pillow, I still couldn't get over my good luck meeting the surfer/plumber of my dreams.

To think that Jim Angelides—a guy who, on a scale of one to ten was a 34—actually wanted to go out with me, Jaine Austen, a gal whose cellulite has been known to throw tailgate parties on her thighs!

Just as I was fantasizing about how marvelous it would be to run my fingers through his spiky blond hair, the phone rang.

"Jaine, sweetie!" Deedee's unmistakable trill came zinging across the line. "Are you sitting down?"

"Yes."

"Is Prozac sitting down?"

"Yes, on my freshly washed pillowcase, as a matter of fact."

"Well, brace yourself, darling. Prozac got the part! She's going to star in the Skinny Kitty commercial!"

"Omigod!" I squealed. "That's fantastic news."

"No, sweetums. That's good news. The fantastic news is that they're paying five grand."

Thank heavens I wasn't eating that Chunky Monkey, otherwise I'm sure I would've choked on it.

"The shoot is next week. I'll e-mail you the address. Just remember. All Prozac has to do is nap and eat."

The easiest five grand I'd ever earn.

"Your little princess is headed for stardom," Deedee assured me. "I just know it. I've got infallible star-dar!"

I hung up in a daze.

First Jim. Now this. The gods were surely smiling on me.

"Wake up, Pro!" I said to my precious furball, who was now snoring atop my pillow. "You got the part in the Skinny Kitty commercial!"

"She did?" asked a disembodied voice, seemingly from out of nowhere.

No, it wasn't a ghost. It was Lance, shouting at me from his bedroom. Thanks to our paper-thin walls, and Lance's X-ray hearing, the guy can practically hear me putting on my makeup.

"Yes, Lance," I called back, with more than a hint of smugness in my voice. "The cat you said would never make it in show biz has landed a part in a commercial."

"Really? I'll be right over!"

Two minutes later, he was sailing into my apartment in his pajama bottoms, his six-pack abs buffed to perfection.

I hate it when guys have skinnier waists than I do.

"So Prozac actually got that part?" he asked, not even trying to hide his disbelief.

"Yes, she did. And it pays five thousand dollars."

At this his jaw literally hung open.

"Omigod, that's wonderful!" he cried when he finally recovered his powers of speech. "Just wonderful!"

I have to admit I was touched. Lance was happy for me and Prozac, after all. He cared about us and had stopped by to share in our good news.

"If Prozac can land a commercial," he said, his eyes gleaming with unadulterated ambition, "then my Mamie is destined to be a major motion picture star!"

Scratch that empathy.

"All I need is your agent's name and contact info."

Of all the nerve! Asking for my help, after how little faith he'd shown in Prozac.

Reluctantly, I scribbled a phone number on a piece of paper and handed it to him.

"Thanks, hon! And congrats on the Skinny Kitty job," he added, wrapping me in a warm hug. "I'm thrilled for you guys."

And he actually seemed to mean it.

I sure didn't see that one coming.

In fact, I was so touched, I was beginning to feel bad about giving him my chiropractor's phone number.

YOU'VE GOT MAIL!

To: Jausten
From: Shoptillyoudrop
Subject: The Perfect Bathing Suit!

Aloha, sweetheart!

Fabulous news! I found the perfect bathing suit for our trip to Hawaii. Only $62.49, plus shipping and handling, from the Home Shopping Channel. An adorable turquoise tankini with a lei embroidered around the scoop neck. I mean, nothing says Hawaii like a lei on your tankini, right? Anyhow, it was so darn cute, I ordered one for you in Outrageous Orange. I just know you're going to love it.

Frankly, honey, I'm counting the days till we go. Daddy has been driving me crazy, training for the upcoming annual Tampa Vistas Scrabble Tournament.

He took one look at the 14-karat gold championship ring on display at the clubhouse and threw his hat in the ring. He's dead set on beating the reigning champion, Lydia Pinkus. Talk about your mission impossible! Not only is Lydia president of the homeowners' association and just about the smartest woman I know, but she also happens to have her master's degree in library sciences, which means she knows practically every word in *The Oxford English Dictionary*.

But for some idiotic reason, Daddy's convinced he can beat her, and has been busy memorizing all sorts of ridiculous words. Like *syzygy* (an alignment of three celestial bodies, a potential 93 points), *muzhik* (a Russian peasant, 128 points), and *quetzal* (the national bird of Guatemala, 374 points). I've spent hours giving him spelling tests. Only in our house it's not called testing. It's called "quizzifying" (a potential 419 points).

And to make matters worse, he refuses to take off his ghastly plaid golfing cap, the one with the red pom-pom on top. He insists it's his "Lucky Thinking Cap" and that he's never lost a game with it. Which technically is true, since the only person he ever plays with is me, and I let him win all the time.

Well, must run and order a Za (short for *pizza*, a potential 62 points).

Had no time to cook. Too busy quizzifying.

Love and XXX,
Mom

To: Jausten
From: DaddyO
Subject: A Shoo-In to Win

Dearest Lambchop—

Have you heard the exciting news? I've entered the annual Tampa Vistas Scrabble Tournament. And

I'm a shoo-in to win. I've been hard at work memorizing the Scrabble dictionary, playing Scrabble on my iPhone, and fortifying myself with strategically timed Power Naps. And thanks to my Lucky Thinking Cap, my mind has been a virtual steel trap. I swear, your old DaddyO has become a walking, talking word machine!

Lydia Pinkus has been champion for years, and it's time somebody knocked her off her throne. Just because she has a degree in library science, she thinks she invented the English language. I can't wait to see the look on the old battle-axe's face when I walk away with the prized Scrabble championship ring.

Wish me luck, Lambchop!

Love 'n' snuggles from
DaddyO

Chapter 5

Mom's "lei" bathing suit arrived the next day, a hunk of industrial-strength latex with hidden "tummy tuck panels." The kind of suit last worn by Mamie Eisenhower at Camp David. Mom bought it for me in a ridiculously large size, and clearly the garment was mislabeled because the hideous thing actually fit.

I made up my mind to lose ten pounds promptly, so I'd have a decent excuse to return it.

It's a well known fact in Austen family lore that Mom is addicted to the Home Shopping Channel. In fact, she actually made Daddy retire three thousand miles across country to be near the shopping channel headquarters in Florida, under the mistaken notion that her packages would be delivered faster that way.

You might conclude from this that Mom is the family eccentric. You'd conclude wrong. That honor goes to Daddy, a man who attracts trouble like freshly washed cars attract rain. As Mom so often says about him: "He doesn't have ulcers. He's just a carrier."

I only hoped Daddy wouldn't drive Mom too crazy prepping for his Scrabble tournament. On the other hand, the more he kept her busy with the tournament, the less time she'd have to buy me "fun" outfits from the shopping channel.

I was standing at the foot of my bed that morning, trying to wriggle my way out of my Outrageous Orange Lei Tankini, when the phone rang.

Deedee's voice came sailing over the line.

"Guess what, sweetie?" she trilled. "I'm taking you to lunch. At the Peninsula Hotel!"

The Peninsula? The swellegant hotel in the heart of Beverly Hills, where rooms started at six hundred dollars a night? What a quantum leap from my usual Quarter Pounder at Mickey D's.

"Meet me there at noon! We'll sign your contract and toast darling Prozac with a bottle of Dom Pérignon."

"That's awfully nice of you, Deedee."

"Pish tosh! It's my pleasure."

With not much time to spare, I zipped into the bathroom for a quick shower and then dolled myself up for the occasion in skinny jeans, white silk blouse, suede blazer, and my one and only pair of Manolo Blahniks.

"See you later, my little money maker!" I called out to Prozac as I headed for the door.

She looked up from where she was lolling on the sofa.

Don't forget. I want my five grand in bacon bits.

Fifteen minutes later, I was pulling up to the Peninsula Hotel valet parking area. Under normal circumstances, I'd drive around endlessly looking for a spot on the street before forking over money for valet parking. Especially at an outrageously expensive joint like the Peninsula. But what the heck? Deedee was treating. For once, I'd spring for valet parking.

The valet who ambled over eyed my ancient Corolla as if I'd just driven up in a four-door cockroach.

"Deliveries in the back," he said.

"I am not making a delivery," I informed him with more than a hint of frost in my voice. "I'm here for lunch."

Blinking back his disbelief, he reluctantly got in my car and zoomed off into the underground lot, no doubt determined to park deep in its bowels, in order to avoid contaminating any of the luxury cars.

I found Deedee out on the patio of the hotel's garden restaurant, seated in a sun-dappled corner beneath a magnolia tree, waving to me merrily with a flute of champagne.

"Jaine, darling!" she cried, bangles jangling. "So wonderful to see you!"

Today she was swathed in neon green gauze, crystal necklaces twinkling on her bosom, gold lacquered chopsticks popping out from her bun.

"Have some bubbly, hon!" she said, pouring me a glass of Dom Pérignon. "Here's to darling Prozac! I'm going to make that adorable furball the biggest animal star since Morris the Cat!"

We clinked glasses and took a sip. Well, I took a sip. Deedee glugged hers down like a sailor on shore leave.

Having downed her bubbly, she poured herself some more and then handed me a menu.

"Order whatever you want, sweetie. The sky's the limit."

I looked at the prices, eyeballs rolling. Would you believe twenty dollars for a burger? But that didn't stop me from ordering it. Deedee topped me by ordering a lobster salad. (A nosebleed expensive twenty-nine smackeroos!)

After our waiter left with our orders, Deedee whipped out a contract from her purse and slid it across the table to me.

"Just sign at the Xs," she said, flourishing a DEEDEE WALKER, AGENT TO THE ANIMAL STARS ballpoint pen.

I signed the contract, my eyes spinning in delight at the spot where Deedee had typed in my five-thousand-dollar payment.

Yes, indeedie. This was a Dom Pérignon day, all right.

The luncheon drifted by in a happy glow, Deedee yapping about her famous animal clients. (Lassie's great-granddaughter. Benji's nephew. The cover parrot on *Parrots Today* magazine.) I just nodded on auto-pilot, scarfing down my burger and picturing the zeros on my paycheck.

In spite of the fact that she'd been talking nonstop, somehow Deedee managed to inhale every last morsel of her lobster salad. Not to mention most of the champagne.

"By the way," she said when she finally ran out of animal stories, "the Skinny Kitty people want you to stop by their offices today and pick up some cat food so you can rehearse Prozac's eating scene at home."

Five grand *and* free cat food. Life just kept getting better and better.

"Will do," I assured her.

Finally, after she'd practically licked the last drop of champagne from her flute, Deedee signaled our waiter.

"Check please," she trilled.

Minutes later the check appeared at our table on a tiny silver tray.

Deedee reached into her purse, and suddenly her eyes widened in dismay.

"Oh, my dear!" she cried. "I can't believe it. I've left my wallet at home. How silly of me. You don't mind picking up the tab, do you, hon? I'll pay you back when I cut you your paycheck."

I smiled weakly and assured her I didn't mind. But of course I did mind, especially when I saw the amount of the bill. Two hundred and six dollars. About two hundred dollars more than I usually pay for lunch. God knows how much that champagne cost.

Oh, well. I forced myself to focus on the five grand winging my way.

I gave the waiter my credit card, hoping it wouldn't be turned down. And thank heavens the friendly folks at MasterCard came through for me. They okayed the charge, and all was well in our sun-dappled corner under the magnolia tree.

Deedee and I air kissed each other good-bye, and I headed out to the lobby. Deedee said she wanted to stay behind to say hello to some friends. But when I turned back to wave to her, I could swear I saw her dumping a basket of rolls in her purse.

As I waited for the valet to retrieve my car from where he'd parked it—somewhere in Nevada, no doubt—I began to wonder if Deedee was nearly as successful as she claimed to be.

First, getting on that bus when she pretended to be driving. Then sticking me with the bill. And finally, swiping those rolls! Oh, well. So what if she was in a bit of a slump? She managed to get Prozac a gig worth five grand. And that's all that mattered.

That's what I kept telling myself, anyway.

When I showed up at the Skinny Kitty offices, there was no sign of the receptionist I'd seen the day of Prozac's audition. Instead a young guy was sitting at the reception desk. At first I didn't recognize him, but then I realized it was Zeke, the writer, one of the gang I'd met in the conference room.

Tall and lanky, he sat hunched over a book, his sandy hair flopping onto his forehead. I wondered what he was doing out here, playing receptionist.

He looked up from the book he was reading, which I now saw was something called *The Marshall Plan for Getting Your Novel Published.*

"Can I help you?" he asked, raking his hair off his forehead.

"I'm Jaine Austen. I was here the other day with my cat, Prozac."

"Of course!" he said. "Prozac! The eater. I've never seen a cat suck up so much food so fast."

"She's got a gift, that's for sure."

"We were all very impressed," he grinned.

"You're the guy who wrote the Skinny Kitty commercial, right?"

"Guilty as charged."

"What are you doing out here at the reception desk?"

"Just filling in while the receptionist gets her nails done."

Clearly, Zeke was not ranked high on the Skinny Kitty totem pole. And as if to prove it, the door to the inner offices swung open just then and Dean Oliver, the inventor of Skinny Kitty, came storming out, spray tanned to within an inch of his life, a salon's worth of gel on his hair.

"Where the hell is my coffee?" he roared at Zeke.

"It's still brewing," Zeke replied with a put-upon sigh.

He pointed to a nearby coffee maker, which indeed was still in the process of dripping coffee into a carafe.

But by now Mr. Slick appeared to have forgotten about the coffee and had turned his attention to yours truly, gazing at me with a bit too much interest.

"Ms. Austen, isn't it?" He took my hand in his and shot me his version of a seductive grin.

"Right," I said, wriggling free from his grasp.

"How can we help you?" he asked, beaming at me from behind his spray tan.

"I'm here to pick up some Skinny Kitty for my cat."

"Ah, yes, the voracious Prilosec."

"Actually, her name is Prozac."

"Whatever." Then, whirling on Zeke, he barked, "Where's the cat food?"

"Over here." Zeke pointed to a shopping bag behind his desk. "It's all set to go."

"Okay," Dean nodded curtly. "Just be sure you bring me that coffee the minute it's ready. "Nice seeing you again," he said to me, shooting his finger at me like a gun.

Then off he disappeared, back into his inner sanctum.

Zeke shook his head in disgust the minute Dean was gone.

"If I've learned one thing from this job," he said, "it's never work for a relative."

"You two are related?"

"First cousins," he nodded. "We grew up together in Ohio. You should have seen him back then. Talk about your nerds. Glasses held together with duct tape. Zits the size of Mount Vesuvius. Now he thinks he owns the world. The minute I make my first sale, I'm outta here."

"Your first sale?"

"I don't intend to be writing these crummy commercials my whole life. No way. I'm working on a novel. And some short stories. And a screenplay, of course."

Of course. This was L.A. Scratch a receptionist, find a screenwriter.

A pinging sound came from the coffeemaker. I looked over and saw the machine had stopped gurgling; the carafe was full.

"Looks like your coffee's done," I said.

"I suppose I'd better bring it to him, or all hell

will break loose. Here's your cat food." Zeke started to get me the Skinny Kitty when the door to the back offices opened again and the mousy producer I'd met at the audition came out into the reception area.

"Hi, Linda!" Zeke said, his eyes lighting up.

Just like the other day, she wore jeans and a T-shirt, her hair swept back in a headband, those god-awful harlequin glasses perched on her nose. Not a speck of makeup on her face. I still couldn't see her married to a slickster like Dean.

"Hi, Jaine," she chirped. "Dean told me you were here. So nice to see you!"

Then she turned to Zeke, who, I couldn't help noticing, was gazing at her much like I gaze upon a freshly delivered pepperoni pizza.

"Coffee ready yet?" Linda asked.

"Yes," Zeke gulped in reply. "I was just going to pour a cup for Dean."

"Don't bother, hon," Linda said. "I'll do it. And thanks for taking over the reception desk. I don't know what we'd do without you."

She flashed him a smile, exposing a slight over-bite, and I could practically feel Zeke's knees go weak.

"Aw, it's nothing," he mumbled.

He watched her as she went to the coffee machine, his eyes filled with longing.

Clearly there was one part of his job that Zeke was madly in love with.

Chapter 6

I spent the next few days rehearsing with Pro, and for once in her life, she was actually cooperating with me.

She gobbled up her Skinny Kitty. She napped on cue. She did everything I asked, with only the occasional belly rub as a reward. It was as if the little ham knew there was a pot of gold at the end of the rainbow and was determined to get her claws on it.

Maybe Deedee was right. Maybe Prozac had a future as a TV star, after all.

Between rehearsals, I spent way too many hours making lists of what I was going to buy with our new-found riches. (Plasma TV. A brand new used car. Platinum Level Fudge-of-the-Month Club. And all the bacon bits my princess could eat.)

Of course, these were hours I should have spent working on the Touch-Me-Not toilet brochure. But my heart simply wasn't in it. There'd be plenty of time for toilet bowls after the shoot.

At last the big day arrived.

Prozac clawed me awake for her breakfast, and right away I was faced with a dilemma. If I fed her now, she wouldn't be hungry for the shoot. And yet there was no way I was going to get away without giving her something for breakfast.

So I put the tiniest dab of Skinny Kitty in her bowl. This would have to tide her over until the cameras were rolling.

After scarfing it down in milliseconds, she looked around, confused.

Okay, I finished my appetizer. Where's the main course?

"You want to be hungry for the shoot, Pro. You want to gobble up that Skinny Kitty and earn us five grand, don't you, honey?"

An impatient thump of her tail.

Yes, but first I want my breakfast.

"I promise you'll thank me later."

Scooping her up in my arms, I plopped her on the living room sofa and tossed her an old cashmere sweater to distract her. Sure enough, within minutes, she was ripping it to shreds. A small sacrifice for that five-thousand-dollar paycheck.

Then I hustled over to my computer and printed out the call sheet Deedee had sent me with the address of the studio where the shoot was to take place. As I laid it beside my purse, my heart did a tiny somersault. How thrilling it was to see my name along with all the other members of the production. People in "the biz"—like Ian Kendrick, the director, a man who'd shot actual movies! True, most of them had gone straight to video, but who cared? Prozac was on the brink of national stardom, and that was all that counted.

By now I was dying to nuke myself a cinnamon raisin bagel but was afraid to go anywhere near the kitchen, lest Prozac follow me there in search of food.

So, like Pro, I went hungry for the sake of the pot of gold at the end of our rainbow.

Dreaming of a cheese Danish dripping with butter, I headed for the bedroom and proceeded to get dressed. I was just blowing out my bangs when there was a knock on my door.

It was Lance, muscles buffed to perfection in cutoffs and a tank top.

"Today's the big day, right?" he grinned. "Just stopped by to wish you good luck!"

Of course, he hadn't been nearly so sunny the other day, when he realized I'd given him my chiropractor's phone number instead of Deedee's. Then he'd come storming into my apartment, Mr. Drama Queen, accusing me of high treason, screeching about how I was Lucrezia Borgia, Tokyo Rose, and Mata Hari all rolled into one.

What with all those theatrics, I had no other choice but to give him Deedee's phone number, after which he was all smiles.

Just as he was this morning.

"I just know Prozac's going to do great today!" he gushed.

Not for one minute did I believe him. I remembered his harsh words about my princess's lack of talent. They were forever etched on my cerebellum, and I was determined to prove him wrong.

"Break a paw, kiddo!" he called out to Prozac, who sat on the sofa in a Buddha-like pose, having abandoned my cashmere sweater.

She looked up, slightly irritated.

Not now! I'm trying to get centered.

Checking my watch, I saw it was time to go. So I grabbed my purse and gathered Prozac in my arms. Once again, I'd decided to leave the cat carrier at home, unwilling to risk upsetting my little moneymaker on the drive over to the studio.

Shoving my call sheet in my purse, I bid Lance adieu and headed out to my Corolla.

When I settled Pro in the car—miracle of miracles—she actually sat still on the passenger seat. No dancing around my gas pedal, no leaping onto the backseat like a Flying Wallenda.

No, this morning she was cool and poised, Grace Kelly on her way to meet Hitchcock.

If she could have reached it, she would've been primping in my rearview mirror. Instead, she sat staring out into space, a dreamy look in her eyes.

This was one cat who was ready for the red carpet.

I found the studio on a forsaken street in a tree-less stretch of Hollywood where hookers were as plentiful as parking meters. (And a lot cheaper.)

After scoring a primo spot in the parking lot, I grabbed my purse and scooped Prozac out from the car. She gazed at the stucco bunker of a building, with the words KLEINMAN PRODUCTIONS painted over the door, clearly unimpressed.

Not exactly MGM, is it?

Inside, a bored receptionist with a massive bubble of black hair sat behind a desk, reading *Entertainment Weekly*.

"I'm here for the Skinny Kitty shoot," I informed her.

Barely looking up from this week's movie grosses, she waved me down a hallway. To my right was a warren of small offices, and to my left an oversized steel door leading to the soundstage.

A frisson of excitement shot through me. How many famous stars had stood before doors just like this before getting their first big break?

I looked down at Prozac nestled in my arms.

"This is it, kiddo. Showtime."

My plucky little trouper looked up at me with bright green eyes.

So when do I get my Oscar?

Taking a deep breath, I headed inside.

At one end of the cavernous room were a buffet bar and a makeshift conference table surrounded by folding metal chairs. The other end of the soundstage had been set up for the shoot with a chaise longue and overstuffed armchair. Lights hung from the ceiling; a camera stood at attention, waiting to be called to action.

Glancing around, I saw Ian, the silver-haired director, sitting at the conference table and taking a slug from his Starbucks thermos. And over at the buffet, Linda was chatting with a fresh-scrubbed blonde in an apron, while Zeke lingered nearby, his eyes riveted on Linda.

As I made my way into the room, Deedee came rushing toward me in a blur of turquoise gauze and silver bangles, ebony chopsticks poking from her bun.

"Jaine darling!" she cried, taking a bite of a luscious cheese Danish.

I would have liked nothing better than to grab a Danish for myself, but I couldn't risk going near the buffet table and whetting Prozac's appetite.

"Here's our little star!" Deedee cooed, waving the Danish in my face as she leaned over to pet Prozac. It was all I could do not to rip it out of her hand. "You two are just in time! We're about to go over the script."

She led me over to a seat at the conference table.

I settled myself in, with Prozac on my lap, nodding hello to Ian, who was still glugging from his Starbucks thermos. I couldn't help but notice he was looking a bit bleary-eyed, no doubt waiting for his caffeine to kick in.

Dean sat at the head of the table, hair slicked back with gel, talking intently to a striking brunette at his side. The reed-thin woman, who could have been anywhere from thirty-five to seventy (only her plastic surgeon knew for sure) was dressed head to toe in pink. From her Chanel suit to her Louboutins to the boatload of pink sapphires accessorizing her outfit, the gal was a one-woman Festival of Pink.

On her lap sat a sleek tabby cat with what looked like a pink diamond collar around her neck. True, the collar could've been made of rhinestones, but I'd bet my bottom Pop-Tart that cat was wearing something straight from Van Cleef & Arpels.

Prozac looked at the diamond-encrusted kitty through slitted lids.

Who invited her?

Deedee, following my gaze, whispered in my

ear: "That's Camille Townsend. Aka the Pink Panther. Positively rolling in dough. Inherited boatloads when her hubby died. Dean met her at a pet charity function and stuck to her like Velcro ever since. From what I've heard, she's bankrolling this whole production."

Dean was patting the Pink Panther's arm as they talked, lingering just a little too long with each pat.

"They seem awfully chummy," I said.

"Chummy? That's putting it mildly. They've been boffing each other for months now.

"Poor Linda," she said, nodding at Dean's wife, still busy chatting with the blonde in the apron. "She supported Dean for years while he worked on his inventions, and now, from what I hear on the grapevine, he's about to dump her for Ms. Moneybags."

Dean interrupted Deedee's stream of gossip just then to summon everyone to the conference table.

"Hello, everybody," he said, rising to greet his minions. "I'd like to welcome you all to the first of what I'm sure will be many Skinny Kitty commercials to come. That's because Skinny Kitty just happens to be the world's most delicious diet cat food. "I'm proud and humbled," he said, not looking the least bit humble, "to have come up with the recipe in my very own test kitchen."

He paused and waited. Across from us, Linda picked up his cue and led the rest of us in a round of applause. His ego sufficiently stroked, Dean then went around the table and introduced us.

It turned out the fresh-scrubbed blonde in the

apron, a gal named Nikki Banks, was the food stylist, whose job it was to make Skinny Kitty look as luscious as filet mignon.

When Dean got to me, he said, "This is Jaine Austen and her delightful cat, Prozac, whose ability to suck up food is truly astounding."

In my arms, Prozac preened.

That's nothing. You should see me claw cashmere into ribbons.

"You all know Ian Kendrick, our esteemed director," Dean continued.

Ian flicked two fingers in a limp wave.

"And my wife, Linda. Thanks, hon, for picking up the delicious deli spread for the buffet."

Linda smiled shyly, still hiding whatever good features she possessed behind her hideous harlequin glasses.

"Oh, yes," Dean said, almost as an afterthought. "There's my cousin Zeke, author of our script. Even though I had to rewrite most of it myself."

He laughed as if he was kidding, but everyone knew he meant it, and across the table, Zeke was doing a slow burn.

"And finally, I'd like to introduce the woman whose generosity has made this shoot possible, my dear friend and colleague, Camille Townsend."

The Pink Panther gave us all a regal nod.

"And, of course, her exquisite cat, Desiree."

Camille held up her furry accessory for all to admire.

In my lap, Prozac snorted.

What a cream puff.

"Let's all give Camille a big round of applause,"

Dean commanded. "Without her, we wouldn't be here today."

Across the table, Linda applauded enthusiastically. If she had any idea about her husband's affair with the Pink Panther, she showed no signs of it.

"Okay, everybody," Dean said, having paid homage to his benefactress. "Time to run through the script."

I picked up the piece of paper in front of me. In fact, this was the first time I'd ever seen a copy of the script. So far, all I'd been doing was honing Prozac's eating and napping skills.

Dean began narrating our little cat food drama. "The commercial starts out with a voice-over announcer asking, 'Is your cat fat? Lazy? Too stuffed to move? Does she turn her nose up at ordinary diet cat food? Well, it's time you tried Skinny Kitty, the diet cat food cats really like!'

"We'll show the 'Before' cat," Dean said, pointing to Prozac, "looking fat and lazy, first refusing to eat Brand X cat food, then digging into the Skinny Kitty. Then the announcer will say, 'After only three weeks of eating Skinny Kitty, your cat will look like this.' And we'll cut to a shot of Desiree."

Camille smiled proudly and held up her sleek little princess.

The *Before* Cat? Prozac was the *Before* cat? I couldn't help but feel a tad insulted.

And in my lap, Prozac was none too happy. Scoff if you want, but I swear that cat understands English.

She glared at Dean, fire in her eyes.

I demand a rewrite!

Oblivious to Prozac's dirty look, Dean continued narrating his chef d'oeuvre.

"Then we're going to wrap up the commercial with a line that's sure to go down in advertising history: *My Skinny Kitty is so delicious, I eat it myself!* "That's right, everybody!" he beamed. "I will actually eat my own cat food. It really is that delicious."

"He eats his own cat food?" I whispered to Deedee.

"According to Linda," Deedee nodded, "he has no sense of smell. Hasn't tasted food in decades."

"Let's take a short break," Dean said, "while our cameraman and lighting director set up the first shot."

Two burly guys, whose names I'd already forgotten but would come to think of as Big and Bigger, thumped off to do their job.

"While everything's getting set up," Dean announced, "Camille and I will be in my dressing room, tweaking the Skinny Kitty ad campaign."

Just as Deedee was rolling her eyes and betting that the only things Dean and the Panther would be tweaking would be each other, a woman's voice came blaring out over the PA system. *Will the owner of a crummy white Corolla with bird poop on the windshield please move their car immediately. You're parked in the owner's spot.*

Okay, so she didn't really call my Corolla crummy and she didn't mention the bird poop on the windshield, but the annoyance in her voice was palpable.

"Oh, dear. That's me," I said, thrusting Prozac into Deedee's arms. "Watch her, will you, while I go move my car?"

"My pleasure!" Deedee cooed. "Deedee will take good care of your precious cargo."

Grabbing my purse, I sprinted down the hallway, past the receptionist, who looked up from her magazine and gave me the stink eye. Out in the lot, I quickly moved my Corolla from its coveted spot near the front entrance—I should've known it was too good to be true—to a far less enviable location next to the studio dumpster.

When I returned to the studio, the receptionist was busy applying press-on nails.

And to think, some people actually have to work for their money.

Heading back down the hallway, I happened to glance into one of the small offices and saw that it was a kitchen. Standing there at a prep table was Nikki, the food stylist, arranging cat food in a bowl. Written on the bowl were the words *Brand X.* Hadn't the script said something about the Before Cat turning up her nose at ordinary diet cat food? This was no doubt the stuff that Prozac would refuse to eat.

Nikki was carefully sculpting it with a spoon, standing back to admire the effect, much like Rodin must have looked as he was putting the finishing touches on *The Thinker.* Pleased with the final result, she then absentmindedly reached for a spray can. Just as she was about to give a spritz, I realized it was a can of Raid.

"Stop!" I cried. "That stuff is poison!"

Nikki looked at the insecticide in her hand and gasped. "Gosh!" she cried. "It looked just like the lemon oil I spray on the Brand X cat food to make it unpalatable for the cats."

She pointed to a spray can of lemon oil, which did indeed bear a striking resemblance to the pest killer. "Thank God you were passing by. What if I'd sprayed the Raid by mistake and your poor kitty ate it? She could have died."

"That's okay," I assured her. "You didn't spray it. All is well."

But I have to admit, I was shaken. I shuddered at the thought of Prozac, hungry from no breakfast, digging into Brand X, laced with Raid.

"The studio's been having troubles with ants," Nikki said, putting the Raid aside on a shelf. "I should have never kept it on the prep table."

Then she picked up the lemon oil and sprayed the Brand X cat food.

"Are you sure that stuff really keeps cats away?" I asked. "I hardly gave my cat any breakfast this morning, and I'll bet she's starving. What if she tries to eat it?"

"No worries," Nikki assured me. "Cats hate lemon oil. Once she smells it, she'll never touch the food."

I had my doubts. After all, we were talking about a cat who's been known to nibble on rancid gym socks.

"Voilà!" Nikki said, holding up the bowl. "Brand X, destined to be rejected."

It was then that I noticed an adorable pink ring, shaped like a hibiscus, flashing on her middle finger. What a perfect accessory for my trip to Hawaii!

"That's such a cute ring!"

"It is, isn't it?" She flashed it to and fro, making it twinkle in the overhead fluorescent lighting. "I picked it up for only ten bucks at Venice Beach."

Making a mental note to pop on down to Venice and do a little vacation shopping, I bid Nikki farewell and headed back to the soundstage.

The first thing I saw when I got there was Deedee, talking on her cell phone—Prozac no longer in her arms.

Where the heck was her "precious cargo"?

Looking around, I groaned to see Prozac perched on the buffet table! When I raced over, I found her chowing down on some rare roast beef. Which, by the way, looked mighty fantastic.

Thank heavens there was no one else at the buffet to witness her crime.

"What do you think you're doing?" I said, whisking her up in my arms and grabbing a cheese Danish while I was at it. "Mergfleflugaffleflillwhoppersofeffer?"

Well, what I meant to say was, "Have you no willpower whatsoever?"

But my mouth was full of Danish at the time.

At which point Deedee approached.

I gulped down the rest of my Danish and sputtered, "I thought you were supposed to be watching Prozac!"

"Sorry, hon. I had to set her down while I took an emergency call from a client. Pierre, my star parrot," she gasped with all the angst of a Shakespearean tragedienne, "has mange!"

I failed to offer her my condolences, fighting the urge to throttle her instead.

"Oh, dear," Deedee now piped up. "Is that roast beef I smell on our princess's breath? Has she been a naughty kitty and been raiding the buffet table?"

"Yes, I'm afraid she has."

"I hope she hasn't ruined her appetite."

"You and me both," I muttered.

"I'm sure our little trouper will pull through for us," Deedee enthused. "I can tell by the determined look in her eyes."

Prozac had a determined look in her eyes, all right. She was now staring at the baked ham, determined to get a bite.

But just then Dean strode onto the soundstage, followed by Camille with Desiree in her arms. Was it my imagination, or was the Panther buttoning one of the buttons on her blouse?

By now Big and Bigger had done their job. The lights were set; the camera was ready to roll.

"Okay," Ian called out. "We need the 'Before' cat."

In my arms, Prozac's tail thumped in annoyance.

Don't call me the 'Before' Cat! I happen to be the star of this commercial!

I headed over to where Ian was standing at the chaise longue.

"In the first scene, we'll have your cat spread out on the chaise, napping. She can do that, right?" Ian asked, treating me to what seemed like more than a hint of gin on his breath. Suddenly I wondered exactly what he'd been toting around in his Starbucks thermos.

"Absolutely, she can nap," I assured him, praying Prozac would get over her snit fit about being the Before Cat and snooze on command.

My prayers were answered.

I set Pro down on the chaise, where, no doubt

drowsy from all the roast beef she'd just sucked up, she instantly proceeded to stretch out.

Before I even had a chance to whisper my knock-out mantra (*Oh, Pro. Wait till I tell you about the miserable day I've just had…*) she was snoring like a buzzsaw.

Big, the cameraman, wasted no time and zoomed in to get some footage.

Nearby Deedee gushed, "Isn't she fantastic! Such a natural!"

"She sure can snore," Dean said, eyeing her in wonder.

After Prozac's triumphant portrayal of fat and lazy, Big and Bigger reset for the next shot: Prozac turning her nose up at Brand X.

We moved to a large square of linoleum—on this rather thrifty production, meant to represent a kitchen floor.

Nikki came bustling in with the bowl of Brand X cat food glistening with lemon oil. She set it down on the linoleum, careful to make sure it was positioned so the camera picked up the words *Brand X*.

"Are we ready?" Ian called out.

I set Prozac down next to the cat food and waited with bated breath, hoping she wouldn't swan dive into the bowl.

But thank heavens Nikki had been right about the lemon oil. The stuff was kitty kryptonite.

Prozac took one sniff and instantly recoiled.

For the first time in recorded history, my champion chowhound actually turned away from a bowl of food.

"My God!" Deedee cried. "I haven't seen an animal this talented since *Beverly Hills Chihuahua*!"

Then it was time for Prozac's big moment. Her final shot of the commercial—eating the Skinny Kitty.

Another break while Big and Bigger set up the shot. When they were finally ready, Nikki brought out the Skinny Kitty in a gorgeous crystal bowl, no doubt part of the Pink Panther's dinner service.

What with all the setups and footage Big had been shooting, it had been well over an hour since Pro had scarfed down that roast beef. With any luck, enough time had passed for my feline garbage disposal to have worked up an appetite.

By now, my confidence was growing. Prozac was on a roll. She could smell that five grand and all the bacon bits it could buy. I felt certain she'd put on the feed bag and suck up that cat food.

Nikki set down the crystal bowl. She'd done a great job of styling the Skinny Kitty, making the chunks of mystery meat look like something straight out of a Martha Stewart cookbook.

Prozac sniffed at it hungrily. She was all set to chow down.

And then Dean went ahead and opened his big mouth.

"As soon as we're through with 'fatty' here, we'll set up for our star, Miss Desiree."

That's when everything went to hell.

I told you Pro understands English. She looked up from the Skinny Kitty, fury flashing in her eyes.

Fatty? He called me Fatty? That's it. I'm outta here.

"Forget about him, Pro," I whispered in her ear. "Just take a bite."

Nothing.

"I'm begging you."

Still nothing.

"Just think of all those juicy bacon bits."

But it was no use. Her jaws were clamped tighter than a chastity belt in the Middle Ages.

"Hey, what's the holdup?" Dean groused.

"Not a problem, Dean," Ian said, stepping up to the plate. "I've got this. I work with animals all the time. They always listen to me."

He crouched down and started to whisper in Prozac's ear, but one blast of his breath sent her skittering away.

Whoa, Nelly. Somebody had a Gin McMuffin for breakfast.

"Nice work, Cecil B," Dean snapped. "Now what are we supposed to do?"

"Don't worry, Dean," Deedee said, hustling to his side. "This is just a minor hiccup. Prozac is a trained professional. I guarantee she'll give the performance of a lifetime. Animals often need a moment of reflection before throwing themselves into their roles. Isn't that so, Prozac, honey? Aren't you just about to throw yourself into the role?"

At which point, Prozac did sort of throw herself into the role. The role of a Psycho Kitty. With a mighty swipe of her paw, she sent the crystal bowl of cat food skittering across the stage and crashing into a floor light, where it promptly shattered to smithereens.

"That's my good Waterford!" cried the Pink Panther, turning as pink as her sapphires.

Dean kneeled down and looked Prozac straight in the eye, oozing rage from every pore.

"Why, you no-talent little flea ball!"

Prozac oozed right back at him.

*Better a flea ball than a sleazeball. And, by the way,
Dippity-do called. They want their gel back.*

Then, as the coup de grâce, she reached out
and landed a nasty scratch on his arm.

And right before my eyes, I saw my five grand
going bye-bye.

If you think, as I thought at the time, that I'd hit
rock bottom, that things couldn't possibly get any
worse, think again.

Because just then, the doors to the soundstage
opened and Lance came strolling in, with Mamie
in tow.

"Hi-ho, everybody! I'd like you all to meet Mamie,
the most talented dog in the world! Is this a good
time?"

Chapter 7

Lance skipped across the room, Mamie trotting behind him, an adorable white fluffball with a fake daisy in her hair.

"You must be Jaine's agent!" Lance cried, making a beeline for Deedee. "Jaine's told me so much about you. And Mr. Kendrick," he said practically salaaming to Ian, "I'm such a fan of your work. I just adored *Attack of the Lemming People*!"

The little toady must have seen my call sheet this morning and wasted no time doing his homework.

"A pleasure to meet you, too, Mr. Oliver," he said, pumping Dean's hand with gusto. "I've brought you pictures of my amazing dog, Mamie. Say hello, Mamie."

Right on cue, Mamie gave a perky little yap.

"Here she is," Lance said, passing out photos, "as a cowgirl. As Cleopatra. And as a licensed registered nurse—"

Dean, no doubt pissed at getting third billing in the introductions, had had enough.

"We don't have time for this nonsense. We're trying to shoot a commercial. With a cat who refuses to eat the cat food."

"Really?" Lance's eyes lit up. "I'm sure Mamie would eat it. She adores cat food. And I bet she could pass as a cat if you shot her in really soft focus."

Dean stared at him, incredulous.

"Will somebody get this clown out of here?"

For once, Dean and I were on the same page.

Big and Bigger materialized at Lance's side, grabbed him by the elbows, and hauled him out the door, Mamie scampering happily in their wake.

By now Dean had worked himself up into quite a frenzy, his face an unbecoming shade of puce.

"What a freaking mess!" he cried, pointing to the Skinny Kitty splattered all over the fake kitchen floor. "It's all your fault," he said, whirling on me. "You and your no-talent cat. I'm gonna sue you for every cent you're worth."

Oh, gulp. The last thing my anemic checking account and I needed was a lawsuit.

"And you," he said, turning his wrath on Ian. "You call yourself an animal director? What a joke. You couldn't direct a flea to a dog."

"That's not quite fair," Ian protested. "You've got to admit, Prozac's a bit bonkers."

"Stop making excuses," Dean snapped. "You can't direct because you're too damn drunk! I could smell the gin on your breath from the parking lot. When's the last time you actually had coffee in that thermos of yours? I'm going to personally see to it that you never work in this town again."

Ian blanched, fear shining in his bloodshot eyes.

"Now, Dean," Deedee said, putting her bangled wrist on his arm. "Let's all take a deep breath and calm down. I'm sure all Prozac needs is a few minutes to center herself, and we'll be up and running."

"Shut up, Deedee," Dean said, slapping her hand away. "I should've never worked with you in the first place. You haven't represented a decent animal act in decades."

"That's not true!" Deedee cried. "Why, my parrot Pierre just shot the cover of *Parrots Today*."

"I've made a few phone calls about you, hon, and rumor has it you've swindled quite a few clients out of their commissions."

"That's a vicious lie!" Deedee cried, chins quivering in indignation.

"Yeah? Well, you can tell your side of the story to the authorities. Because I'm going to report you to the D.A.'s office the first thing tomorrow morning."

Deedee gulped in dismay.

And I must say, I was a bit shaken myself.

Was it possible that Dean was right, and that all along Deedee had been planning to cheat me out of my five grand?

By now the tension was so thick, you could cut it with a weed wacker.

Nikki and Zeke were huddled together, along with Big and Bigger, waiting for Dean to spew his anger on them, but by this point, he seemed to have run out of steam. He just stood there, fists clenched, his face still that unbecoming shade of puce.

It was then that mousy little Linda stepped up and saved the day.

"Why don't we all take a break, hon?" she said to Dean, smiling that serene smile of hers. "It's almost time for lunch anyway. When we come back up, we can shoot the last scene in the commercial, the one where you eat the cat food. In the meanwhile, we can send out for another crystal bowl, and Jaine can work with Prozac. I'll help her. I'm sure, between the two of us, we can get Prozac to gobble up the Skinny Kitty."

Like magic, her words seemed to calm him down.

There was something about her voice, so soft, so reassuring that even I, who had given up all hope of ever seeing a paycheck, was beginning to believe that maybe things would work out, after all.

"Okay, Linda," Dean said, at last unclenching his fists. "We'll give it a try. Now I think I'll go rest in my dressing room."

"Good idea, sweetheart."

"I'll go with him," the Panther piped up, not exactly happy at this loving exchange between husband and wife. "There are some more details we need to go over for the ad campaign."

Linda watched them trot off together, her smile frozen on her lips. Surely, she must have suspected something was going on between the two of them.

"Zeke!" Dean called out as he was leaving. "Clean up the cat food mess."

Zeke nodded, gritting his teeth.

As soon as Dean and the Panther were gone, Zeke got to work cleaning up the cat food, muttering curses under his breath. Meanwhile, Nikki left to buy a new crystal bowl, and Big and Bigger ambled off to set up the next shot.

Ian and Deedee, still shaken from Dean's threats, went out to the parking lot for a breath of fresh air.

"Time for us to get to work with Prozac," Linda said, turning to me, her comforting smile back in place again. "Let's try to get her to exercise, so she can work up an appetite."

We headed over to the chaise longue where Prozac had shot her napping scene.

"Dean's just got the patent on his latest invention—a catnip-infused ball of yarn." She reached into her purse and took out what looked like a simple ball of yarn. "The catnip scent is infused into the yarn and sealed in there so it stays fresh indefinitely. It's really a breakthrough in the world of cat toys. "Let's see if Prozac likes it," she said, tossing the yarn onto the chaise.

I plopped Prozac down next to it, but she just stared at it disdainfully.

Puh-leese. If you think I'm about to play with a silly ball of—Oh, Mama! What's that I smell? Yummity yum yum yum!

By now her little pink nose was sniffing in overdrive, and she was rolling around on the chaise with that ball of yarn like a stripper wrestling in a vat of Jell-O.

"I've never seen her so excited about a toy," I marveled.

Linda beamed with pride.

"We call it Yarn-Nip. Dean and I think it's going to be a top seller."

"Thanks so much for coming to our rescue," I said as we watched Prozac prance around with the Yarn-Nip. "If you hadn't stepped in, I'm sure Dean would have kicked us out the door."

"It was nothing, honey," she shrugged. "After sixteen years of marriage I know how to defuse Dean. Underneath all his swagger and explosions, he's really a good guy."

"Dean . . . a good guy?" Zeke scoffed as he sidled up to join us. "You're a saint to put up with him, Linda. And everybody knows it."

"Stop it, Zeke," Linda said sharply. "You know I don't like that kind of talk."

"Sorry," Zeke mumbled like a puppy who'd just been swatted on the head with a newspaper.

Zeke continued to hang out with us as we watched Prozac have intimate relations with her ball of yarn, gazing at Linda with pure longing in his eyes.

After a while, Nikki returned to the soundstage.

"Mission accomplished!" she said, joining us. "I found a crystal bowl at a thrift shop just a few blocks away. The Skinny Kitty's all prepped for Dean. I left it in the kitchen, safe from mischievous paws," she added with a sidelong glance at Prozac, who by now, in several states, was undoubtedly legally married to the ball of yarn.

Nikki then headed off to reward herself with a snack from the buffet table, accompanied by Linda and Zeke.

I would have loved to join them and swan dive into some baked ham, but didn't dare let Prozac out of my sight.

Eventually, Big and Bigger announced that they were ready to shoot, and Ian and Deedee were summoned from the parking lot.

Ian staggered back onto the soundstage, weaving unsteadily on his feet, clearly three sheets to the wind, gulping gin from his Starbucks thermos. He was soon followed by Deedee, who came marching in with a self-assured smile, brow unfurrowed under her ebony chopsticks.

"Are you guys okay?" Linda asked, eyeing Ian with concern.

"Fine," Ian muttered

"I'm perfectly well, thank you," Deedee said. "Your husband may have issued some ugly threats, but I've got nothing to be worried about. Not now. You see, I've taken care of him forever."

And with those enigmatic words, she bopped over to the buffet table and helped herself to a bear claw.

Linda, looking somewhat taken aback at Deedee's pronouncement, summoned Dean and the Pink Panther from their latest "work" session.

"Camille helped me with my makeup," Dean said as he and the Panther sauntered over to join us.

I'll just bet she did, I thought, eyeing a smudge of foundation on the Panther's thigh.

"Okay, everybody. Quiet on the set!" Ian called out as Dean crossed to the stage and took a seat in the armchair that had been set up for the shot.

"You ready?" Ian snapped, glaring at Dean.

"Probably the only person on this soundstage who is," Dean shot back.

Ian took a defiant slug from his thermos and called out: "Where the hell's the cat food?"

At which point, Nikki came rushing in with a freshly styled bowl of Skinny Kitty, along with a tiny silver fork.

"That bowl isn't real crystal," the Panther sniffed.

"It'll have to do," Linda said, steely-eyed.

"Yes, let's get this thing over with," Dean said, grabbing the bowl and fork.

"Okay," Ian shouted. "Action!"

And just like that, Dean morphed from monumental grouch to personable spokesman, all smiles, Mr. Rogers in Armani.

"My Skinny Kitty cat food is so delicious," he said, spearing a forkful, "I eat it myself."

He held up the chunk of cat food, admiring it as it shimmered in the studio light. Then he popped it in his mouth and, true to his word, ate it.

He was just about to dig in for another bite when suddenly he clutched his stomach, his face drained of color. The silver fork came clattering to the floor, followed by the bowl of cat food. Seconds later, Dean joined them with a thud, coiled in a fetal ball, moaning in pain.

For a minute, everyone just stood there, frozen.

"What's wrong?" Ian finally managed to ask.

"I've been poisoned, you idiot," Dean gasped, in what turned out to be his genial last words.

"Someone call 911!" Linda cried.

Zeke dug out his cell phone and made the call as Linda raced to Dean's side.

"Hang in there, honey," she crooned, cradling him in her arms. "You're going to be okay."

But for once Linda couldn't make things right.

Dean was dead and gone long before the paramedics showed up.

"And that," Ian said, as they carted Dean's body out the door, "is a wrap."

YOU'VE GOT MAIL!

To: Jausten
From: Shoptillyoudrop
Subject: Scrabble Central

I can't wait till this dratted Scrabble tournament is over. Daddy has commandeered the dining room (now known as Scrabble Central), where he sits in his Lucky Thinking Cap, memorizing words with *x*'s and *q*'s, playing Scrabble on his iPhone, and taking Power Naps every seven and a half minutes.

The other day he came home from the market with a jumbo jar of gherkin pickles. Apparently he read on some wacky Web site that pickles help boost brainpower, and he's been stuffing his face with gherkins ever since.

What with all that acid, I'm afraid he's going to give himself an ulcer. I've told him he's asking for trouble, but does he listen? Of course not! He just sits there, trying to figure out how he can work "oxyphenbutazone" into a game for 1,778 points.

Oh, dear. Someone's at the door. Must run. More later—

XOXO,
Mom

To: Jausten
From: Shoptillyoudrop
Subject: The Most Exciting News!

Jaine, sweetheart, I've got the most exciting
news. Guess who's going to be the special guest
presenter at the Scrabble Championship Awards
Luncheon? World-renowned game show host
(and silver fox) Alex Trebek!

Lydia Pinkus just stopped by with the news. It
turns out her old college roommate is a friend of
Alex's fourth cousin once removed. At any rate,
Lydia wrote him one of her persuasive letters, told
him how much we all adore *Jeopardy*, and that
darling man agreed to come to Tampa Vistas!

I absolutely must order a new dress for the
luncheon. Which reminds me, honey. Did you ever
get that Outrageous Orange tankini I sent you?
Isn't it the cutest thing ever?

Love you oodles.

XOXO,
Mom

To: Jausten
From: DaddyO
Subject: Last Days of the Scrabble Queen

I suppose Mom has told you the good news,
Lambchop.

Alex Trebek is going to be giving me my championship ring at the Scrabble awards luncheon. Pretty darn exciting, huh?

You know, I've always wanted to be on *Jeopardy*. When this Scrabble thing is over and I get back from Hawaii, I just may give it a try.

Lydia was so full of herself when she was here just now, bragging about how she'd convinced Alex to come to Tampa Vistas. But I could tell, deep down she was scared. She saw me in my Lucky Thinking Cap and knew she didn't stand a chance in the tournament. I could see the fear in her beady little eyes. Her days as Scrabble Queen are coming to an end, and she knows it.

Well, I'm off to the market to buy some gherkin pickles. Did you know pickles are brain food, Lambchop? It's true. I read it on the Internet!

Love 'n' snuggles from
Your Scrabble-tastic
DaddyO

To: Jausten
From: Shoptillyoudrop
Subject: Peace & Quiet

Daddy's at the market, getting more gherkins, and I must admit I'm enjoying the peace and quiet. No pop spelling quizzes. No cursing at the iPhone Scrabble game. Just blissful silence. I took advantage of the lull to order the most adorable dress for the Scrabble awards luncheon. Navy blue, scoop neck, three-quarter sleeves, with a flouncy skirt and tasteful smattering of bugle beads at the neck. (Just $69.95, plus shipping and handling!) They had it in a beautiful fuchsia color, which might be fun for one of your L.A. cocktail parties. What do you think?

Oops. I hear Daddy at the front door. I'll pretend I'm napping, in case he wants me to give him a spelling quiz. Oh, dear. Now he's hollering about something. I'd better go see what's wrong.

XOXO,
Mom

To: Jausten
From: DaddyO
Subject: Infamy!

Today, Lambchop, is a day that will live in infamy!

My Lucky Thinking Cap is missing! And I know who took it. That snake in the grass, Lydia Pinkus. I saw her eyeing it when she was here earlier.

I foolishly left the door unlocked when I went to the market, and she must've snuck in while I was gone and stolen it in a scurrilous attempt to rob me of my mental acuity.

But her devilish plot will be foiled! I'll get my cap back, if it's the last thing I do.

Love 'n' snuggles from
DaddyO

To: Jausten
From: Shoptillyoudrop
Subject: Oreo Therapy

Of all the idiotic nonsense. Daddy's misplaced his "Lucky Thinking Cap," and he's convinced Lydia Pinkus stole it. How absurd. He's out "casing her town house" for evidence right now.

Honestly, I bet that cap is sitting right here in the house somewhere. Although I must admit, I've looked everywhere and can't find it.

Must run, honey. Am in desperate need of Oreo Therapy—

XOXO,
Mom

Chapter 8

The next few days passed by in a blur of grief. Not over Dean, of course. I barely knew the guy. And what little I knew, I sort of hated.

No, I was mourning the loss of my five grand and all the goodies it would have bought. There'd be no new TV in my future. No new used car. No Platinum Level Fudge-of-the-Month Club.

I returned to my old life with its anemic checking account, dreaming of things that might have been and wondering, not incidentally, why the heck I'd never heard from Phil Angelides's cutie pie nephew, Jim.

My life was in a sinkhole, all right. And I was not alone.

I was certain Daddy would drive Mom crazy searching for his Lucky Thinking Cap. It was so typical of him to assume Lydia Pinkus had stolen it. Daddy has always had it in for Lydia, always ready to lay the blame for anything amiss in his life at Lydia's size EEE feet.

Something told me Mom was in for a whole lot more Oreo therapy in the days to come.

Even worse was poor Prozac. Ever since the shoot she'd been moping around, in a deep funk over her aborted career as a TV commercial star. Never had I seen her so glum. Gone was the kitty who lived to claw my cashmere sweaters to shreds, to snag the pepperoni from my pizza, and to hog my pillow at night. In her place was a sluggish shell of a cat, lying listlessly on the sofa with soulful Brando eyes and piteous little mews that seemed to be saying: *I coulda been a contenda.*

I only hoped she'd snap out of it eventually. In the meanwhile, I was spoiling her rotten with chicken tenders and belly rubs. (The latter received with none of her usual writhing in ecstasy—just a glazed look in her eyes and a dispirited thumping of her tail.)

Dean's murder, of course, had been all over the news.

Toxicology tests had shown that he'd been poisoned with Fragrance-Free Raid. Apparently, the killer had given the Skinny Kitty a spritz of the stuff when Nikki left it unattended to grab a bite at the buffet.

So far the police hadn't named any suspects. But my mind was buzzing with them.

First and foremost on my list was Deedee. Hadn't she returned to the studio, boasting that she'd gotten rid of Dean forever? And what about Ian? He certainly had motive. Dean had been threatening to torpedo his career.

And finally, there was Zeke. Anyone could see the young writer detested his cousin. With Dean out of the way, Zeke would have an unencumbered path to Linda, the woman he so obviously adored.

The one person I never thought the cops would suspect was me.

Which is why I was so stunned when, a few days after the murder, there was a knock on my door and I opened it to find two homicide detectives standing on my doorstep.

Both wore ill-fitting suits and not a trace of a smile.

Flashing me their badges, they asked if they might have a few words with me about Dean's murder. Reluctantly, I ushered them in, wishing I were wearing something a bit more confidence inspiring than my grungy sweats with the grape jelly stain on the sleeve.

Settled side by side on my sofa, they asked me how well I'd known the deceased (not very) and whether or not I'd liked him (not much).

"Dean was sort of difficult," I explained. "A bit of a temper."

"So we've heard," said one of the cops, a bulldog of a guy with a barrel chest and a most disconcerting scar on his cheek. "In fact," he said, checking his notes, "it appears that shortly before his murder, Mr. Oliver threatened you with a lawsuit."

"He said he was going to sue you for every cent you were worth," added his partner.

I saw where this was going.

"You're not accusing me of killing him to stop his lawsuit, are you?"

"We're not accusing you of anything," Scarface assured me. "Not yet, anyway."

"Do you have any witnesses who can confirm

you were on the soundstage while the poisoned cat food was left unattended?" his partner asked. "That would be from approximately eleven thirty a.m. to noon."

I thought back to the day of the murder, when Nikki, having prepped the cat food for the final shot, had shown up at the soundstage to grab a snack. Linda had been with me up until then, but she and Zeke soon left me to go to the buffet table, leaving me all by my lonesome, up a creek without an alibi.

"No," I admitted. "I was alone with my cat."

Prozac looked up from where she had been moping on my keyboard.

I was almost a star, you know.

I saw the cops exchange a look. For all they knew, I could have easily trotted across the hall and blasted the Skinny Kitty with Raid.

"Just don't leave town," they warned me as they got up to go.

"Oh, hell," I moaned once I'd shut the door behind them. I was a murder suspect.

Again.

Yes, this wasn't the first time. Just last year I'd been a suspect in a murder at a teenage beauty pageant (a harrowing saga you can read all about in *Death by Tiara*, now available in paperback and on all the usual e-gizmos).

"Darn it, Pro," I sighed, slumping down onto the sofa, still warm from the cops' fannies. "What am I going to do?"

A world-weary glance from her perch on the keyboard.

Personally, I'm thinking of joining a convent.

I'd just gone to the kitchen for a restorative dose of Oreos when my frazzled nerves were shaken by another knock at my door. Had the cops changed their mind and returned to arrest me on the spot?

But thank heavens it was only Lance, who, unlike me, was in the sunniest of moods.

"Who were those two guys I saw walking down the path?" he asked, sailing into the living room.

"The police. They think I might have killed Dean Oliver."

"I don't believe it!" he cried, horrified.

"I know. It's awful, isn't it?"

"Is that what you wore to talk to the police? Those grungy sweats with the grape jelly stain on the sleeve? It's no wonder they suspect you of murder."

"Hey, a little less fashion critique and a little more sympathy, if you don't mind."

"Of course, hon," he said, taking my hand in his. "You know I worry about you. If you get suspected of one more murder, we're gonna have to buy you a getaway car." Then, seeing the stricken look in my eyes, he added, "But don't worry, sweetie. I'm sure they'll find the real killer. And besides, you've got to look on the bright side."

"Which is?"

"I was nowhere near the studio at the time of the murder and have an airtight alibi!"

"Yeah, that's the bright side, all right."

"Well, here's something that'll really cheer you up."

"You're leaving me alone and going back to your apartment?"

"Now, now, we mustn't be bitchy just because

we're a suspect in a murder case. Guess where I just came from? Lunch with Deedee! She signed Mamie on as a client! She says she's going to make her the most famous show biz dog since Lassie. And she practically guaranteed her a co-starring role in a new Brad Pitt movie! Is that unbelievable, or what?"

"It truly is unbelievable," I said, with the brightest fake smile I could muster. "So you had lunch with her, huh?"

"At the Peninsula. It was absolutely glorious!"

"She stick you with the check?"

"As it happened, she forgot her wallet, so I picked up the tab. But she assured me she'd pay me back with my first paycheck. Well, must dash and tell Mamie the good news. She'll be so excited. And try not to worry about that murder thing, hon. Once Mamie lands this part with Brad Pitt, I'll get you the finest lawyer money can buy. Ciao for now!"

And off he dashed, with three of my Oreos.

I was just reaching into the bag to grab one for myself when I flashed back on what the cops said right before they left. Those three miserable words:

"Don't leave town."

This murder could take months to solve. If I couldn't leave town, I'd have to kiss my Hawaiian vacation good-bye.

No way was that going to happen.

Somehow, someway, I would find the killer in time to soak up the Maui sun.

In the meanwhile, I did the next best thing and soaked up some Oreos.

Chapter 9

As luck would have it, I got a chance to start my investigation the very next day.

While leafing through the *L.A. Times*, I saw there was to be a memorial service for Dean that morning at St. Paul's Church in Westwood.

And so, after an hour cranking out ideas for the Touch-Me-Not toilet ("Look, Ma! No hands!"), I gussied myself up in my funereal best: black slacks, black tee, black blazer, and my one and only pair of Manolos. True, the T-shirt, a Home Shopping Channel gift from my mom, sported the slogan "Crazy Cat Lady," but nobody need know about that if I kept my blazer buttoned.

After wrestling my mop of curls into a sedate bob, I popped on a pair of silver hoop earrings, grabbed my purse, and headed for the door.

"See you later, hon," I called out to Prozac.

She didn't even look up from where she was sprawled out on the sofa, next to a pair of panty hose I'd left for her to play with. Normally, they'd have been in ribbons by now, but today she'd totally ignored them.

Poor thing was still deep in her funk.

I got in the Corolla and drove over to St. Paul's, ruing the day I'd ever gotten her involved in that damn Skinny Kitty commercial.

Trying to find a parking spot in Westwood is like panning for gold in the Sahara. After circling around for what seemed like eons, I finally managed to nab a spot about six blocks from St. Paul's and clomped over to the church, cursing my Manolos every step of the way.

I headed inside and was surprised to find the large, wood-beamed chapel almost full.

Somehow I hadn't pictured Dean as the kind of guy with friends.

All the mourners were seated toward the front of the church, leaving the last few rows empty.

I spotted Linda up front, with Zeke at her side, his shoulder almost touching hers. I bet he was one happy camper, sitting so close to his heart-throb.

A few rows behind Linda, the Pink Panther was seated—for once, all in black—her surgically enhanced profile peeking out from under a wide-brimmed black hat.

I slipped into the last pew, empty except for a guy with a shopping bag in his lap.

Up at the pulpit, the priest was in the middle of his eulogy.

"Although I didn't know Dean well," he was saying, "he was a generous contributor to the church building fund and a dynamic presence in the congregation."

And by "dynamic presence," he undoubtedly meant "pain in the butt."

"The person I really knew well was Dean's wife, Linda," the priest went on, shooting her a sorrowful smile. "My heart and prayers go out to her in her time of need."

A soft murmur of approval rippled through the audience.

He then asked if anyone wanted to say a few words about Dean.

A few people got up to speak, all of them friends of Linda, all of whom spouted some token niceties about Dean and then, like the priest, went on to talk with great feeling about what a wonderful wife Linda had been.

In death, as in life, Linda was the popular one in that marriage.

After a while, I glanced over and was shocked to see the guy next to me pulling out a bottle of champagne from his shopping bag.

Unlike the other mourners, he was not dressed in black, but in jeans and a sweatshirt, a baseball cap clamped on a headful of frizzy red hair.

Aware of my glance, he sidled over next to me and opened the twist-top bottle.

"A bit of bubbly?" he whispered, pouring some into a plastic glass.

I shook my head no.

"More for me then," he said, taking a healthy glug.

"You realize that this is a funeral service, right?" I whispered.

"Yep," he nodded. "I just dropped by to make sure Dean was really dead." Now he reached into his shopping bag and pulled out a pastry. "Care for a cheese puff?"

Honestly. Did he really think I was crass enough to eat a cheese puff at a funeral service?

(It was delicious, by the way.)

"Artie Lembeck," he said, handing me his business card. "You know that diet cat food Dean claimed he invented?"

"Skinny Kitty," I nodded.

"He didn't invent it. I did. The bum tricked me into signing over the rights to the recipe. Sold it to him for only five hundred bucks. Then Dean turned around, ramped up production, and started making a fortune on it. Cut me off at the knees. "So here's to Dean," he whispered, holding up his champagne glass. "May he rot in hell forever."

At which point, a woman a few rows in front of us turned around to give us an angry "Shhhh."

But I hardly noticed, boggled as I was over Artie's little tirade.

Quite the eulogy, wasn't it?

It was enough to make me wonder if I'd just been sharing a pew with Dean's killer.

I left Artie glugging down the rest of his champagne and clomped the six long blocks back to my Corolla.

The priest had wrapped up the funeral service by inviting us all to a reception at Linda's house. And now, armed with directions I'd picked up from a church attendant, I got in my Corolla and took off.

As I drove, I thought about my chat with Artie. The guy clearly detested Dean and was thrilled to see him dead. But had he been the one to spritz that fatal blast of Raid?

Was it possible Artie knew about the shoot and went to the studio to have it out with Dean? Had he overheard Dean's temper tantrum? Had he then hidden in some empty office, waiting until he saw Nikki leave the kitchen, and dashed in to poison the Skinny Kitty?

I had to admit it seemed pretty unlikely. But anything was possible. Especially with a guy who brought cheese puffs to a funeral.

I found Dean and Linda's house in a modest pocket of Westwood, on a tree-lined street filled with 1930s bungalows. It was a charming cottage, tasteful and understated.

I figured Linda was the one who'd picked it out.

I headed up a brick pathway lined with roses, past an open wrought iron gate. The front door was unlocked, so I let myself into the living room where Linda sat in an armchair, surrounded by well wishers. Zeke stood on guard behind her chair in a dark blue suit, his sandy hair flopping onto his forehead, his cheeks flushed with excitement. He was trying to look somber, but I could tell he was loving every minute of his new role as Linda's protector.

I looked around the living room, with its original sconces and crown molding. On an end table beside me sat a framed picture of Dean and Linda taken years ago on a sandy beach. I picked it up to get a closer look. Dean smiled winningly into the camera, his hair free of gel and blowing in the wind, not a trace of the arrogance I'd come to know. Linda, looking boyish in a one-piece bathing suit, smiled up at him adoringly.

By now, the crowd around Linda had thinned, and I walked over to pay my respects.

"Jaine," Linda said, with a wan smile. "How nice of you to come."

Poor Linda. Her face was mottled; behind her harlequin glasses her eyes were red-rimmed with tears.

"I'm so sorry about Dean," I said.

And at that moment, of course, I was sorry. Sorry he was dead, sorry Linda was in so much pain, and most of all, sorry I was a suspect in this whole darn mess.

"It's been a terrible shock," Zeke said, still trying his best to look like someone who gave a damn.

"Is there anything I can do to help?" I asked.

"We'll be fine," Zeke assured me. Accent on the *we*.

"Please help yourself to something at the buffet," Linda added, pointing to an adjacent dining room.

A fresh batch of mourners had lined up behind me, so after offering my sympathies one final time, I skedaddled over to the dining room, where I was happy to find a lovely spread of deli cold cuts, pasta salad, kosher pickles, and assorted cookies.

Still a bit full from the cheese puffs I ate at the funeral (if you must know, I had three), I reined myself in and made myself the weensiest roast beef sandwich, with just a smidgen of pasta salad and the tiniest sliver of a cookie.

As I stood there, scarfing down my chow, I listened to the chatter of the mourners around me.

Poor Linda. Such a wonderful woman.

How she put up with Dean, I'll never know.

I'm surprised they had the service in a church. The only thing Dean ever worshipped was himself.

Ouch.

I only hoped Dean couldn't hear us in hell.

I was just polishing off my sandwich when I looked up and saw Nikki Banks walk in the front door and make her way over to Linda. Without her food stylist's apron, she looked surprisingly sophisticated in a black sweater and slacks.

Linda shot her the same wan smile she'd given me, chatted for a bit, then waved her over to the buffet.

"Hey, Nikki," I called out as she approached. "Good to see you. Sorry it's under such sad circumstances."

"I know," Nikki tsked. "I tried to make it to the memorial service, but I was stuck at work. I'm styling a burger shoot. God, it's tough keeping lettuce crispy."

Then, turning to the buffet, she cried, "Food! Wonderful! I didn't have time for lunch."

"The roast beef's great," I said.

She looked down at the spread and frowned. "Parsley garnish," she said, picking up a sprig from the deli platter. "How passé."

Then she turned to me and grinned. "Sorry. Occupational hazard of being a stylist."

As she whipped together a turkey on rye, I decided to toss a few questions her way.

"I still can't get over what happened to Dean," I said.

"It's so awful," Nikki agreed, spreading some mustard on her rye. "And I feel so guilty. If I hadn't left the cat food alone in the kitchen, he'd still be alive today."

"You mustn't blame yourself. You had no idea there was a killer in the studio. Speaking of which, did you happen to notice anyone hanging around in the corridor when you left the kitchen?"

I eagerly awaited her reply, wondering if perhaps she'd spotted Artie, the vengeful inventor.

But, alas, she'd seen nothing.

"Like I told the police, I didn't see a soul. And I didn't see anyone leaving the soundstage while I was at the buffet, either."

"What about Linda and Zeke? Were they with you the whole time you were at the buffet?"

"No, they wandered off. But I wasn't paying attention to anyone. I was too busy worrying about whether Dean would have another hissy fit before the shoot was done.

"What a horrible day that was," she said, arranging some pasta salad on her plate in a perfect mound. "And to top everything off, I lost my ring. Remember the pink hibiscus ring you liked so much? I took it off to wash my hands at the kitchen sink and forgot to put it back on. When I called the studio to see if anyone found it, they insisted no one had turned it in. But I don't trust that dingbat receptionist. If you ask me, she's probably wearing it as we speak."

I remembered the receptionist with the big hair

and bigger attitude and figured Nikki might well be right.

"Do you have any idea who may have wanted to kill Dean?" I asked, easing the conversation away from costume jewelry and back to the murder.

"Take a number," Nikki said, swallowing a mouthful of turkey sandwich. "Dean made enemies like I make brownies—by the dozen."

I briefly wondered if Nikki could have done it, but it seemed hard to believe she'd want to kill Dean just because he was hard to work with. If everybody ran around killing impossible bosses, half of corporate America would be tucked away in their crypts.

Having come to a dead end with Nikki, I was debating whether or not to reach for another cookie when I suddenly became aware of a wave of whispers rippling through the room.

I looked around and saw everyone's eyes riveted on the front door, where Camille Townsend, aka the Pink Panther, had just made a grand entrance, her hourglass figure swathed in designer black, her wide-brimmed hat cutting a dramatic swash across her cheekbones.

Linda's face hardened at the sight of her.

Now the whispers stopped, and the house was so quiet, you could hear a kosher pickle drop.

As the Panther tottered over to Linda on her Louboutins, Zeke rushed out from behind Linda's chair, papa bear protecting his cub.

But Linda stopped him.

"No, Zeke," she said, standing up. "I'll take care of this."

The Panther would have to be brain dead not to sense the hostility oozing her way.

"I'm so sorry for your loss," she said, smiling stiffly.

"Really?" Linda shot back. "How about sleeping with my husband? You sorry about that, too?"

"I don't know what you're talking about," the Panther said, blushing under the brim of her hat.

"Everyone knows you two were having an affair. You may have made a fool of me while Dean was alive, but not anymore. Please leave. You're not welcome here."

The Panther, clearly unaccustomed to being called out in public, lobbed Linda a look of sheer malice and stormed off.

Linda watched her go, a satisfied smile on her face.

Well, whaddaya know? It looked like mousy little Linda had just sprouted a pair of claws.

Chapter 10

The next day, I decided to pay a return visit to Kleinman Productions for a tête-à-tête with the receptionist. As I recalled, she had a peripheral view of the hallway from her desk. And I was hoping she might have looked up long enough from *Entertainment Weekly* to see the killer sprinting into the studio kitchen.

This time when I showed up, I found her with her nose buried in *The Hollywood Reporter*, reading an article about Beyoncé.

I hadn't paid much attention to her the day of the shoot, so caught up had I been in my dreams of Prozac's stardom. But today I took in her jet black bubble of hair, goth-white skin, and squinty eyes circled in liner so thick she looked like a punk raccoon.

I checked her fingers for hibiscus rings but saw only a couple of silver snakes slithering up to her knuckles.

"Can I help you?" she asked, tearing herself away from her magazine.

A rhinestone-lettered necklace dangling in her cleavage informed me that her name was Angie.

"I sure hope so, Angie. I was here last week for the Skinny Kitty commercial."

"Yeah, I remember you. First you parked in Mr. Kleinman's parking spot. And then your cat screwed up the commercial."

"Guilty as charged," I said, just barely managing to fake a smile.

"So what do you want?" she snapped.

Looked like somebody skipped receptionist school the day they were teaching The Polite Way to Greet Visitors.

"Actually, I was wondering if you could answer a few questions about Dean Oliver's murder."

At which point, I could practically feel a curtain slam down between us.

"Forget it. I already talked to the cops, and that was bad enough. I didn't like their attitude, not one bit. Just because a gal has a DUI or two, that doesn't make her a criminal, for heaven's sake. And that shoplifting charge was never proven!"

"I'm sure it wasn't," I said in my silkiest voice. "And I'm not a cop," I hastened to assure her. "I'm a part-time semi-professional PI."

"I thought you were an animal handler."

"Like I said, the PI thing is just part-time."

"Forget it. I'm not talking to anybody." And with that, she hunched her shoulders and went back to Beyoncé.

"I really need your help," I said, throwing myself

on her mercy. "The cops think I might have killed Dean."

I gave her my most beseeching look, the kind Pro gives me when she's all out of bacon bits.

Without batting an eyelash, she replied: "That's too bad, honey. Better lawyer up."

A regular heart of gold, huh?

And once again she returned to *The Hollywood Reporter*, moving her lips every syllable of the way.

I was about to give up and head out the door when I got an idea.

"I see you're reading about Beyoncé," I said. "You a fan?"

For the first time, I saw a hint of a smile on her pinched little face.

"Totally! I just love her."

"She's coming to Staples Center in a few weeks," I pointed out. A fun fact I'd picked up from an ad on the back of the magazine.

"Yeah, I know," Angie sighed. "It's sold out already."

"It just so happens I work security at Staples Center."

"Really?" The raccoon eyes lit up.

"You betcha. I get free passes to all the concerts."

"You do?"

"Absolutely. I can get you in to see Beyoncé's show."

"You can?"

"Sure!" By now, my lies were flowing like ketchup on the Fourth of July. "All you have to do is answer a few questions."

"Omigod! That's wonderful." Then her brow furrowed in suspicion. "Let me see the passes first."

What a distrustful little worm.

"I don't get them until the concert opens," I said, hanging tough.

"Oh, all right," she caved. "What do you want to know?"

"Just this. Did you happen to see anyone, anyone at all, slip into the studio kitchen between eleven thirty and noon on the day of the murder?"

"Nope," she said.

"You sure?"

"Absolutely. Mr. Kleinman went off to a meeting, so I skipped out to have a pedicure. I wasn't even here."

Foo. All that lying for nothing.

"So you have no idea who might have poisoned the Skinny Kitty that day?"

"Sure. I know who did it."

What a delightful young woman!

"Who?"

"The agent. That Deedee lady."

"Really? What makes you so sure?"

"When I was coming back from the nail salon, she was out in the parking lot, talking on her cell phone. And I heard her say, 'Don't worry. I know exactly how to do it. When I'm through, Dean won't ever bother me again.' "

Whoa. Talk about your damning testimony.

"Did you tell that to the police?"

"I sure did. I'm surprised they haven't arrested her yet."

"Thanks so much," I said, starting for the door. "I really appreciate your help."

"Hey, wait!" she called out after me. "What about the free concert passes?"

"I'll drop them off as soon as I get them."

With a cheery wave good-bye, I scooted out to the parking lot, making a mental note to send her a Beyoncé CD for her troubles.

In the meanwhile, I had more important matters to attend to.

Jumping in my Corolla, I headed over to see Deedee, my kitten-doping, bill-shirking agent.

Something told me she might have just added "cold-blooded killer" to her résumé.

At first I thought I got Deedee's address wrong.

When I walked up to what was supposed to be her office, all I saw was a Chinese restaurant. A dingy hole in the wall called the House of Wonton.

I got there in the middle of the lunch rush, which at the House of Wonton wasn't much of a rush. Only about a third of the tables were filled.

A middle-aged hostess in what looked like a capri set straight from the Home Shopping Channel held out a menu.

"Just one?" she asked.

"Actually, I'm not here for lunch. I think I'm at the wrong address. I'm looking for Deedee Walker, the animal agent."

"You're at the right place," the hostess replied. Was it my imagination, or did she roll her eyes at the mention of Deedee's name? "She's here. Down the hall, past the kitchen and the ladies' room."

Deedee worked out of a Chinese restaurant? Clearly, my agent to the animal stars was going through some hard times.

I walked through the dimly lit restaurant with its

cracked leather booths, down a hallway redolent of fried onions, past a steamy kitchen filled with shouting cooks and clanging pots. Then, just beyond the ladies' room, as promised, I found a door with Deedee's name on it.

Poking my head inside, I saw Deedee sitting at a desk awash with papers, Chinese take-out cartons, and a stack of *Parrots Today* magazines. I figured the bright green critter on the cover was Deedee's star parrot, Pierre.

Behind her, the walls were lined with framed photos of cats, dogs, birds, and the occasional hamster.

"Hi, Deedee," I said, stepping inside.

"Oh, God," she moaned, staring glassy-eyed into space. "I'm doomed." Her face ashen, she held out the shards of a fortune cookie in her hand. "Do you know what this means?" she asked.

"You just had Chinese for lunch?"

"There was no fortune in my fortune cookie. That's a very bad omen." Another moan as she stared down at the cookie shards.

"I just know the police are going to arrest me!" she wailed, her bangles jangling in a Greek chorus of despair. "They heard what I said about Dean before he was killed, that I'd 'taken care of him forever.' And I could tell by the way they were looking at me that they think I'm the one who sprayed his cat food with Raid."

At that point, I couldn't help thinking the same thing.

"But I'm innocent!" she cried, as if reading my thoughts. "I never went near the damn cat food. After Dean made his ridiculous accusations against me—which were totally false, by the way; I have never ever so much as cheated my clients out of a single penny—I went out to the parking lot and called Emmy, my Reiki healer. She gave me instructions on how to exorcise Dean's evil spirit from my body. That's what I meant when I said I'd taken care of him forever. You believe me, don't you?"

"Of course," I fibbed, still not convinced that she wasn't the killer. Or that she hadn't been cheating her clients. I hadn't forgotten that humungous bill she'd saddled me with at the Peninsula.

"I'd never hurt anyone," Deedee insisted. "Ever. Reiki is all about channeling positive energy. Have you ever tried it?"

"No, I haven't."

My preferred method of channeling positive energy, FYI, has always been chocolate.

"Emmy is the most wonderful Reiki healer. And she's fabulous with weight loss. You really ought to give her a try to trim down those hips of yours. She works with animals, too. If you don't mind my saying, I think darling Prozac could use a little help in the anger management department."

Of course, I did mind her saying, especially that crack about my hips, but I swallowed my irritation.

"What a wonderful idea!" I chirped. "Do you have her card?"

"In fact, I do," she said, rummaging around in her desk. "Here it is!" she said, handing me a business card stained with what I suspected was a blot of soy sauce.

I'd be contacting Emmy, all right, not for weight loss or animal anger management, but to check

Deedee's alibi and find out if she was really on the phone while the Skinny Kitty was left unattended.

"Speaking of the murder," I said, cranking the conversation back to where I wanted it, "I don't suppose you noticed anyone slipping into the kitchen during the break."

"No. Like I told the police, I was out in the parking lot."

"Was Ian with you the entire time?"

"I don't know for sure. I thought I saw him in his car, slugging back some gin, but I was so busy exorcising Dean from my psyche, I lost track of him."

She gazed at me earnestly.

"When I'm in a Reiki healing state, I see nothing. I hear nothing. That's why it's so effective. You really ought to give it a try, Jaine. Your hips will thank you."

If she made one more crack about my hips, I'd swat her with a copy of *Parrots Today*.

But I refrained from physical violence and managed to stay focused on the matter at hand.

"Dean was pretty rough on Ian that day. He threatened to ruin his career. Do you think Ian might have killed him to shut him up?"

"Far be it from me to cast suspicion on anyone—I know how painful that can be—but rumor has it Ian's desperate for work. He really couldn't afford to have Dean running around bad-mouthing him."

"So you think he's the killer?"

"Possibly. But why speculate about Ian when it's me the police suspect? Oh, Jaine! I don't know what I'm going to do. What if they haul me off to jail? I'm way too attractive to go unmolested."

Hello? Earth to Deedee. Have you looked in a mirror lately?

I felt fairly certain that a fifty-something woman with a spare set of chins would be safe from unwanted advances behind bars.

"But I've got to stop panicking," Deedee said, taking a deep breath. "I must remain calm, at peace with my inner chakras. I must drink from life's pool of serenity. I must bathe in the shower of love. I must—

"Holy Mackerel!" she cried, jumping up and pointing at something over my shoulder.

I whirled around, thinking maybe the killer had shown up to dash off a quickie double homicide.

But no. I now saw Deedee was pointing at a shiny brown bug scampering up her wall.

"Damn the House of Wonton and their miserable cockroaches!"

She reached into her purse and pulled out a can of Raid, blasting the critter to oblivion.

When my heart finally stopped fibrillating, I thanked Deedee for her time and headed out to my Corolla. It wasn't until I was back in the bright light of day that I realized the significance of what I'd just seen.

Deedee carried around a can of Raid in her purse! If she was the killer, maybe she didn't even need the Raid in the studio kitchen.

Maybe she came prepared with her very own murder weapon.

Chapter 11

"**P**rozac, honey. I'm begging you. Just have a teeny bite."

I was sitting in bed with Prozac later that afternoon, trying to hand-feed her freshly sautéed chicken tenders. But she was lost in another world.

"Fatty." He called me "fatty." I may never eat again.

"You've got to eat something, honey. Or you'll waste away."

If only I had a working index finger, I could be a bulimic.

"Yummy chicken!" I crooned, taking a bite. "Yummy, yummy, yummy!"

And indeed it was yummy. Before I knew it, I'd scarfed down three tenders.

Roused from her reverie, Prozac lobbed me a look of stern disapproval.

Clearly, I've learned all my bad eating habits from you.

Turning away, she gazed at the TV just in time to see a cat food commercial. She watched in disgust as a computer-generated cat did the cha-cha.

Feh. You call that acting?

"Oh, Pro," I moaned. "What am I going to do with you?"

I'd called Dr. Madeline earlier that afternoon, thinking maybe she'd give Prozac a kitty antidepressant. But Dr. M. explained that antidepressants are used to treat anxiety in animals, not depression. So there'd be no Prozac for Prozac.

Dr. M. advised me to lavish Prozac with even more attention than I was already giving her, which hardly seemed possible. That cat gets more attention than a stripper at a bachelor party.

Now I thought about Emmy, Deedee's Reiki healer. Deedee said she worked with animals. I sincerely doubted Prozac would respond to any New Age mumbo jumbo, but I had nothing to lose. Besides, it would be a good excuse to meet Emmy and check out Deedee's alibi.

I made a mental note to call her and was just about to bite into another chicken tender when there was a knock on my door.

Leaving Prozac glaring at the TV, I shuffled off to get it.

It was Lance, who came sailing in like an extra from *West Side Story*, in tight jeans and a black leather jacket.

"What do you think?" he asked, whirling around. "I'm going for the bad boy look."

"If you're going for bad boy, I'd lose the ascot."

"Don't be silly, Jaine," he said, fluffing a foulard ascot around his neck. "I'm a bad boy with impeccable taste. I thought I'd wear this outfit to Mamie's Brad Pitt movie audition. I have a feeling Brad is into black leather.

"I can see it now," he said, gazing off into an imaginary future. "I walk into the room, and Brad and I lock eyeballs. Cupid shoots his arrow, and before you know it, it's pffft to 'Brangelina' and hello to 'Brance'!"

"I hate to bust your bubble, Lance, but Brad Pitt isn't gay."

"Maybe not in your fantasies."

"And besides," I pointed out, "he probably won't even be there."

"Don't be such a Debbie Downer. Even if Brad doesn't show up, you never know who will be there. I've always wanted to date someone in the movies. Other than an usher, of course. And who knows? Maybe I'll get discovered. Frankly, I've always thought I'd make a fabulous actor."

The next thing I knew, he'd be nominating himself for an Academy Award.

"I saw Deedee today," I said, trying to tether him back down to earth. "She's terrified she's going to be arrested for Dean's murder."

"I know," Lance said. "I spoke to her earlier. I've been worried sick."

Whaddaya know? A little empathy from Mr. Moi.

"You think she can work on my contract from jail?"

So much for empathy.

"Lance, for once in your life, can you think of somebody other than yourself?"

"What're you talking about? I'm always thinking of others. Why, just last week I donated an old tuxedo to a homeless shelter."

"How very thoughtful."

"Anyhow," he said, plopping down on my sofa, "I just hope this whole murder thing gets wrapped up soon. Do you have any idea who might have done it?"

"I hate to say it, but so far, my leading suspect is Deedee. She had motive, and a can of Raid."

"Your leading suspect? Don't tell me you're doing your PI impersonation again."

"It's not an impersonation, and yes, I'm doing it."

"For crying out loud, Jaine. You almost got bumped off last year, tracking down the killer at that beauty pageant. Did you not learn anything from that whole experience?"

"How to tape a bathing suit to your tush so you don't get a wedgie."

"Seriously, Jaine," he said, his eyes wide with concern. "You've got to promise me you'll be careful."

"I promise."

"Do you want my help? I could come along and protect you. Along with my impeccable fashion sense, I've got remarkably keen powers of deduction."

Oh, glug. The last thing I needed was Lance playing Poirot at my side.

"Thanks, Lance. But I can handle this."

"Just don't get yourself hurt. I don't know what I'd do without you, sweetie."

With that he took me in his arms and wrapped me in a fuzzy bear hug.

See? Moments like these are why I put up with the guy.

"Oops. I'm crushing my ascot," he said, breaking away from our embrace. "Must run. I'm off to the salon to add more highlights to my hair. I can't decide which color to go with: Sun Kissed or Ash Blond. What do you think?"

"Ash Blond."

"Sun Kissed, it is!"

And off he sailed, my aggravating bestie.

I headed back to the bedroom where I found Prozac staring at the bedspread, her chicken tenders still untouched.

New Age or not, I really had to give that Reiki healing thing a shot.

As I settled down next to Pro, scratching her behind the ears, the phone rang.

I picked it up to hear:"Hey, Jaine. It's me. Jim Angelides."

Omigosh. Phil's cutie pie nephew. I'd just about given up on him.

"I know it's the last minute, but I was wondering if you're free for dinner tomorrow."

Forget about it. Absolutely not. I knew the rules. I couldn't possibly let him think I was available at such short notice. I'd play it cool and tell him I was sorry but I had other plans.

You know where this is going, right?

"Pick me up at seven," were the words I actually uttered.

Maybe when the Reiki healer showed up, she could work on my backbone.

YOU'VE GOT MAIL!

To: Jausten
From: DaddyO
Subject: Still Missing

Dearest Lambchop—

Your diligent daddy has been hard at work trying to memorize the Scrabble dictionary, but it's just not the same without my Lucky Thinking Cap, which, I'm sorry to say, is still missing.

I know Lydia has it stashed away somewhere, but so far I've had no opportunity to retrieve it. Unfortunately the battle-axe has recently installed a high-tech security system, thwarting my efforts to bust into her stronghold and do a thorough search of the premises.

But today, at last, I got a lucky break. As I was driving back from the market with a fresh supply of gherkins, I passed Lydia's townhouse and saw her taking out her trash. And she had a mighty shifty look in her eyes when she was doing it.

Dollars to doughnuts my thinking cap is sitting there in her garbage, along with her prune pits, dental floss, and empty Metamucil jars.

And I intend to rescue it ASAP!

Love 'n' snuggles from
DaddyO

To: Jausten
From: Shoptillyoudrop

Good heavens!

Daddy thinks Lydia has tossed his Lucky Thinking Cap in her garbage can. Did you ever hear of anything so idiotic?

XOXO,
Mom

To: Jausten
From: DaddyO
Subject: A Tad Disappointed

Dearest Lambchop—

For some unfathomable reason, your mother is being very unsupportive. She thinks the battle-axe walks on water, and refuses to believe Lydia had anything to do with the disappearance of my Lucky Thinking Cap. Moreover, she says she refuses to cook me dinner if I go looking for my cap in Lydia's garbage.

I must admit I'm a tad disappointed in her.

Oh, well. Mom's planning to make meat loaf tonight, and you know how I feel about your mother's meat loaf. So I'll just wait until after she's asleep to go out on my garbage raid.

Love 'n' hugs from
Your determined
DaddyO

Chapter 12

I had a hard time digesting my cinnamon raisin bagel the next morning, having been foolish enough to open my e-mails and read about Daddy's plans to go rooting around in Lydia Pinkus's garbage.

Honestly, I was so distraught, I could barely finish my second bagel.

But eventually, I regained my equilibrium and called to make an appointment with Emmy, the Reiki healer, who agreed to stop by my apartment later that week.

I did some heavy-duty gulping when she told me her fee—a hundred bucks an hour—but at that stage I was willing to try anything to get my forlorn furball back in good spirits.

"Good news, Pro," I said when I hung up. "The Reiki healer is coming to see us."

Prozac just stared down at a spot under my chintz armchair.

Kill that dust bunny for me, will you? I don't have the energy.

If left to my own devices, I would have spent the rest of the day giving Prozac belly rubs. Or primping for my upcoming date with Jim. Or perhaps shopping for some strappy sandals to wear on my Hawaiian vacation. But I had to focus on the murder and clear my name if I intended to actually go on said vacation.

So I decided to pay a visit to Linda.

I hadn't forgotten how angry she'd been during her dramatic face-off with the Pink Panther at Dean's funeral reception. Angry enough, I now wondered, to have doctored her husband's cat food with a fatal dose of Raid?

It was time to find out.

I drove over to Linda's place in Westwood, hoping she'd be there when I showed up.

But, alas, no one came to the door when I rang the bell.

So I settled down to wait for her in my Corolla with a free copy of *War and Peace* I'd downloaded on my phone. It was going to be quite a challenge reading *War and Peace* three sentences at a time on the phone's tiny screen, but I was up for it. It was a book I'd always meant to tackle. And now was the perfect opportunity.

I clicked open the book and began to read:

> *War and Peace*
> *By Leo Tolstoy*

I was really quite proud of myself, using this otherwise wasted time to expand my mind, to broaden my horizons, to stretch my literary muscles—

"Jaine! Are you okay?"

Someone was tapping at my car window.

My eyes flew open, and I felt drool on my chin. Good heavens. I must've dozed off somewhere on the copyright page.

I looked up to see Linda standing outside my Corolla, peering down at me through her harlequin glasses.

"I saw you lying there with your mouth open, and I thought maybe you'd passed out."

"No, no. Just resting," I said, surreptitiously wiping away my chin drool. "Actually, I came to talk to you."

"Sure. Come on in the house."

I followed her into her charming bungalow, where she kicked off her shoes and curled up on her living room sofa, gesturing for me to take a seat on the other end.

"Just got back from my therapist," she said with a sigh. "These past few days haven't been easy."

"I can imagine."

"You want anything to eat? I've got deli leftovers from the funeral reception in the fridge."

Actually, I would have liked nothing better than to scarf down some cold roast beef, but Linda seemed so wiped out, I didn't have the heart to put her to the trouble.

"No, thanks. I'm fine."

"Thank God. I don't think I can manage the trek to the kitchen." She sank deeper into the sofa cushions, her arms limp at her sides. "So how can I help you?"

"Actually, I'm investigating Dean's murder. The police think I may have killed him, and I'm trying to clear my name."

"Why on earth would the police think you killed Dean?"

"Because he was threatening me with a lawsuit."

"But Dean was always threatening to sue people," Linda said with a dismissive wave. "Half the time he was just blowing off steam."

"Well, the police are taking his threat seriously, so I'm doing what I can to track down the killer."

"Anything I can do to help, just ask. The sooner Dean's killer is caught, the happier I'll be."

"For starters, did you see anyone slip out of the soundstage while Nikki left the Skinny Kitty unattended?"

"No, after I left you and Prozac, I grabbed a bite at the buffet and went over to the conference table to check my e-mails. I wasn't really paying attention to what was going on around me."

"What about Zeke? Was he with you the whole time?"

"No, I don't think so. I vaguely remember him wandering off somewhere, but like I said, I wasn't paying attention."

So Zeke had wandered off. And Linda was alone at the time the Skinny Kitty was poisoned.

Which meant neither the grieving widow nor her worshipful admirer had alibis for the time of the murder.

"Can you think of anyone who might have wanted to see Dean dead?"

"Too many, I'm afraid. There's Ian and Deedee. Dean was threatening to ruin their lives. And there was Dean's old partner, Artie Lembeck. Artie's convinced Dean stole his cat food recipe. Dean insisted he didn't steal it, that he tweaked the recipe and made it better. I wanted to believe Dean. But who knows? Maybe he really did cheat Artie, and Artie was out for revenge."

"Anyone else?" I asked.

"Of course, there's me."

"You?" I said, careful not to mention my train of thought had been chugging along that exact same track.

"I'm sure the police must have me on their suspect list. After all, everyone knew about Dean's affair with Camille. I had the perfect motive: The scorned wife. But believe me," she said, "the only person I wanted to kill in that triangle was Camille."

She picked up the picture of her and Dean on the beach, the one I'd seen at the funeral reception, the one where they both looked so impossibly young.

"Those were the good days," she said wistfully. "Dean was so sweet. So funny. He really loved me then."

She gazed deeply into the picture, as if longing to escape into the frame, back to the days when her husband really loved her.

"I wanted to go to law school, but I scrapped all my plans and worked two jobs so Dean could follow his dream and devote himself to his inventions. And how did he repay me? By cheating on me. He's had women on the side for as long as I can remember. Camille wasn't the first. Not by a long shot. There were plenty of others. Like Nikki, the food stylist, to name just one."

Whoa! Dean had been boinking Nikki?

"They first met when Nikki styled some cat food for the Skinny Kitty Web site. Nikki fell head over heels in love with Dean. But as soon as Camille came along, he dumped her like a hot potato. That's the kind of guy he was."

She looked up at me with tears shining in her eyes.

"And the worst thing is—after all these years, after all his affairs, I still loved him. How sick is that?"

She started sobbing then, great heaving sobs.

And at that moment, it was hard to believe that Linda could have poisoned Dean.

The poor thing had actually loved the bum.

I gave her some comforting pats on her hand, assuring her she had nothing to be ashamed of, that she'd been brave and loyal under the most trying circumstances.

Then I thanked her for her time and asked if she'd mind e-mailing me the contact list for everyone on the shoot.

"Not a problem," she said with a weak smile.

I headed back to my Corolla, my mind abuzz with the news flash Linda had just unleashed about Nikki's affair with Dean. If Dean had dumped Nikki like a hot potato, she had every reason to want him dead.

I may not have gotten any deli leftovers that morning, but I was walking away with a hot new murder suspect.

Chapter 13

Working on the theory that Hell Hath No Fury Like a Food Stylist Scorned, I called Nikki the minute Linda e-mailed me the Skinny Kitty contact list. She agreed to see me that afternoon. And after a nutritious lunch of Cheerios and Oreos (from the ever-important "O" food group), I headed over to the Culver City photography studio where she was working.

A doe-eyed receptionist with an impressive display of nose rings led the way to the studio kitchen. En route we passed a photographer shooting a mouthwatering bowl of ice cream. At least, I thought it was ice cream.

"It's really mashed potatoes," the receptionist informed me. "Real ice cream would melt under the camera lights."

Ice cream. Mashed potatoes. Either one worked for me.

"Here we are," the receptionist said, dropping me off at the kitchen.

I stepped inside to find Nikki stuffing paper towels into a chicken.

That's right. Paper towels. I watched in disbelief as she bent over the bird—her apple-cheeked face flushed with perspiration—stuffing it with Bounty's finest.

"Hi, Jaine," she said, catching sight of me.

Then, no doubt noting the look of incredulity in my eyes, she explained, "I always use paper towels to stuff chickens. It's a food stylist trick. Makes them look nice and plump. Then I undercook them so they don't shrink, and give them some color with food coloring. Finally, for that perfect roasted-to-perfection look, I use this!"

With that, she reached under the counter of her cooking island and brandished a blowtorch.

Good heavens, I thought, gazing at the poor Bounty-stuffed bird. It was enough to make a person go vegetarian.

Her chicken plumped up to her satisfaction, Nikki put it in the oven and climbed on a stool at her cooking island.

"Have a seat," she said, pointing to another stool.

Once my fanny was hoisted in place, she asked, "What's up?"

This was going to be awkward, so I had to be very tactful and choose my words with the utmost of care.

"I know all about your affair with Dean."

Quick. Somebody enroll me in Tact 101.

"It's not something I'm proud of," Nikki said, blushing clear up to the roots of her blond shag cut.

"Linda told me Dean dumped you for Camille Townsend."

"That he did," she said with a bitter laugh.

"I guess you must have been pretty angry."

"Hey, wait a minute!" she cried, waving her blowtorch. "If you're suggesting I killed Dean in a fit of anger over the Pink Panther, you're crazy!"

I didn't like the way she was holding that blowtorch. I just hoped she didn't go pyromaniac on me.

"Sure, I was upset when Dean left me, but I never dreamed of killing him. And besides, Dean dumping me was the best thing that ever happened to me. If he hadn't let me go, I'd have never hooked up with my boyfriend. He's ten times the man Dean ever was. So no, I didn't kill Dean, if that's what you're suggesting."

"I wasn't suggesting. Just asking."

Thank heavens she'd stopped fiddling with her fire shooter.

"No," she said, going over to the refrigerator and taking out a bunch of carrots. "I got over Dean ages ago. Why, it didn't even bother me when I heard him and Camille giggling and cooing in Dean's dressing room on the day of the murder."

"You heard them?"

"Unfortunately, yes. Dean's dressing room was right next to the kitchen. And the walls were paper thin. It was disgusting having to listen to them," she said, starting to peel the carrots. "But not upsetting. To tell the truth, I felt sorry for Camille. Sooner or later, Dean was bound to dump her, too. That's the kind of guy he was."

"Did you hear anything they said?"

"Trust me, Jaine. They weren't doing much talking."

"Too bad. It might've given us a clue to the killer."

Nikki looked up from her carrots and shot me an appraising look.

"You're awfully interested in this murder. What're you? Some kind of cop?"

"Actually, I'm a part-time semiprofessional PI."

"Really? A detective? In that outfit?"

One of these days I've got to stop wearing my CUCKOO FOR COCOA PUFFS T-shirt to work.

"Yes, really," I said, trying to give off my best Tough Gal vibes.

"You ever look for lost things? Like, say, my pink hibiscus ring?" She stared down at her naked finger wistfully. "I'll pay you twenty bucks if you find it."

"I'm afraid I don't do costume jewelry searches."

"Too bad."

"Right now all I want to find is Dean's killer. Are you sure you don't have any idea who might have done it?"

"Frankly," she said, abandoning her carrots to open the gossip floodgates, "I'm surprised the police haven't arrested Ian Kendrick."

"Why Ian?"

"This isn't the first time someone died on one of his productions. Years ago, back when he was doing A-list movies, he got into a fight with his lead actor, who threatened to have him fired. Three days later, the actor wound up getting killed when some explosives accidentally detonated on the shoot. Lots of people at the time thought that it wasn't an accident and that Ian was responsible, but there wasn't enough evidence to convict him. He never did jail time, but he never got hired on another A-list movie again."

Well, well. Another juicy tidbit to add to my files.

"Thanks for the lead," I said, getting up to go.

"You sure you don't want to track down my ring?" she asked, batting her baby blues. "I'll bump up the reward to thirty bucks."

Thirty bucks? For an entire investigation? Was she crazy? There was no way a woman of my semi-professional standing was going to work for that kind of money. (Well, not unless I really needed it.)

"Why don't you just go down to Venice and buy another ring?"

"I already tried, and they're all sold out."

"Wish I could help," I said, "but I've got my hands full with this murder thing."

"Well, good luck," she said, going back to her carrots. "And before you go, would you mind passing me that deodorant?"

She pointed to a spray can of deodorant on a shelf behind me.

Why on earth would she need deodorant? I wondered as I handed it to her.

"I use it to spray the carrots," she said, seeing the puzzled look on my face. "Keeps them looking nice and shiny."

That did it. The woman had officially ruined chicken dinners for me forever.

Thank heavens she hadn't been styling a pizza.

Chapter 14

Back home, I spent the next several hours toiling away on the Toiletmasters Touch-Me-Not brochure. Okay, so it wasn't exactly several hours. More like twenty minutes. After which I tossed all thoughts of hands-free toilet flushing to the winds and headed for the tub, where I proceeded to luxuriate in a strawberry-scented bubble bath, daydreaming about my upcoming date with the hunkalicious Jim Angelides.

Dating a plumber had never exactly been high on my wish list, but then, I'd never seen eyes as blue as Jim's. Now plumbing seemed like quite the dashing profession. Just think, when we were married and living in our charming little cottage by the sea, I'd never have to worry about a clogged drain ever again!

I let my mind wander down fantasy lane, drifting off on moonlit walks on the beach, romantic getaways in the Bahamas, and lingering kisses on the deck of our yacht.

What can I say? I like to dream big.

When the last strawberry-scented bubble had bit the dust, I dredged myself out of the tub and started to get ready for my big date.

After moisturizing, spritzing, spraying, and blow-drying, I slipped into pearl gray slacks, a black cashmere sweater, gold hoop earrings, and my trusty Manolos. I topped it all off with a fabulous black Dooney & Bourke satchel bag I'd picked up half price at Nordstrom.

"So, Pro. How do I look?" I asked, twirling around for her inspection.

She gazed up from where she was sprawled out on my bedspread.

Like the woman who led me to the waters of show biz and then left me to drown.

Dammit. She was still showing no signs of getting better. I just hoped Emmy, the Reiki healer, would be able to help.

I was giving myself a final dab of perfume when Jim showed up, looking even better than I remembered him, très spiffy in chinos and a blue blazer, his surfer hair glistening with streaks of blond, smelling of some positively yummy aftershave.

He stood on my doorstep for an awkward beat as we smiled at each other, not sure of what do to.

"So good to see you," he finally said, breaking the ice with a small but tingleworthy hug. "And who's this?" he asked, looking over at Prozac, who'd just wandered in from the bedroom.

Normally, at the first sign of a cute guy, Prozac morphs into a feline floozy, hurling herself at his ankles, doing her version of a pole dance.

But tonight she just jumped on the sofa and set-tled down into a listless lump.

"Who're you, cutie pie?" Jim cooed, scratching her behind the ear.

She gazed up at him morosely.

A has-been, a nobody, another trampled heart on the mean streets of Tinseltown.

"Does she always look so unhappy?" Jim asked.

"She's been in a bit of a funk lately, but I'm hop-ing she'll snap out of it soon."

"Poor baby," Jim said, giving Pro a sympathy scratch. Then he turned to me and asked, "Ready to go? I've made reservations at Simon's."

You bet I was ready to go! Simon's happened to be one of the most expensive restaurants in town, famous for their fabulous prime rib.

I bid Pro adieu and headed out the door with Jim, visions of prime rib dancing in my head.

Jim's car was parked out front, a sleek, low-slung silver Porsche. And as I sank down into the deca-dently soft bucket seat, I offered a silent prayer of thanks to my darling friend and employer, Phil An-gelides.

I was riding along in the Porsche, watching the palm trees whoosh by, feeling the cool night air on my cheeks, and trying to decide whether to order butter or sour cream with my baked potato, when Jim said, "I hope you don't mind, but before we go to the restaurant, I need to stop off at my apart-ment."

Wait a minute. I didn't care how cute he was. No way was I about to have dipsy doodle with this guy *before* our first date.

"Don't get the wrong idea," he added, as if reading my mind. "I want you to meet my roommate. Arnold and I are very close, and I need to get his approval before I can go out with you."

"What?" He had to be kidding.

"I know it sounds strange, but a while back I got involved with a woman, and it turned out pretty badly. We went through a messy breakup, probably like you and Collier-Curtis."

"Collier-Curtis?"

"Your old boyfriend."

"Right," I nodded, remembering the ridiculous beau I'd made up at Toiletmasters.

"Anyhow, I never want to make that kind of mistake again. Arnold warned me this gal was all wrong for me from the get-go. And he was right. I really trust his judgment, so it would mean a lot to me if you met him."

"Well, okay . . . I guess."

"Don't worry," Jim assured me. "Arnold is sure to love you."

I looked at Jim's gorgeous profile, his lake blue eyes, his surfer hair with the white-blond streaks and tried to tell myself I was on my dream date. But this whole roommate approval thing seemed a bit weird.

And things were about to get a whole lot weirder when Jim pulled into the parking lot of the Sunset Manor Retirement Home.

"I thought we were going to your place," I said, looking around. "What are we doing here?"

"I live here."

"You live in a retirement community?"

"I like the amenities," he said. "Especially bingo night! Well, c'mon! Let's go meet Arnold!"

With sinking heart, I left the luxurious confines of the Porsche and followed Jim into the lobby of the apartment building, where several elderly women were sitting in wingback chairs.

"Playing bingo tonight, Jim?" one of them asked.

"No, I've got a date," he said proudly, pointing to me. "That is, if Arnold approves."

The women nodded and looked at me with what I couldn't help but think was pity.

We rode up in an elevator fitted with handrails and got off on the third floor.

"I've got a fabulous view of the physical therapy pool!" Jim announced as he led me to his apartment.

By now, I was having serious doubts about my dream date. But when Jim opened the door to his apartment, hope flooded back into my heart. The place looked terrific. Hardwood floors, taupe leather furniture, chrome and glass end tables—not a handrail anywhere. This was definitely the pad of a hip young metrosexual.

I chided myself for my earlier doubts. So what if he lived in a retirement community? Maybe the rent was reasonable. And maybe the amenities were terrific. And so what if he was tight with his roommate? It was probably a good thing he could be close with another guy; it showed he was capable of commitment.

"Go ahead," Jim grinned. "Say hello to Arnold."

"Where?"

"He's right over there. On the sofa."

I looked at the sofa but didn't see anything on it. Except for a stuffed teddy bear in a red T-shirt with a big "A"embroidered on the chest.

"Well?" Jim said, picking up the bear and holding him out to me. "Aren't you going to say hello to Arnold?"

Oh, God. He actually expected me to talk to his stuffed animal.

"Um. Hello, Arnold," I managed to say.

"Hi, Jaine," Jim replied as Arnold, in a high falsetto voice. A voice he would slip in and out of all evening as he played the part of Arnold, the Teddy Bear.

"So what do you think, Arnold?" Jim asked, back in his own voice. "She pass inspection?"

"With flying colors!" came his falsetto reply.

Would you believe I was actually sort of relieved? I hadn't been there thirty seconds, and I cared what an inanimate object thought of me.

"Better be careful, buddy," came the high-pitched voice. "I may make a move on her myself."

"Hands off!" Jim cried, as Jim. "I saw her first!"

Then he turned to me with a heart-melting smile.

Good heavens. How could someone so cute be so nuts? Maybe this was all a giant joke. Maybe he was testing me to see if I had a sense of humor.

"Ready to go to dinner?" he asked.

"Absolutely," I said, waiting for him to tell me that he loved to kid around and talk like a teddy bear.

But no, the next thing I heard was "Arnold" saying, "I want to come, too!"

Jim turned to the teddy bear. "Forget it, Arnold. I want to be alone with her."

"But you never take me anywhere!" the falsetto voice whined. "I'm tired of sitting here alone in the apartment listening to Mr. Rosenblatt next door blasting *Hoarders* on his TV."

"Oh, all right," Jim said, with a sigh. "You don't mind, do you, Jaine?"

Of course I minded. The last time I went on a date with a stuffed animal, I was four.

But I just smiled weakly and said, "No, I'm fine."

Jim thrust Arnold into my arms and went to get him a sweater.

"He's so susceptible to drafts," he explained.

Alone with Arnold, I seriously thought about making a break for it and calling a cab. But then I remembered Phil Angelides, my boss at Toiletmasters. I couldn't risk Phil's ire by dumping his nephew in the middle of a date.

Soon Jim returned with a miniature cashmere V-neck for Arnold (I kid you not; it was cashmere!), and we headed out to the elevator.

Waiting there was an elderly lady in a floral housedress.

"Hello, Eloise," Jim said in his normal voice.

She mumbled a curt hello and proceeded to ride down with us in stony silence.

Just before she got off at the lobby, she grabbed my elbow with bony fingers and whispered to me, "Watch out for the bear. He's trouble."

Then she sprinted off the elevator, Jim and I following in her wake.

Crossing the lobby, Jim suddenly stopped dead in his tracks.

"Oh, God!" he gasped. "It's her."

"Who?" I asked.

"My old flame. The messy breakup I told you about."

"Just ignore her," Arnold advised. (By now you know it was Jim talking in his falsetto, right?) "I'll take care of her."

We approached the woman in question. I was expecting one of the staff, a cute young thing—a waitress, a nurse, or one of the administrators. But no, Jim's ex-inamorata was a chubby grandmotherly woman well into her seventies, with china-blue eyes and a nimbus of fluffy white curls.

"Hello, Ida," Jim said coolly.

"Remember the restraining order, Jim," she said, holding out her palm.

"What did you ever see in her, anyway?" came the falsetto voice.

"Oh, hell," Ida groaned. "Not that damn bear again."

"Hey, Ida," the falsetto voice blared on. "You're so old, at your birthday party, the candles cost more than the cake!"

"Now, Arnold," Jim chided in his own voice, "there's no need for unpleasantries, just because she broke my heart."

"No one treats you that way and gets away with it, buddy," the falsetto voice replied.

Holy Moses. Send in the psycho squad!

Beyond embarrassed, I raced out to the parking lot and yanked open the passenger door of Jim's Porsche.

Jim and Arnold came strolling along seconds later.

"I wanna sit up front!" Jim whined as Arnold. "I wanna sit up front!"

Then, turning to me and switching voices, he asked, "Do you mind, Jaine?"

"Fine. Better him than me."

Okay, I didn't say that last part, but I was thinking it, believe me. By now I was eager to put as much distance between me and Jim as humanly possible.

But I soon regretted my decision to give up the front seat as my knees jammed into my chest in the tiny rear seat of the sports car.

I spent the drive over to the restaurant listening to Jim and Arnold argue over which station to listen to (Jim wanted country; Arnold wanted salsa), with an occasional insult hurled by Arnold to nearby motorists.

"Hey, lunkhead! Where'd you learn how to drive? The Braille Institute?"

Invariably, the lunkhead in question would turn and shoot me a rude middle finger, assuming that the high-pitched voice hurling the insult could have come only from moi.

At last we pulled in at Simon's, a vine-covered restaurant with a dark green canopy out front.

Jim turned to me and thrust Arnold into my hands.

"Quick. Put him in your purse."

"I don't wanna go in her purse!" Arnold wailed.

"Stop making a scene in front of Jaine," Jim chided the teddy bear, "or she'll get a bad impression of us."

Too late, brother. That bus had left the station a long time ago.

I stowed Arnold in my purse and stepped out of the car, my knees stiff from twenty minutes of being welded to my chest.

Jim tossed his keys to a valet parker, and as the valet got in the car, Arnold's falsetto voice rang out, "Hey, buddy. Whatever you do, don't fart in the car!"

Naturally, the valet assumed it had been me talking and shot me the filthiest of looks.

Slinking away from the valet, I followed Jim inside the restaurant—a macho man steak place with plush carpeting, dim lighting, and deep burgundy leather booths. The kind of joint that reeked of T-bones and testosterone.

The maître d', a beefy guy with an obvious toupee, stood guard at the reception podium.

"May I help you, sir?" he asked Jim as we approached.

"I have reservations," Jim said.

That made two of us.

"Angelides, party of two."

As the maître d' looked down to check his reservations book, "Arnold" chimed in, "Party of *three*."

The maître d' looked up, puzzled.

"Is that two or three, sir?"

"It's *two*," Jim said, giving my purse the evil eye.

Scooping up some menus, the maître d' led us through the restaurant, past tables filled with rich old men and their stunning young "nieces." He made quite an imposing figure as he strode in front of us, his toupee shining in the glow of the restaurant's soft lighting.

Then a familiar falsetto voice piped up: "Hey, buddy. Is that a toupee on your head or a carpet remnant?"

The maître d' whirled around and glared at me.

Oh, foo. Was I going to get blamed for Arnold's zingers all night?

Still quite miffed, our not-so-genial host led us

to a booth, where he practically hurled our menus at us and stomped off.

"Let me out of here!" Arnold whined the minute the maître d' had gone. "I refuse to sit here next to a half-eaten Almond Joy all night."

I looked down at my open purse, and sure enough, an Almond Joy was visible in the clutter next to Arnold.

Normally I'd be embarrassed to have my date see a half-eaten candy bar in my bag. But with Jim, I didn't give a flying frisbee. By now his blue eyes and sun-streaked hair had lost all their appeal.

"All right," Jim said, plucking Arnold out of my purse and propping him on the table against a pair of oversized salt and pepper shakers. "You can sit here."

"No!" Arnold whined. "I want to sit on Jaine's lap."

"You're not sitting on Jaine's lap!" Jim snapped. "That's how we got hit with that restraining order from Ida."

"Waiter!" he called out, motioning to a guy in a cropped red jacket.

The waiter scurried to our table, only to stare goggle-eyed at Arnold, propped up against the salt and pepper shakers.

"We need a baby seat," Jim said.

"A baby seat, sir?"

"Yeah," Arnold's falsetto rang out. "You got a problem with that?"

"Er . . . no, sir," the waiter gulped.

And off he dashed, no doubt to update his résumé.

Minutes later, he returned with the baby seat,

which, in a stroke of good luck, Jim parked between us. At least there'd be no kneesies to worry about.

"My girlfriend's got a thing about her stuffed animal," Jim explained to the waiter with an indulgent shrug. "She just can't leave him at home."

Oh, for heaven's sakes.

"He's not mine!" I cried.

"If you say so, hon," Jim said, winking broadly at the waiter.

"Can I get you something to drink?" the waiter now asked, trying hard not to stare at Arnold in his baby seat.

"A chardonnay, please," I said. "Just bring the bottle. I don't need a glass."

Of course, I didn't really ask for a bottle. But, oh, how I wanted one.

Jim ordered a martini—and a whiskey sour for Arnold.

After the waiter left, I sat there fuming. I still couldn't believe Jim had the nerve to pawn off his insane teddy bear fixation on me.

And now he'd ordered a martini *and* a whiskey sour. Both of which Jim would no doubt guzzle down. This could only spell trouble. I'd had it with this guy. I had to get out of there. Now. I'd just tell him I had to go. No excuses. Just get up and go.

"Look, Jim. I've really got to—"

And just as I was about to make my break for freedom, I happened to glance down at the menu.

Oh, Lord. Apparently, I'd died and gone to Chow Heaven. There on the parchment-like pages was the stuff dreams are made of. My dreams, anyway. Prime rib au jus. Double-stuffed baked potatoes brimming with sour cream and bacon bits. Creamed spinach. And for dessert, Molten Chocolate Lava Cake—dense chocolate cake with a warm, gooey chocolate center, topped with whipped cream and fudge sauce.

"Jaine?"

I looked up and realized Jim was looking at me questioningly.

"You were saying? You've really got to . . . ?"

"Order this fabulous molten chocolate lava cake. It looks divine."

Yikes! I'd just sold my soul for a chocolate cake! (Are you even remotely surprised?)

"Go ahead," Jim said. "Order all you want. And don't worry about the insanely expensive prices. It's my treat."

I checked out the menu and saw that the prices really were insanely expensive.

"Are you sure?" I asked.

"Not a problem," Jim replied with an expansive wave.

He may have been a nutcase, but at least he was a generous nutcase.

The waiter now returned to our table. I couldn't help but notice a wary look in his eyes, like that of a rabbit approaching a particularly cranky lion.

"Ready to order?" he asked after setting down our drinks.

"Yes," Jim said. "We'll have the chateaubriand for two." Then, turning to me, he asked, "And what would you like, Jaine?"

Good heavens. He actually intended to "share" a chateaubriand for two with his stuffed animal! The guy was certifiable.

I gave the waiter my order, going whole hog with the prime rib, baked potato, and creamed spinach. "And molten chocolate lava cake for dessert," I added, the words tripping off my tongue in happy anticipation.

"You sure can pack it away, can't you?" Arnold commented after the waiter had sprinted away.

But I'd already had a few sips (okay, gulps) of my chardonnay and was thus immune to Arnold's zinger. And I hardly minded when Jim started feeding him bits of French bread, making yummy noises as Arnold "ate."

"So, Jaine," Arnold said between bites, "tell us all about yourself."

"Well—"

"Do you put out on the first date? How do you feel about threesomes? Are you wearing panties?"

"Arnold!" Jim cried. "Cut that out!" Then he turned to me apologetically. "I'm afraid he's had a bit too much to drink."

And indeed, Jim had been putting the whiskey sour to Arnold's lips and making slurping sounds along with his yummy bread-eating noises.

"This is why I don't take you anywhere," he said, turning back to his best buddy.

At which point, I looked up to see the maître d' leading a couple to their table—a gorgeous young thing, all legs and boobs, accompanied by a massive goon of a guy with hair sprouting from his open Hawaiian-print shirt.

"Hey, sweetheart!" Arnold called out. "What's a doll like you doing with Orca?"

The goon stopped in his tracks and stomped over to us.

"Who said that?" he asked, his hands thrust in his pockets, where I'm sure a pair of brass knuckles were waiting to spring into action.

And Jim, with the straightest of straight faces, replied, "I think it was one of the busboys, sir."

It was a mighty tense couple of seconds before the goon decided to buy Jim's story and stalked off to his table.

By now, I'd drained my chardonnay, and was once again considering making a run for it, but I couldn't bear the thought of missing out on that molten chocolate lava cake.

Eventually our food came, and dinner passed by in a surreal blur as Jim fed Arnold pieces of steak, gave him sips of whiskey sour, and took pictures of me and Arnold for Arnold's Facebook page.

Yes, apparently, the bear had a Facebook page. With, according to Arnold, seventy-two friends.

Probably Jim's buddies from the psycho ward.

I even had to pretend to give Arnold a bite of my prime rib.

"Arnold loves prime rib," Jim said.

"Yeah, baby," Arnold crooned. "Lay it on me!"

Reluctantly, I cut a piece and mimed feeding it to him.

"More! More!" Arnold cried.

"Not until you finish your chateaubriand," I said sternly, refusing to play this ridiculous game one more minute.

Somehow I managed to tune out Jim and Arnold and concentrate on my chow.

Which was fantab, I might add. The prime rib. The baked potato. The creamed spinach. And the second glass of chardonnay.

I was sitting there, digesting it all, dreaming of the molten chocolate lava cake to come, when suddenly I realized that Jim and Arnold seemed to be in the middle of a heated argument.

"No, Arnold," Jim was saying. "You can't drive the car home."

"Why not?" Arnold's falsetto rang out in reply.

"Because you've had too much to drink, that's why."

"I am so sick of hanging out with you. You never let me have any fun. Never let me drive. Making me hide in a Bloomingdale's shopping bag when we go to the movies. You're always keeping me under wraps. And you know why? Because you're jealous, that's why! You know I'm so much cuter than you!"

"No way," Jim scoffed.

"I'm twice as cute as you," Arnold's falsetto insisted. "Just ask Jaine. I'm a regular chick magnet, aren't I, hon?"

If truth be told, he did seem a tad more fun than Jim.

"And stop putting the moves on my date!" Jim cried. "She's mine."

"That's what you think, buster. She's had her hand on my thigh all night!"

"*What?*" I shouted.

Jim's face flushed with anger. Good heavens, he actually believed his own little melodrama.

"Why, you ungrateful little twerp," he said, yanking Arnold from his baby chair and shaking him so hard, I thought Arnold's glass eyes might fall out.

But Arnold wasn't down for the count. Not by a long shot.

"So you want to play rough, huh?" came the falsetto voice.

And with that, Jim began hitting himself with Arnold, alternately crying out, "Ouch! Ouch! Ouch!" and then, as Arnold, yelling, "Take that. And that. And that!"

By now everyone in the restaurant was staring at us.

"Jim, please," I said, grabbing Arnold from him. "Everyone's looking."

"Arnold started it," he said, pouting as I put Arnold back in his baby seat.

"Look!" came Arnold's falsetto. "Here comes dessert."

And indeed, a waiter was approaching with two pieces of apple pie (for Jim and Arnold) and my long-awaited molten chocolate lava cake.

Right behind him was our genial maître d'.

"Hey, carpet top!" Arnold cried.

"I'm afraid I'm going to have to ask you to leave," the maître d' said just as the waiter set down my chocolate extravaganza.

"Now?" I asked, eyeing the lava cake, swimming in ice cream and fudge sauce.

"Yes, now."

With that, the maître d' yanked Jim out of the booth.

"Hey!" Jim shouted, toting Arnold in the crook of his arm. "You can't do this to me. I'm a paying customer!"

With reckless abandon, I dug in and managed to nab one mouthful of molten chocolate lava cake before the waiter gently hauled me to my feet.

We were escorted through the restaurant and out the door, "Arnold" shouting, "You'll be hearing from our attorney about this!"

The minute we got outside, however, Jim burst into a fit of giggles.

"It worked again, buddy," he whispered to Arnold.

"You betcha!" he answered himself in Arnold's falsetto. "They kicked us out without making us pay the bill! We racked up another freebie!"

Omigod. That crazy fight was just a ploy to get out of paying the bill.

Jim chuckled all the way back to my duplex and had the nerve to ask if he and Arnold could come in for a nightcap.

"Over my dead body," were the words I muttered to myself as I stomped away from the Porsche, having told Jim I had a splitting headache.

(The truth, by the way.)

The last thing I heard as the dynamic duo disappeared into the night was Arnold whining, "I wanna drive!"

YOU'VE GOT MAIL!

To: Jausten
From: Shoptillyoudrop
Subject: Never Been So Mortified!

You'll never guess who came knocking at my door
at 1:20 a.m. last night. Two Tampa Vistas security
guards. With Daddy in custody, naked below the
waist except for a pair of Scrabble boxer briefs!

I've never been so mortified in all my life!

In spite of promising me he wouldn't go near
Lydia's place, Daddy snuck out of the house to go
rooting around in her garbage can, looking for that
ridiculous Lucky Thinking Cap of his. Of course it
wasn't there. I told him all along Lydia didn't steal
his silly cap.

Anyhow, while he was rummaging around in her
garbage, he came across a pair of hideous plaid
Bermuda shorts. Apparently Lydia's brother (a
delightful man but with questionable taste in
Bermuda shorts) had left them there on his last
trip, and when Lydia discovered some moth
holes in the tush, she threw them out.

Now any normal human being would see a pair of
hideous plaid Bermuda shorts with moth holes in
the tush and say, "Yuck!" But not Daddy! One look,
and it was love at first sight. He thought they'd be
perfect for our trip to Hawaii.

And then he did something that, for the life of me,
I'll never understand. Instead of taking them home
to try them on, he decided to take off his pants
and try them on then and there, right in the middle
of the street. He claims he was just being "practi-
cal," that he didn't want to carry the shorts home if
they didn't fit. And besides, he said, he was certain
no one would see him at one in the morning.

That's where he was wrong, of course. Because
Mrs. Thorndahl, who lives right across the street
from Lydia, had just finished watching a Golden
Girls rerun and was going to the kitchen to fix
herself some warm milk when she heard someone
rattling around outside. She peeked out her living
room window to see what was going on. And that's
when she saw Daddy in the moonlight, rooting in
Lydia's garbage in his Scrabble boxer briefs.

She wasted no time calling security to report a
"perverted prowler," and ten minutes later I was
being roused from a perfectly wonderful dream
(featuring George Clooney and a vat of fudge) to
find Daddy on our doorstep, sandwiched
between two security guards.

After giving him a stern warning about raiding
other people's garbage cans in his underwear, they
hurried off into the night. Frankly, I think they were
thrilled to be rid of him.

I was so mad, I made Daddy sleep on the sofa.
Which, by the way, is where he found his dratted

Lucky Thinking Cap. It was there all along, wedged behind the sofa cushions from one of his Power Naps.

XOXO from
Your unbelievably frustrated
Mom

To: Jausten
From: DaddyO
Subject: Little Run-In

Dearest Lambchop—

I suppose Mom told you about my little run-in with the Tampa Vistas security department.

In my defense, I can only say that I did what any red-blooded American Scrabble player would have done when dealing with an underhanded opponent like Lydia Pinkus. Even though she didn't steal my Lucky Thinking Cap, I bet she *thought* about stealing it. And I simply can't believe that old bat Mrs. Thorndahl had nothing better to do in the middle of the night than loiter at her living room window spying on perfectly innocent citizens.

But on the plus side, I found an exceedingly stylish pair of plaid Bermuda shorts in the trash—perfect for our Hawaiian vacation. True, they have a few tiny holes in the tush area, but if I wear colored briefs, I'm sure no one will notice.

And, saving the best news for last, I found my Lucky Thinking Cap! It was wedged under one of the sofa cushions. Your mom thinks it got stuck there during one of my power naps, but I wouldn't be at all surprised if Lydia hid it there when she was at the house the other day. Oh, no. I wouldn't put it past her. Not one bit.

But no matter. I've got it back, and that's all that counts. Victory will be mine!

Time to get back to Scrabble Central.

Love 'n' snuggles from
Your overjoyed
DaddyO

Chapter 15

I woke up the next morning still reeling from my date with Jim, haunted by the memory of Arnold slinging insults, slurping his whiskey sour, and slugging it out with Jim. Talk about your schizophrenic nightmares.

Prozac, never a fount of empathy, was particularly cool when I told her my tale of woe.

Boo hoo. At least you got prime rib, while all I have are the ashes of my shattered career.

Then, just when I thought my nerves couldn't get any more frazzled, I opened my e-mails from my parents and read about Daddy's raid on Lydia Pinkus's garbage.

Can you believe he actually tried on a pair of Bermuda shorts from the trash?

And how could he have been so foolish to strip down to his undies right across the street from Mrs. Mary "Eagle Eyes" Thorndahl, a woman who, for as long as anyone has known her, has been on round-the-clock lookout for burglars, UFOs, and dogs pooping on her lawn?

Oh, well. There was nothing I could do about it, so I settled down with a cinnamon raisin bagel slathered with butter and extra raspberry jam. I was in the middle of calming my nerves with *The New York Times* crossword puzzle when the phone rang.

"How's my favorite writer?" Phil Angelides's voice came sailing over the line. "Jim told me what a great time you two had last night."

What?? The only wonderful part about that evening was when it was over.

"I can't tell you how happy that makes me, Jaine. Confidentially, Jim has had some troubles connecting with women."

That tends to happen when you're a raving lunatic.

"And I'm so glad you're going to the Fiesta Bowl with him."

"Say what?"

"Jim told me you two were coming to the party together."

Absolutely negatory. No way was I going to the Toiletmasters annual bash with Jim and his fuzzy wuzzy alter ego. I'd just have to tell Phil that Jim was a perfectly lovely schizophrenic, but that we weren't a match, and I'd be coming to the party on my own.

"You are going with Jim, right?" Phil was saying. "You're not going to break his heart like his last girlfriend, are you?"

I'd just be strong and tell him No, and it would all be over. Simple as that.

"Um . . . sure, I'm going with Jim."

Okay, so I'm a world-class coward, a sniveling weakling of the highest order. But all was not lost. I had a plan. I'd just call Phil in a day or two, tell him I'd reconciled with my mythical boyfriend Collier-Curtis, and make some excuse to get out of going to the party.

In the meanwhile, however, I had a murder to solve.

I hadn't forgotten what Nikki told me about Ian Kendrick and the actor who died under mysterious circumstances on the set of his movie.

After filling in the last clue on my crossword puzzle, I hustled over to my computer and Googled Ian. Sure enough, there were several articles about an explosion gone awry on the set of an epic called *Thunderbolt*, resulting in the death of a rising young action star named Gavin Hudson. A few stories mentioned that Ian had been brought in for questioning by the police, but the star's death had ultimately been ruled an accident.

So Dean wasn't the only one who'd clashed with Ian and wound up dead.

I most definitely needed to pay a little visit to the ponytailed Brit.

A half hour later I was tootling over to Ian's house in the Hollywood Hills, wending my way up the steep streets, my ancient Corolla huffing and puffing every inch of the way.

When I finally got to Ian's place, I saw it was a gated estate, obscured from view by a wall of shrubbery.

What rotten luck. I was hoping to catch him unawares. Now I'd have to use the intercom at the gate and announce my presence. I pressed the buzzer, and after some static, Ian's voice, slurred with booze, came on the line.

"You from the maid service?" he asked.

"No, it's Jaine Austen. We met on the Skinny Kitty shoot. I was hoping to talk to you about Dean's murder."

"Forget it. I've said all I'm going to say to the cops."

With that, he cut me off, leaving me nothing but dead air. My interview was over before it began.

I was sitting there, cursing myself for not coming up with an inventive cover story, when another car pulled up behind me and honked. Turning, I saw a bright yellow Volkswagen Beetle with the words MIGHTY MAIDS painted on the hood.

And suddenly I knew how to get to Ian.

I grabbed my purse and hustled over to the Beetle.

Two young women—one blond, one Hispanic, and both in maid's uniforms—were sitting up front. The blonde sat behind the wheel, chewing a wad of bubble gum.

"You ladies here to clean Mr. Kendrick's house?" I asked.

"No, we're here for high tea," the blonde said, blowing a bubble. "Of course we're here to clean."

Looked like the Mighty Maids came fully equipped with mighty mouths.

"Who're you?" her partner asked.

"Actually," I said, "I'm from the board of health." I reached into my purse and flashed them my badge.

Of course, it wasn't a board of health badge, but a USDA meat inspector badge I'd picked up ages ago at a flea market for moments just like this. "I'm afraid Mr. Kendrick's home is quarantined."

"Quarantined?" the blonde asked, eyes wide.

"Chicken pox," I nodded. "No visitors allowed."

"Okay," she said, "but he's still going to get billed for our time."

"It's part of the contract," her partner added. "If he doesn't cancel with twenty-four hours' notice, he pays in full."

"Mr. Kendrick's okay with that."

"Great." The blonde finally graced me with a smile. "C'mon, Sylvia," she said to her partner. "It's margarita time!"

They took off, happy to spend the next few hours at the nearest cantina, and I sprinted back to my Corolla to press the intercom buzzer.

Ian's voice came squawking through the box again.

"Who is it?"

"It's Mighty Maids, sir," I said, disguising my voice, hoping he wouldn't realize it was still me.

"Come on in," he snapped. "You're late."

The gate creaked open, and I drove into what looked like a small jungle, overgrown with trees and long-neglected shrubbery. I headed up a winding pathway, wayward branches brushing against my windshield.

At last I arrived at a magnificent but crumbling old Spanish-style home with cracked red tile roof, stained stucco walls, and aggressive weeds snaking up the sides of the house.

Ian might have been using a maid service, but it

clearly had been decades since this place had seen a landscaper.

I walked up to an ornate wooden door composed of intricately carved panels and, I suspected, an army of well-fed termites.

The rusted doorbell produced a loud chime, and soon I heard the shuffle of feet approaching. Seconds later, the door swung open, and there was Ian in a terry bathrobe, reeking of gin, his feet bare, his face a road map of wrinkles, and his ponytail sporting an extra layer of grease.

In his hand, he held a highball glass.

"It's about time," he sniffed. "Hey, wait a minute. Aren't there usually two of you?"

Then, squinting at me through gin-blurred eyes, he said, "I know you. You're the woman with the impossible cat."

"Look, I just need to talk to you about—"

But before I could get out the rest of my sentence, he was reaching for the door.

Oh, hell. He was about to slam it right in my face.

"Wait!" I cried out. "If you answer some questions about Dean's murder, I'll clean your house."

He hesitated a beat, then continued to shut the door.

"For free!" I added. "I'll clean your house for free."

The door swung back open to reveal a smiling Ian.

"Come in, my dear," he said, his voice plummy with good cheer.

I stepped into a massive foyer, replete with an elaborate wrought iron staircase straight from a

Warner Brothers swashbuckler. Any minute now, I expected Errol Flynn to come leaping over the bannister in velvet tights.

Geez, I thought, looking around, this house was humungous. Cleaning it could take ages. No wonder Ian needed two Mighty Maids.

"Cleaning supplies are in the service porch," Ian said, waving his highball glass vaguely toward the back of the house. "We'll talk when you're through."

Oh, no. No way was I cleaning this mini-coliseum, only to have him change his mind and clam up on me later on.

"Nope," I said, standing my ground. "We talk first. Then I clean."

We locked eyeballs in a stare down, but what with all that gin coursing through his veins, it was clearly hard for Ian to stay focused.

"All right," he said, finally looking away. "But you'd better do a good job on the bathroom grout."

He now led me to a barn of a living room, with Spanish floor tiles and an oversized fireplace. Dusty drapes hung from floor-to-ceiling windows, and large empty squares dotted the walls where paintings once hung.

Why did I get the feeling he was selling off his assets one by one?

The only pieces of furniture in the room were a worn leather sofa, a rumpsprung armchair, and a coffee table stained from decades of sweaty highball glasses.

Ian flung himself down onto the sofa, miraculously managing to keep the flaps of his robe shut, and motioned for me to sit across from him in the armchair. Then he reached for a bottle of gin on the coffee table and refreshed his highball.

"Care for a nip?" he asked, holding out the bottle. "Glasses are in the kitchen. You'll probably have to wash one."

"No, thanks. I'm fine."

"Pardon the way I look," he said. "I was just watching one of my old movies on TV."

And indeed, the end credits were rolling on a bulky old TV on the floor near the fireplace.

Ian stared at the TV, gulping at his gin, as the movie faded out and Turner Classic Movies maven Robert Osborne popped up on the screen.

"That was one of the early films of director Ian Kendrick, who had a successful string of movies in the nineties but, after a fatal accident on the set of *Thunderbolt,* sadly faded into obscurity."

"I'm still here, Bob," Ian said with a bitter smile, snapping off the TV.

"That must have been a terrible time for you," I said as gently as I could.

Ian looked at me with an air of studied nonchalance.

"Why? I had nothing to feel guilty about. If anyone should have felt guilty, it was the special effects guys. They were the ones in charge of explosives. It was a tragic accident, but I had nothing to do with it."

I got the distinct impression he was reciting words written decades ago by a long-gone press agent.

"So Dean is the second person to have died on one of your sets," I pointed out.

"What of it?" Ian huffed. "Just because he died on my set, that doesn't mean I killed him."

"Do you have any idea who did?"

"Why the hell do you need to know?" he snapped, no longer the least bit nonchalant.

"Like you, Ian, I'm a suspect in Dean's murder, and I'm trying to clear my name."

He glared at me, indignant. "Who says I'm a suspect?"

"I'm just assuming you are, since Dean was threatening to ruin your career."

"So I had a motive to kill him. Big deal. So did half the people who ever met him. But I swear I was out in the parking lot the whole time that cat food was left unattended. I didn't go near the stuff."

"If you didn't, who did?"

"If you ask me, it's that pipsqueak writer Zeke. Anyone could see he was dying to get Dean out of the way so he could get his hands on Linda."

"Can you think of anyone else who might've wanted to see Dean dead?"

"I can think of everyone else. Everybody hated the guy. They were probably waiting on line to poison that cat food."

"And you saw nobody going into the kitchen while the cat food was unattended?"

"I already told you, I was out in my car, spending quality time with my Starbucks thermos. Now is that all?"

"It certainly seems like it."

"Okay, then," he said, slamming his highball down on the coffee table. "Time for you to start cleaning."

And clean I did.

I spent the next three hours hauling around an

ancient vacuum, battling dust bunnies the size of honeydews, and scrubbing bathroom grout with a toothbrush. Out of the goodness of my heart, I'll spare you my encounter with The Toilets That Time Forgot.

Three hours later I was sweating like a pig. By then, I didn't care if Ian was the killer; I just wanted to go home and soak my aching muscles in a soothing bubble bath.

I'd finally made my way up to Ian's bedroom, a cavernous lair with a bare mattress on the floor and an ancient TV on a scarred dresser. Like most of the other rooms in the house, it looked like all the good furniture had been sold.

In spite of my fatigue, I began rummaging through Ian's dresser drawers, hoping I might unearth a valuable clue or, even better, some Tylenol.

But all I found were a depressing number of condoms and some magazines, the titles of which are not fit for publication in a family-friendly novel.

It was when I was vacuuming his closet, however, that I struck pay dirt. And I do mean dirt. That closet had a layer of dust thicker than a shag carpet. I was lifting a pile of moldering laundry from the floor to get in and vacuum when I saw a large book peeking out from under some unsavory undies. Plucking the undies aside, I picked up the book, which I now saw was a scrapbook.

I opened it and began turning the pages. All of which were filled with newspaper and magazine clippings. There were a few movie reviews, and pictures of Ian as a young man. (I must admit, he'd been quite a looker.) But most of the book was filled with clippings about Gavin Hudson's murder. *Variety. The Los Angeles Times. The Hollywood Reporter. Newsweek.* Ian had collected them all.

And then, coming to the end of the collection, I turned the page to see the start of a whole new collection: clippings about Dean Oliver's murder. Ian had pasted in what looked like every newspaper and online story he could find.

In spite of the sweat soaking my clothes, a chill ran down my spine.

Was Ian keeping a scrapbook of the murders he'd committed?

I was sitting there, looking down at Dean's face smiling up at me from his obituary, when suddenly the scrapbook was jerked from my hands.

I looked up and saw Ian standing over me, breathing thunder.

"What the hell do you think you're doing?" he said, the veins in his neck throbbing.

"I . . . I found this scrapbook under your laundry," I said, scrambling to my feet, "and I was just dusting it off."

I started backing out of the room, but with every step back I took, Ian took a step forward.

"Didn't anybody ever tell you it's not nice to go snooping in other people's belongings?" he said, his eyes shining with a manic gleam. "A girl could get hurt that way."

By now my heart was pounding. I ordered myself to stay calm and keep backing away. One step after another. And another. And . . . damn! I'd just tripped over the dratted vacuum cleaner.

"I swear I wasn't snooping," I lied, regaining my balance. "I didn't even notice what was in the book."

"Like hell you didn't."

I continued backing up, and Ian continued advancing.

Then something made me turn around. I don't know if it was luck, a guardian angel, or that manic gleam in Ian's eyes. But turn I did and realized with a gasp that I'd backed up to the top of the winding wrought iron staircase. One more step and I'd have gone hurtling down its steep tile stairs.

I reached for the rail and tore down the steps, grabbing my purse from the living room on my way out the door.

Ian didn't give chase, just stood at the top of the steps, his eyes boring into mine.

Outside, I scrambled into my Corolla and took off, grateful I hadn't wound up as another clipping in Ian's murder memory book.

Chapter 16

Back home, I made a beeline for the bathtub, where I spent the next hour soothing my frazzled nerves with a hot bath and a healing dose of Double Stuf Oreos.

Feeling somewhat revived, I slipped into my sweats and tried to work on the Touch-Me-Not brochure. But I simply couldn't stay focused. I kept thinking about how close I'd come to hurtling down Ian's wrought iron staircase.

Finally, I gave up and decided to do some mindless grunt work. It was about time I cleaned my desk, otherwise known as my dining room table, where papers tend to multiply like telemarketers at dinnertime.

I was tossing out an impressive pile of junk mail and long-expired coupons when I came across the contract I'd signed for the Skinny Kitty shoot.

I glanced through the pages, mourning the five thousand dollars I would never earn, when I stumbled on a clause that lit a ray of hope in my heart.

Apparently, those generous folks at Skinny Kitty had promised to pay me one thousand dollars if, for any reason, the commercial didn't get made.

That clause, I knew from prior writing assignments, was known as a kill fee.

At the time I'd signed the contract, I'd been so focused on the five grand, I hadn't even noticed the one-thousand-dollar consolation prize.

Wasting no time, I called Deedee, who, wouldn't you know, didn't pick up.

I left her a message, telling her I wanted to collect my kill fee and asked her to please call me back as soon as possible.

I really wanted that thousand bucks.

I only hoped Deedee hadn't already spent it.

I fell into an uneasy sleep that night, still haunted by the memory of Ian staring down at me from the top of his staircase with that maniacal gleam in his eyes.

Soon I was dreaming that I was back in Ian's bedroom, his murder memory scrapbook in my hands. I was turning the pages, fingers trembling, when I heard footsteps down the hall. I dashed into the closet and pulled the door shut, shuddering as the footsteps grew nearer and nearer.

"I know you're in there, Jaine," I heard Ian saying in a ghastly singsong whine, "and I'm coming to get you. There's going to be a whole chapter about your murder in my scrapbook!"

By now he was at the closet door. He tried to open it, but I held fast.

"Let me in!" he cried, pounding on the door,

louder and louder, till the noise was roaring in my ears.

Then I felt a ferocious yank and lost my grip on the doorknob. The door was opening! Any second now he was going to kill me!

And that's when I woke up, sitting up in bed with a jolt, clammy with sweat.

Thank heavens it was only a dream.

I was just about to sink back down in my pillows when I saw someone standing in the shadows at the foot of my bed. Oh, hell! The knocking I'd heard in my dream had been real! It was probably Ian. Somehow he'd forced his way in. The crazed director was out to kill me, after all!

Adrenaline rushing through my veins, I reached for my cell phone on my night table and hurled it at him.

"Hey!" A woman's voice called out in protest. "Are you crazy? You could've hurt me with that thing."

A wave of relief washed over me as I realized it wasn't Ian—but Kandi.

I switched on the light, and sure enough, Kandi was standing at the foot of my bed, her hair rumpled, a feverish look in her eyes.

"Kandi!" I cried, checking my clock radio. "It's two a.m. What the heck are you doing here? And how did you get in?"

"I knocked for ages, but there was no answer. So I let myself in with the spare key you gave me in case of an emergency."

"Emergency? What emergency? Is something wrong?"

Once again, I noticed the feverish look in her eyes.

"Kandi, honey." I leaped out of bed and rushed to her side. "What is it?"

"You've got to help me!" she said. "I need to borrow your credit card, just for a few minutes."

"My credit card?"

"Yes, I saw the most fabulous boots online at Neiman Marcus, suede knee-highs on sale, fifty percent off, and I absolutely must have them! C'mon," she said, grabbing me by the wrist. "Let's go to your computer and order them. I can pay you back right now. I brought cash."

She reached into her jeans pocket with her free hand and waved a wad of bills in my face.

Prozac, who had been snoring on my pillow, was now fully awake and shooting us dagger glares.

Some of us are trying to sleep, you know.

"Kandi!" I cried as she dragged me out to the living room. "Get a hold of yourself! Remember the new leaf you turned over. You're a recovering shopaholic. You can't do this stuff anymore."

"And I won't do it anymore. Not after tonight. Not ever again. Just this once. So hurry up. Give me your card. I'll take anything. Visa. MasterCard. Amex. Even Discover."

By now, she'd hauled me to my computer at my dining room table.

"Kandi, sweetheart," I said, tugging her back over to my sofa. "You've got to be strong and resist the urge. Hang in there, honey!"

"Just one more pair of boots!" she pleaded. "That's all I ask."

I shook my head firmly.

"One is too many, and a hundred's not enough."

She blinked in confusion.

"What the heck is that supposed to mean?"

"It's a classic line from *The Lost Weekend*. Remember? Ray Milland? The crazed alkie trying to give up booze?"

"For heaven's sakes, Jaine. Must you compare me to some actor who's been dead a million years? Couldn't I at least be Sandra Bullock in *28 Days*?"

"The point is, Kandi," I said, pulling her down on the sofa, "you don't need another pair of boots, not when you've got a whole closetful sitting in your condo at home."

I shot her my sternest no-nonsense look (a little something I'd picked up from Prozac).

"Okay, okay," she said, abashed. "You're right. I won't order the boots."

See? All it took was a firm hand and an iron will. I was really quite proud of myself.

"How about a pair of slippers? I saw a cute pair at Zappo's for under forty bucks."

"You can't order anything, Kandi. That's what it means when you're a recovering shopaholic."

"How about socks? Ones with little pom-poms on the ankle?"

"There'll be no boots. No slippers. No socks with pom-poms. What you need is a great big hug and a bowl of Chunky Monkey."

As it turned out, I was the one who needed the Chunky Monkey. All Kandi needed was the hug and a nap.

She tumbled into bed alongside me (and a snoring Prozac). When I woke the next morning, I found a note from her on my night table.

Darling Jaine—
Thank you for saving me from myself.
How can I ever repay you?
XOXO,
Kandi
P.S. I know! How would you like a beautiful
hand-knit cell phone cover?

Chapter 17

I sprang out of bed that morning, ready to forget yesterday's angst and face the new day with a smile. Which is what I did. For a whole twenty-seven seconds, until I padded to the front door for my newspapers and discovered *The New York Times* was missing.

As far as I'm concerned, there are only three things that make life worthwhile: Chocolate, chocolate, and *The New York Times* crossword puzzle.

I simply can't start my day without it.

I searched under the jasmine bush next to my front door, thinking maybe the newspaper delivery guy tossed the paper there by mistake. But it was nowhere in sight.

Grumbling and cursing, I stomped off to the kitchen and fixed Prozac her morning Minced Mackerel Guts.

She nibbled at it listlessly, very Blanche DuBois dining at the Kowalskis.

After nuking myself a CRB and making do with the *L.A. Times* crossword, I turned my attention back to where it belonged: Dean Oliver's murder.

Given yesterday's harrowing encounter with Ian, I was ready to lock him up and throw away the key. But I couldn't ignore that pesky "innocent until proven guilty" thing our justice system is so fond of.

Which meant I'd have to keep on investigating.

I remembered what Nikki said about hearing Dean and the Pink Panther through the paper-thin walls that separated the kitchen from Dean's dressing room. Now I wondered if the Pink Panther had heard anything on the day of the murder that might lead me to the killer.

Checking in with my pals at Google, I discovered that the Pink Panther, aka Camille Townsend, had worked as a fashion model until she hooked up with a Silicon Valley honcho and walked away with a bundle in a divorce settlement.

Could I risk calling her and going with the truth, telling her that I was investigating Dean's murder? Did I really have to resort to a sneaky subterfuge to see her? After all, the Panther was one of the few people who actually liked Dean. Surely she'd want to help me find the killer.

For once, I decided to stick with the truth. And after waiting until a decent hour, I called the Pink Panther's phone number on Linda's contact sheet.

A soft-spoken woman with a Hispanic accent answered.

"Jaine Austen," I said in my most professional voice, "calling for Ms. Townsend."

"I'm sorry, but Miss Camille isn't taking any phone calls."

Okay, time for the sneaky subterfuge.

(I'd had one warming on the back burner of my brain all along.)

"Can you tell her I'm a writer with *Cat Fancy* magazine, and we want to feature her cat Desiree in our first ever centerfold?"

After years of being a writer, I've found that most people simply can't resist the temptation of seeing themselves—or their significant others—in print.

A moment of silence while my soft-spoken friend thought over my offer. Then, finally, the words I longed to hear:

"Hold, please."

And hold I did, drumming my fingers on the dining room table, trying to ignore Prozac hissing at the mention of Desiree's name.

Finally, the woman got back on the line.

"Can you be here at one o'clock?"

Sometimes it pays to be sneaky.

The Panther's magnificent Bel Air estate, Casa Rosa, lived up to its name, its impeccably landscaped grounds awash in pink roses and peonies. The house itself was a white sandstone wonder, with turreted roofs and a front portico so grand, I almost expected a doorman to come racing out and take my car.

Instead, I parked in front of one of the mansion's five (yes, five!) garages.

The soft-spoken woman I'd talked to on the

phone came to the door in a spotless white maid's uniform and ushered me into a foyer fragrant with the heady aroma of Stargazer lilies, a huge bunch of which were on display on a table by the front door.

"Miss Camille is in her bedroom," the maid said, leading me up a flight of marble stairs, which, I must admit, gave me the heebie jeebies, reminding me as they did of my recent brush with death at Ian's place.

Soon I was being ushered into a palace of a bedroom. I'd expected it to be done up in pink, but it was all pristine white—white plush carpeting, white satin bedding, white chaise longue, and white lacquered furniture—the perfect backdrop for the sprays of pink roses and peonies strategically dotted around the room.

Off to the side was a walk-in closet the size of a small airplane hangar. Good heavens. The woman had more clothes than my local Bloomie's.

The Panther was reclining on the chaise in a pink velvet jog suit, with Desiree in her lap, staring down at her hands.

Lying sprawled on her white satin bed were two German shepherds decked out in collars studded with pink bling.

I marveled at the two dogs, wondering how they made it across the snowy white carpeting and onto the satin bedding without leaving a single speck of dirt. Did the Panther have a special maid on tap just to dustbust after her dogs?

"Miss Austen to see you, ma'am," the maid announced.

The Panther looked up from her reverie.

"Thank you, Sofia."

It was easy to see that she had once been a model, with her fabulous cheekbones and flowing mane of glossy brown hair. Lithe and willowy in her jog suit, she'd not gained an ounce since the days she'd walked the runway. And any hint of a wrinkle on her face had been Botoxed to oblivion.

Over on the bed, the German shepherds, now roused from their nap, took one look at me and began snarling.

"Tristan! Isolde!" the Panther scolded. "Behave yourselves."

And just like that, they put their heads back down and resumed their naps.

I gazed at them wistfully, thinking how nice it must be to have pets who actually do what you tell them to.

The Panther turned to me now and blinked in confusion.

"Aren't you the woman from the Skinny Kitty shoot? The one with the obstreperous cat?"

"She's not so much obstreperous as strong willed," I said, leaping to Prozac's defense.

"But you told Sofia you were a writer."

"It's true. I'm a freelance writer. The Skinny Kitty job was actually the first time I took my cat on a commercial shoot. And probably the last," I added with a rueful smile.

"Anyhow," I said, launching into the tiny fib I'd fabricated for the occasion, "I sometimes write for *Cat Fancy* magazine, and when I heard they were looking for a cat for their new centerfold feature, I immediately thought of your Desiree. I just knew she'd be perfect for the job."

"Isn't that nice, Desiree?" the Panther cooed, stroking the beauty in her lap. "How'd you like to be a centerfold?"

The cat yawned in reply. I guess it was a bit of a comedown from national TV.

"All I have to do is take a few photos and send them on to my editor. Once she sees Desiree, I know she's going to love her. Do you mind?" I asked, taking out my cell phone.

"Go right ahead," the Panther replied. "Desiree loves having her picture taken."

And indeed the cat preened as I snapped her picture, posing like the pro her mistress had once been.

"Thanks so much for stopping by," the Panther said when I was done playing Magazine Photographer. "Let me know if your editor likes the pictures."

Clearly my cue to go. But I couldn't leave now. I hadn't even begun to question her about the murder.

"Um. I'm supposed to get a few facts for the centerfold. You know. Desiree's turn-ons. Turn-offs. Favorite scratching spots. Stuff like that."

"Of course," the Panther said. "Have a seat." She gestured to the chair at her mammoth vanity.

I pretended to record our interview on my phone as the Panther told me all about Desiree's turn-ons (filet mignon, Perrier, Porthault pillow-cases), turnoffs (canned cat food, tap water, domestic caviar), and favorite scratching spot (Mommy's antique armoire). Finally I'd run out of inane questions to ask.

"Well, thanks for stopping by," the Panther said.

Once again, I ignored her cue to leave.

"It's such a shame we had to meet under such tragic circumstances," I tsked. "I still can't get over what happened to poor Dean."

"Such a wonderful man," she said, shaking her head. "So amazing in bed."

Okay, so she didn't say "in bed," but trust me, I could read between the lines.

"Dean and I met at a charity gala and clicked right away. I knew the minute I met him we were destined to be lovers."

Okay, she said "friends."

"We grew incredibly close in a very short time. "Confidentially," she said, stroking Desiree, "I think he was lonely. He told me he no longer loved his wife, that he'd outgrown her."

"Oh?"

"Yes, Dean and Linda met when they were quite young. Dean became a man of the world. But poor Linda stayed the same provincial girl Dean dated in high school."

"Do you think Linda knew she was losing him? Do you think she might have snapped under the emotional pressure and killed him?"

"I doubt it," the Panther said. "She loved him too much to kill him. But I suppose anything's possible."

"Do you have any idea who might have done it?"

She shook her head, dazed at the very thought.

"God, no. Who'd want to kill a charismatic man like Dean?"

Yikes. Somebody sure had been drinking the Kool-Aid in that relationship.

"I ran into Nikki the other day," I said, "and she

told me that Dean's dressing room was right next to the kitchen at the Skinny Kitty shoot. I don't suppose you saw or heard anybody in the kitchen on the day of the murder? Someone who might have tampered with the cat food?"

"I didn't hear a thing. Dean and I were way too preoccupied working on our ad campaign."

By which, of course, she meant going at it like bunny rabbits.

"But I did *see* something."

At last. A lead!

"I took a break from our work session to go the ladies' room, and just as I got there, I thought I saw Zeke, the writer, slipping into the kitchen. Of course, it might not have been Zeke. I'm extremely nearsighted, and the ladies' room was way down at the other end of the hall. For all I know, the person I saw wasn't even going into the kitchen, but into another room down the hallway. I thought about telling the police, but I didn't want to get Zeke in trouble. He seems like a sweet young man, and I can't believe he'd kill his own cousin."

I, on the other hand, had no trouble whatsoever picturing Zeke as a cold-blooded killer.

And I made up my mind to have a chat with him ASAP.

In the meanwhile, I thanked the Panther for her time and left her as I'd found her—reclining on her chaise longue, staring down at her hands.

I wondered what she was thinking about.

Her lost love? The fragility of life?

Or simply whether it was time for a manicure.

Chapter 18

Checking the Skinny Kitty contact list, I was sur-prised to see that Zeke's address was the same as Linda's. At first I thought it was a typo. But when I called Linda to ask her about it, she explained that Zeke lived in a guest cottage at the back of her property.

And so twenty minutes later, I was walking up the flagstone path to Zeke's guest quarters, a charming cottage with shutters at the windows and a profusion of pansies out front.

Zeke came to the door in jeans and a T-shirt, his sandy hair tousled, holding a can of Red Bull.

"Hey, Jaine!" he cried. "Linda told me you were investigating Dean's murder. Wow! That is so cool! Who'd a thunk it? You? A PI? Talk about casting against type!"

It looked like somebody had been nipping just a tad too much Red Bull.

"Entray, entray!" he said, waving me inside his tiny home—a single room with a futon, TV, and a large desk; the latter jammed with a laptop, piles of papers, and a giant thesaurus.

Off to the side was a tiny kitchenette.

"Have a seat," he said, gesturing to his futon.

As I sank down into its marshmallow depths, I noticed something very interesting hanging over Zeke's desk: a well-worn dartboard with Dean's picture on it. Several darts were piercing the dearly departed's nose.

"Nice decorating touch," I said, gesturing to the wall art.

Zeke had the good grace to blush.

"I suppose I should get rid of it, but I can't bring myself to do it. Too many happy memories."

"Doesn't Linda mind?"

"I make sure she never sees it."

With that, he pulled out the darts and flipped the board over, revealing a mirror on the other side.

"Very clever."

"It's kept me from being evicted, that's for sure. So, can I get you something to drink? I'm afraid all I've got is Red Bull."

"No, thanks. I'm fine."

"Me too," he said, taking a big slug from his can. "More than fine. I'm great!"

Then he flung himself into the swivel chair from his desk and scooted it across the room to face me.

"I've been on a writing marathon ever since Dean died, working on my novel. My creative juices have been positively flowing! I realize now that Dean was holding me back, always criticizing me, and taking nasty shots. It's a wonder I was able to write a single syllable."

With that, he jumped up and raced to his desk.

"Look!" he said, holding up a stack of manuscript pages. "Just look at all the pages I've written!"

He grinned proudly, flush with the excitement of a writer who's been churning out pages—or perhaps a killer who's been getting away with murder.

"And it's not just my life that's improved," he said, scooting back to his swivel chair. "Linda's so much better off with Dean gone. The guy treated her like dirt. Cheating on her with the Pink Panther right under her nose. Why, I remember one night not long ago I saw Camille sneaking in the side door of the main house after midnight.

"Poor Linda," he tsked. "Upstairs sleeping while God knows what was going on downstairs in her own house. "But that's all over now," he said, taking a final slug of Red Bull and crushing the can in his fist. "Linda won't have to put up with that crap anymore. Dean won't ever be able to hurt her again."

Time for the big question.

"Are you the one who made sure he'd never hurt her again?"

"If you're asking if I killed him, the answer is no. I hated the guy, but I'm not a killer."

The jury was still out on that one.

"Actually," I said, "I was just talking to Camille Townsend, who said she saw you outside the studio kitchen at the time the cat food was poisoned."

"That's a lie!" he said, his face flushed with

anger. "I went to the men's room. But that's it. I went nowhere near that kitchen!"

He was so forceful in his denial, I was tempted to believe him.

Then, just when I was considering writing him off as a suspect, his cell phone rang.

"What's up?" he said, answering it. "Okay, sure. I'll be right there."

"That was Linda," he said, bounding out of his chair, his anger forgotten. "The mail just came. I got a letter from *The New Yorker*. I bet they're buying the short story I sent them! Be right back."

He was out the door like a shot.

And the minute he was gone, I was at his desk, snooping.

I checked out the first few paragraphs of his manuscript (I sure hoped he wasn't counting on a yes from *The New Yorker*) and rummaged around the detritus of his desk. Sitting on top of a pile of bills was a mushy greeting card with two kittens cuddling on the front cover. Inside it said, *You had me at "meow."*

It was signed, *To Linda, XOXO, Zeke.*

Not exactly a Shakespearean sonnet, but clearly Zeke was about to make his moves on his beloved.

Then, unable to resist the lure of his open laptop, I clicked on Zeke's recent search history.

Whaddaya know? There among "literary agents" and "sex toys" were three recent searches—for poisons.

And just like that, Zeke went from would-be author to could-be killer.

* * *

Later that night I was stretched out in the tub, thinking about Zeke, who—in case you're wondering—didn't sell his short story to *The New Yorker*. He'd come back to his cottage, tossing his rejection letter into a wastebasket crammed, I suspected, with many other like-minded missives. But, still fueled by Red Bull, he shrugged off this temporary setback and practically pushed me out the door, eager to resume work on his novel.

Now I wondered if Zeke had used some of his unbounded energy to zap a bit of Raid on Dean's Skinny Kitty. Surely those online poison searches were a tad incriminating.

And yet, if he really had killed Dean, would he be foolhardy enough to blab about how happy he was to be rid of him? Wouldn't he try faking some grief?

And what about my other suspects du jour? There was Ian and his Murder Scrapbook. And my unscrupulous agent, Deedee, who trotted around with a convenient can of Raid in her purse.

"Oh, Pro!" I sighed. "So many suspects, so little proof."

Prozac, who was perched on the toilet tank, merely stared at me, glassy-eyed.

How I longed for the days when I'd pour my heart out to her, only to have her yawn in reply. Now the poor thing didn't even have the energy to open her mouth.

I was lying there, wondering if she was ever going to be her old self again, when I heard Lance knocking at my front door.

"Open up, Jaine. It's urgent!"

Of course, Lance's idea of urgent is a BOGO

sale at H&M. Nevertheless, I wrenched myself from the tub.

"Hold on!" I cried. "I'll be right there."

Minutes later, I was in my robe, leaving damp footprints on the floor as I hurried to get the door.

"Hey, sweetie," he said, sailing in, clad in faded jeans and an I ❤ MAMIE T-shirt. "Here's your *New York Times*. Hope you don't mind. I borrowed it this morning."

So that's where it went!

He held it out gingerly by the edges. Quickly I grabbed it from him, only to discover it was covered with wet, slimy stuff.

"What's this wet goo?" I asked.

"Dog spit," Lance replied. "Mamie's been rehearsing with it all day. The Brad Pitt gig fell through, but Deedee lined up an audition for a Polish sausage commercial. Mamie is up for the part of the family dog who brings in the morning paper. You should see her carrying that paper in her little mouth. She's such a pro. I just know she's going to be a star!" His eyes shone with dreams of glory and six-figure paychecks. "Today Polish sausage. Tomorrow the world!"

But I was only half listening to his babble. All I cared about was my puzzle. It wasn't too late to fill it in. It would be my special after-dinner treat.

I opened the paper eagerly, hoping that inside, the puzzle would be dry. But when I finally fished it out, I groaned to see the squares obliterated by dog spit.

Grrr.

"And look at all these great new publicity photos!" Lance gushed. By now, he'd settled on the sofa and was holding out a bunch of glossies. "Here's Mamie as a doctor." (Mamie with a stethoscope around her neck.) "Here she is as a flamenco dancer." (Mamie with a rose clenched in her teeth.) "Here she is as a ballet dancer." (Mamie in a tutu.) "Isn't Mamie just the cutest doggie you've ever seen?"

Prozac, who'd wandered in from the bathroom, looked up at Lance with jaded eyes.

The cuter they are, the harder they fall.

"And here's one more," Lance said, whipping out a final photo. "Me, as a doctor. The photographer let me wear Mamie's stethoscope. He said he'd take more pictures of me, in case I decide to go into show biz. Which, as you know, I'm seriously thinking of doing. Tell me, is it just me, or do I bear an uncanny resemblance to Laurence Olivier?"

"It's just you."

But he was oblivious to my barb, too busy staring at himself as a doctor.

"Well, gotta run, hon," Lance said, finally tearing himself away from his head shot. "You don't mind if I take your paper again tomorrow, do you?"

"Touch my paper, and you're a dead man."

"Okay, okay," he said, palms out in self-defense. "If that's how you feel, I won't take your paper. I've learned my lesson."

Thank goodness for that.

"I'll take Mr. Hurlbutt's paper across the street. He doesn't seem like much of a reader to me."

"Why can't Mamie rehearse with *this* paper?" I asked, holding out the paper he'd stolen that morning.

"Ick, no. It's got spit all over it. Who'd want this?"

"Well, thanks so very much for returning it."

"No problem, hon. That's what friends are for."

And with that, Lance sailed out the door, a five-letter word for the most irritating man in the world.

Chapter 19

By now Prozac had reached the depths of her depression, slinking around the apartment like an extra from *Invasion of the Body Snatchers*, a lifeless automaton, a shell of her former self.

She clawed me awake for her breakfast the next morning, barely grazing my nightgown, looking down at me with glazed eyes.

Time to feed me, I guess. But if you want to sleep an extra twenty minutes, go for it.

I gulped in dismay. What happened to my pampered princess, stomping on my chest, demanding her chow?

Thank heavens Emmy, the Reiki healer, was stopping by that afternoon. I only hoped she'd be able to rouse Prozac from her funk and bring back the fractious furball I knew and loved.

I actually did roll over and fall asleep again, and for the first time in I don't know how long, I slept until ten. I must admit, it felt divine.

At this point, the old Prozac would have been

yowling for her breakfast at ear-shattering deci-
bels. But today she just followed me as I padded to
the kitchen and sloshed some minced mackerel
guts in her bowl.

Leaving her pecking at her chow, I headed for
the front door where I was happy to find my unsul-
lied newspapers—along with a box of Krispy Kreme
doughnuts and a note from Lance.

> *So sorry about taking your paper yesterday. Here's*
> *half a dozen chocolate glazed doughnuts with*
> *sprinkles on top. Love & kisses, Lance.*

See? Lance may be a tad self-centered at times,
but his heart's in the right place. That's why I love
the guy.

> *P.S. I ate most of the sprinkles.*

Damn that man!

Back in my kitchen, I nuked myself some instant
coffee, then settled down with *The New York Times*
crossword puzzle and a single Krispy Kreme doughnut. Yes, that's all I was going to allow myself. One
chocolate glazed doughnut with most of the sprinkles missing. Not a bite more.

Twenty minutes later, I'd finished the puzzle
and both doughnuts.

Okay, so I had two. You would have, too. They
were scrumptious. And they couldn't have been
very fattening, what with all the sprinkles missing.

And besides, I'd make up for the extra calories
with a superlight lunch. I'd order the bacon ranch
salad at McDonald's. Only 190 calories!

Come to think of it, as long as I was saving so many calories at lunch, there was no reason I couldn't have another doughnut now, right? With all those sprinkles missing, it was practically a diet doughnut. . . .

This is why you should never bring me doughnuts.

After scarfing down half a third doughnut, I finally tore myself away from the Krispy Kreme box and headed for my bedroom to get dressed.

I comforted myself with the thought that the chocolate on my doughnuts was filled with energizing endorphins.

And that morning, I was going to need all the energy I could get. Because I'd made up my mind to confront Deedee and demand the thousand bucks she owed me.

I'd left Deedee about half a dozen messages, none of which she'd returned. Which left me no alternative but to drive out to Hollywood and corner her at work.

When I showed up at the House of Wonton, they were just getting started on the lunch crowd. The hostess, clad in a turquoise capri set with sequined butterflies flitting across her chest, waved me through to the back.

Marching across the restaurant, I was determined to hang tough with the ever-elusive Deedee. I'd simply tell her I wanted my thousand-dollar kill fee, and I wanted it *now*.

I stomped down the hallway past the kitchen, picking up a few choice curse words from the cooking staff, and arrived at Deedee's door. I knocked sharply. Then, without waiting for permission to enter, I flung the door open to find Deedee sitting at her desk, her chopsticks askew in her hair, eyes closed, clutching a crystal to her chest.

"Deedee?" I said.

No response.

"Deedee?"

Still no response.

If she thought she could get out of paying me my money with some sort of fake meditation act, she was nuts.

Just as I was about to reach over and yank the crystal from her hands, her eyes flew open.

"Jaine! How long have you been standing there? I've just been communing with my crystal in my never-ending search for inner peace."

Yada yada. Blah blah blah. What a load of poo poo.

"Thank heavens you stopped by!" she added, with what looked like a genuine smile.

I must admit, I was taken aback. I was expecting a rat caught in a trap, not someone who actually seemed happy to see me. Maybe getting my kill fee wouldn't be so tough, after all.

"I know who killed Dean!" She beamed with pride.

"You do?"

Well, this was good news. I could wrap up this case and concentrate on getting a decent pair of strappy sandals for my trip to Hawaii.

"Who was it?"

"Dean."

Huh?

"I'm convinced it was suicide," Deedee said, with a confident nod. "Dean was an evil man, cheating on his wife, threatening to ruin my career and Ian's. So careless with other people's lives. It all caught up with him. Somewhere deep in his soul he had a spark of conscience. A spark that grew over time into an unbearable burden. Then, overcome with remorse over his evil ways, he decided to end it all."

"So he killed himself by poisoning his own cat food?" I asked, oozing skepticism.

"Admittedly an unusual way to go, but people do strange things."

She picked up her crystal and gazed into it, a faraway look in her eyes.

"Dean reminds me a lot of my ex-husband. El-more. A selfish man, thought only of his own carnal desires. Started having affairs almost from the day we got married. Then one day a tall redhead named Ursula walked into our office. She had a poodle she wanted to get into show business. The dog was terrible. Could barely find his own tail. But Elmore signed the dog anyway. I should have known then it was all about Ursula. Before long, he'd left me for her. A year later he had the nerve to invite me to their wedding.

"He never thought I'd show up. He just sent me the invitation to rub salt in my wounds. That's the kind of person he was. But I went with my head held high. I wasn't going to give him the satisfaction of seeing me unhappy.

"When he saw me at the reception, something powerful happened. After all those years of being selfish, his conscience finally kicked in. I could see it in his eyes. He knew he'd done wrong. He knew he'd sinned."

Her eyes shone with a feverish intensity.

"I wasn't surprised when he keeled over at the wedding dinner. They said it was a heart attack. But I knew better. It was his conscience. He couldn't live with the despicable human being he'd become. The stress of it all killed him. He did it to himself. Just like Dean killed himself."

Wow. This was serious loony tunes chat. Any minute now, she'd be telling me her chopsticks were receiving signals from outer space.

"That's my theory anyway," she said modestly.

"I'll be sure to keep it in mind. But actually, Deedee, there's another reason I stopped by. The same reason I left those seven messages on your phone."

"You left me seven messages?" She blinked in fake confusion. "Well, gosh. I never got them. Darn cell phone. Always on the fritz. Last time I ever buy my electronics at Toys'R'Us. Haha."

"I want to talk to you about my kill fee from the Skinny Kitty shoot. According to my contract, you owe me a thousand dollars."

"Oh, that," Deedee said with a wave of her caf-tanned arm. "Honey, you can't get paid until Dean's estate is settled. That could take weeks or months. Maybe even years."

At which point, she started shuffling papers on her desk, pretending to look them over. I could tell it was all an act, because the paper she was studying so intently was upside down.

"I promise to call the minute I hear anything about your money," she said, her eyes refusing to meet mine.

"You do that."

"And think about my suicide theory."

"I'll give it all the thought it deserves," I assured her.

Which was, of course, none.

I headed back out into the restaurant, seething. The nerve of that woman, yapping about her husband's lack of conscience when clearly hers had disappeared some time along with the Tyrannosaurus rex.

I was muttering a colorful stream of four-letter words I'd picked up from the cooking staff when suddenly I noticed a customer in a Miami Dolphins baseball cap. I didn't much care about the guy. Or his cap. What my eyes were riveted on were the steaming fried rice and egg rolls on his plate.

Good heavens, they looked dee-lish.

But I couldn't possibly think of eating Chinese food, not after the two and a half doughnuts I had for breakfast. No way! Absolutely not! As soon as I left the restaurant, I was heading straight for McDonald's and a 190-calorie bacon ranch salad.

Reluctantly I tore my eyeballs away from Mr. Dolphin and continued toward the front of the restaurant.

As I approached the reception desk, the hostess smiled at me, her sequin butterflies glittering in the sunlight streaming in from the street.

"Have a nice day," she said.

"Okay, you talked me into it. I'll have some fried rice and an order of egg rolls."

She blinked, puzzled.

"What's that?"

"I'd like to order some food. Fried rice and egg rolls. To go."

"Fine," she said, nodding.

"And throw in some fortune cookies!"

Oh, Lord. I can't take me anywhere.

The hostess wrote out my order and handed it to a passing waiter. Then she turned to me and asked, "You're Deedee's client, aren't you?"

"Sort of," I nodded.

"Watch out," she warned. "She'll rob you blind."

"I figured as much."

"Untrustworthy lady," she tsked. "Always late with her rent. I let her stay here only because I feel sorry for her. Her husband left her for another woman. Then he died. Terrible tragedy."

"I know. She was just telling me. He had a heart attack."

"Heart attack?" She shook her head vehemently, sending her sequined butterflies aflutter. "No, no heart attack."

"Then how did he die?"

"Food poisoning. Just like the Skinny Kitty man."

Well, how do you like them wontons?

Ten minutes later, I left the restaurant with my fried rice, egg rolls, and a hotter-than-ever murder suspect.

Chapter 20

You'd expect a Reiki healer to be a New Age-y gal in yoga pants, dripping with kabbalah bracelets, right? Not Emmy. I blinked in surprise when she showed up at my doorstep, a frumpy fortysomething with tightly permed hair and a housedress straight out of the Ethel Mertz collection. She strode into my apartment in no-nonsense orthopedic shoes, a massive tote bag slung over her shoulder.

"So nice to meet you," she said, grabbing my hand in a firm handshake.

Then instantly she pulled away, frowning.

"What's that goo on your hand?"

"So sorry. I was eating an egg roll. I'm afraid my hands are a little greasy."

"Egg rolls, eh?" she said, giving my body the once-over. "In case you're interested, I also do special healing for weight loss and appetite control."

"Oh?" I replied, more than a hint of frost in my voice.

"Just something to consider."

With that, she tossed her tote down on my sofa and took out an oversized appointment book.

"I never go anywhere without this baby," she said, tapping it with pride. "Don't believe in computers. Soul-sucking hotbeds of negative energy."

Cancel that grant from the Bill Gates Foundation.

"Now, let me see," she said, riffling through the pages of her appointment book. "If I remember correctly, I'm here for . . . ?"

"Prozac."

"Why on earth would I need any Prozac?" she bristled. "I'm perfectly happy, thank you very much."

"No, Prozac is my cat."

"Really? Most unusual name," she said, eyebrow raised in disapproval. "If you ask me, pharmaceuticals are an insidious crutch destroying the moral fiber of this nation."

She certainly was chock-full of opinions, n'est-ce pas?

Then, consulting her appointment book, she said, "I see here that Prozac is depressed."

"Very. She was supposed to star in a cat food commercial, but everything fell apart, and she hasn't been the same since. In fact, your client Deedee was there at the shoot. She's the one who referred me to you."

"Deedee," Emmy beamed. "Such a lovely woman. Such a noble spirit."

Could she possibly be talking about the same unscrupulous cat doper who'd conned me out of a pricey lunch at the Peninsula?

But then I realized that this was a golden opportunity to confirm Deedee's alibi.

"Deedee told me she had a phone appointment with you the day of Dean Oliver's murder. In fact, she was on the phone with you when Dean was killed, right?"

Emmy shot me a steely glance.

"I'm sorry, but I never give out confidential information about my clients. I'm sure you'll come to appreciate that if you ever consult me about your eating issues."

The woman was really beginning to get on my nerves.

"Now where's your kitty?" she asked, tossing her appointment book back in her tote.

"In my bedroom."

I'd left Prozac lounging on the bed next to a cashmere sweater, hoping the lure of the expensive wool would stir her out of her funk.

"Right this way," I said, leading Emmy to my bedroom, where we found Prozac sprawled out on the bed, staring dully off into space in Stepford Kitty mode, my cashmere sweater untouched at her side.

"Prozac, honey," I cooed. "Look who's here. It's Emmy, the Reiki healer."

Emmy's pinched face softened at the sight of her.

"Oh, my," she tsked. "That's one sad little cat."

At this, Prozac seemed to take umbrage, lobbing Emmy a withering glare.

Talk about sad. Where'd you get your outfit? A thrift shop in Odessa?

"Well, let's get started," Emmy said, scooting Prozac to the edge of the bed. "With human patients, I usually do hands-on healing. But with animals, I don't make contact with the body. My hands will just hover over your beloved animal, transmitting the healing energy from my palms."

She held out her arms, palms cupped over Prozac, eyes shut in concentration.

Prozac sniffed the air, her pink nose twitching.

Hey, lady. Ever hear of deodorant?

Emmy continued to hold her hands over Prozac, moving them above her body, in a trancelike state.

Prozac looked up at her, baffled.

All this hand hovering, and no belly rub? What good is she?

Something told me this Reiki thing was going to be a bit of a bust.

But it needn't be a total waste of time. I remembered the appointment book in Emmy's tote bag, where she made notes about her patients. A quick peek inside would tell me if Deedee was really on the phone with her at the time of the murder.

"Excuse me," I whispered, eager to get back out to the living room. "I've got something in the oven I need to check on."

Of course, the only thing I ever used my oven for was to warm my socks on a cold winter's day, but Emmy didn't need to know that.

"For Pete's sake," she snapped, eyes springing open. "You've broken the healing chain. I need absolute silence for this to work."

From the bed, Prozac practically rolled her eyes.

For this to work, lady, you're going to need a miracle.

Apologizing profusely for breaking Emmy's

healing chain, I scooted out, promising there'd be no more interruptions.

Once in the living room, I made a beeline for her tote.

So eager was I to get at Emmy's appointment book that I whipped it out with just a bit too much fervor. Oh, crud. I watched in dismay as the massive tote tipped over, sending its contents clattering to the floor.

"What the hell was that?" Emmy shouted from the bedroom.

"So sorry!" I cried out. "Just dropped a pot. No more noise from now on. I promise!"

I spent the next few minutes on my hands and knees, retrieving lipstick, tampons, tissues, Diet Coke, and—of all things!—a bag of Reese's Pieces.

(And she had the nerve to make cracks about *my* eating habits!)

At last I'd shoved everything back in the tote. Grabbing the appointment book, I thumbed through the pages until I got to the day of the murder.

Sure enough, between eleven thirty and noon, I found Deedee's name. So she *had* been on the phone with Emmy.

And then I saw, scrawled under Deedee's name, the cryptic letters "KD."

I began to ponder what this could possibly mean when I heard Emmy clomping down the hallway from my bedroom.

Quick as a bunny, I bolted over to her tote to stash the book away. But I was not quite quick enough. Just as I was shoving it inside the tote, Emmy came barging into the living room.

"All through!" she chirped. "The treatment

doesn't take much time with small animals like Prozac."

Then she saw me frozen to the spot, still clutching her purloined appointment book.

"Hey, what're you doing with that?"

With the dazzling sangfroid I'm known for, I replied: "Um . . . er . . . uh . . ."

Suspicion oozing from every pore, Emmy stomped to my kitchen and flung open the oven door.

"So this is what you were cooking?" She held up a pair of long-forgotten gym socks. "What are you going to serve them with? A side of shoelaces?"

She stood scowling at me, arms clamped across her ample chest.

"You didn't come out here to check anything in your oven. You came out here to snoop in my appointment book."

"Okay," I confessed. "I needed to find out if Deedee was really on the phone with you on the day Dean Oliver was killed. I'm a suspect in his murder, and I'm trying to track down the killer."

She thought this over and must have decided I was telling the truth.

"Yes, Deedee was on the phone with me," she conceded. "Satisfied now?"

"Almost. Just one more question. What does 'KD' mean?"

"Karmic Detox. I was giving Deedee instructions on how to purge Dean's negative karma from her body. Is there anything else you'd like to know? Details from my sex life, perhaps?"

"*You* have a sex life?" were the words I barely stopped myself from blurting out.

"No, thanks. I'm fine. You've been very helpful, and I'm very grateful."

"You can show me your gratitude with a check for a hundred dollars, please."

I took out my checkbook and wrote the check. Just as I was handing it to her, Prozac came wandering into the room, dragging her paws, still in full tilt Stepford Kitty mode.

"She doesn't look very peppy to me," I said.

"No worries," Emmy said. "I've cured her. She may not show it right away, but one of these days she'll be her old self. I guarantee it."

Yeah, right, I thought, watching my hundred bucks eddy down the drain.

Slinging her tote over her shoulder, Emmy bid me farewell and headed off to wave her hands over her next patsy (I mean, client).

No doubt about it. This Reiki thing had been a total waste of money.

But on the plus side, at least I was able to check Deedee's alibi. She had been on the phone with Emmy, as claimed. Of course, for all I knew, their conversation lasted five minutes, leaving her plenty of time to dart over to the studio kitchen for a quick spritz of Raid.

And what about "KD"? Did it really mean Karmic Detox, as Emmy claimed? Or had Emmy been covering for her client?

Was it possible the initials "KD" really meant *Kill Dean*?

YOU'VE GOT MAIL!

To: Jausten
From: DaddyO
Subject: The Big Day

Today's the big day, Lambchop! The Tampa Vistas Scrabble Championship. I just finished a power breakfast of Cheerios and gherkins, and now I'm off to trounce The Battle-Axe once and for all!

Love 'n' snuggles from
DaddyO

To: Jausten
From: Shoptillyoudrop

Would you believe that crazy father of yours just ate pickles for breakfast!!?!

XOXO,
Mom

To: Jausten
From: Shoptillyoudrop
Subject: Poor Daddy!

I know Daddy's been driving me nuts getting ready for the Scrabble tournament, but now that it's over, my heart's breaking for him.

He showed up so full of confidence, with his Lucky Thinking Cap and his jar of gherkins. And much to my surprise, he sailed right through the early elimination rounds, devastating his opponents with words like *whizbang*, *jezebel*, and *jukebox*.

Then it was just him and Lydia. I thought for sure it would be a bloodbath, but Daddy stood his ground (with *flapjack*, *maximize*, and *exorcise*).

True, Daddy was chomping down on his gherkins while it was Lydia's turn, hoping to throw her off her game with his munching, but brilliant player that she is, Lydia refused to be distracted.

Daddy and Lydia were going at it neck and neck, and believe it or not, toward the end of the game, Daddy was fifteen points ahead of Lydia. It looked like he was actually going to win. But then, when all Daddy had left were some useless o's and u's, Lydia used all her tiles on a triple-word score that swept her to victory with 180 points.

And the word she used? *Gherkins!*

Poor Daddy! What tragic irony. The pickles he'd been counting on to put him over the edge were the agent of his defeat!

Somehow he managed to shake Lydia's hand and not pout too much. Honestly, honey, I felt so darn sorry for him, I hardly even minded those hideous plaid Bermuda shorts he insisted on wearing to the tournament.

I'm going to cook him a lovely pot roast for dinner tonight. With scalloped potatoes and a martini for dessert.

XOXO,
Mom

To: Jausten
From: DaddyO
Subject: Miserable News

Miserable news, Lambchop. The battle-axe "won" the tournament.

I wrote "won" in quotes because I wouldn't put it past her to have cheated her way to victory. If you ask me, she probably had a list of high-scoring words written on the insides of her orthopedic socks.

Yes, La Pinkus seems all prim and proper on the outside, but I'm sure she's the one who snuck into the house and hid my Lucky Thinking Cap. The stress of which, incidentally, cost me valuable days of training.

She's not to be trusted, that's for sure.

Oh, well. At least I've got my stylish new Bermuda shorts to console me.

Love 'n' hugs from your
Victorious in spirit
DaddyO

To: Jausten
From: Shoptillyoudrop

P.S. I thought for sure Daddy would refuse to go to the Scrabble awards luncheon, but I just asked him, and he's agreed to go. Talk about your gracious losers!

To: Jausten
From: DaddyO

P.S. I just promised your mom I'd go to the stupid awards luncheon. The only reason I'm going, of course, is to meet Alex Trebek. Once he and I get a chance to chew the fat, I'm sure I'll be a shoo-in for *Jeopardy!*

Chapter 21

The next day Prozac was still so deep in her funk, she didn't even bother to wake me. Once again, I slept in, jolted to consciousness at 10:30 by the phone ringing at my bedside.

I picked it up to hear Kandi's excited voice.

"Guess what, hon? I've got the most fantastic news!"

"What is it?" I asked, shoving Prozac's tail from my nose.

"I'll tell you all about it at lunch. Meet me at the Westside Tavern at noon. Oops. Gotta run. The cockroach is having a hissy fit."

I assumed that the cockroach to whom she referred was the lead insect on Kandi's show, *Beanie & the Cockroach*. Leaving Kandi to her cockroach wrangling, I hung up and turned to Prozac, who was staring listlessly at a pair of panty hose I'd left out on the bed for her.

To think there was a time I found these playthings amusing.

"Good morning, honey," I said, stroking her behind her ears. "How'd you like some nice human tuna for breakfast?"

Human tuna—two words that normally sent her into a feeding frenzy. But today? Nada. Zippo. Zilch.

Hustling to the kitchen, I scooped some Bumble Bee into her bowl, praying she'd show some interest. But, alas, she did her Blanche DuBois bit, nibbling at it with faint disdain.

I cringed to think of the hundred bucks I'd spent on Emmy, the Reiki healer. Waving her hands over Prozac had done absolutely nothing except give Emmy's arm flab a workout. Not for a minute did I believe her guarantee that Prozac would soon be back to her old self.

After reading about Daddy's tragic loss in the Scrabble tournament (beaten by his beloved gherkins!), I settled down with some coffee and a generously buttered cinnamon raisin bagel and whiled away the next fifteen minutes with the crossword puzzle.

I'd just filled in the last clue and was heading to the bedroom to get dressed (okay, I was heading to the kitchen for another cinnamon raisin bagel) when Lance showed up, sailing into my living room with Mamie in tow, a shopping bag dangling from his arm.

"Today's the big day, Jaine!" he cried, all duded up in a designer suit, his blond curls moussed to perfection. "We're off to our audition!"

At this, Mamie gave an excited little yap.

"Doesn't she look adorable?" Lance gushed, the proud stage papa.

And, indeed, Mamie had been groomed to within an inch of her life, her white fur spotless and adorned with a polka dot bow.

"Look!" Lance said, pointing to his tie. "Our polka dots match."

Sure enough, his mauve and white polka dot tie was the same fabric as Mamie's hair bow.

Prozac, who'd finished her breakfast and was now stretched out on my chintz armchair, belching tuna fumes, yawned in disgust.

What a ham. And I don't mean the dog.

"I'm so proud of my little star," Lance gushed. "She's got her newspaper shtick down pat. And wait till you see the special new trick I've taught her. It's going to impress the heck out of the casting people!

"Voilà!" he said, taking a small purse out of his shopping bag. "An imitation Hermès handbag. The original cost twelve grand!"

My God, twelve thousand dollars for a purse? Something to hold used tissues and linty Life Savers? Had the world gone mad?

"I've taught Mamie how to pick it up and carry it."

He put the purse down on my coffee table and called out to Mamie. "Look, Mamie! There's your Hermès purse!"

Mamie, who had been busy sniffing Prozac's tail, looked up, interested.

"Go get it, girl!"

Lance pointed to the bag, and sure enough, Mamie left the exotic scent of Prozac's rear quarters and trotted over to the coffee table, where she snatched the purse in her mouth.

Then she strutted around the room, dangling her faux Hermès, loving every minute of her fashion glory.

"Isn't that just the cutest thing you've ever seen?" Lance said, beaming. "Talk about your designer doggies!"

From her perch on the armchair, Prozac gazed at Mamie with world-weary eyes.

Enjoy it while it lasts, kiddo. One day you're a star, and the next, you're back on the sofa, sniffing for old pizza crusts.

But Mamie was still prancing around, oblivious, prepping for the runway in Milan.

"I'm bringing my head shot, just in case," Lance said, flashing the eight-by-ten glossy of himself sporting a stethoscope. "And I've had more pics taken, too," he added, whipping a sheaf of photos from the shopping bag. "Here's my preppy look. My truck driver look. And my cowboy look. What do you think?"

"Lance, I can honestly say this is the first time I've ever seen a cowboy with a monogrammed pocket hankie."

"I know. Super touch, isn't it?"

I could only nod weakly.

"And look at the business cards I've made up."

He fished out a business card from his shopping bag, bordered in tiny paw prints, which read:

MAMIE, THE WONDER DOG!
THE MERYL STREEP OF THE CANINE WORLD
LANCE VENABLE, MANAGER
1-800-I BARK 4U

I stared at it, gobsmacked. Not at the Meryl Streep comparison, although heaven knows that was cheeky enough. I simply could not get over the 800 phone line.

"You had a special phone number set up?"

"Of course."

"What if she doesn't get the part?"

"She will. No doubt about it. My Mamie is headed for doggie stardom. Nothing but the best for us from now on. Limos, fine wine, gourmet kibble. Top of the line all the time! Oh, by the way. Can you loan me six bucks for valet parking?"

Mamie might or might not come back as a star, but one thing I knew for sure: Lance would always come back as the most irritating man in the world.

Chapter 22

"**A** present for you, sweetheart."

I was sitting across from Kandi at the Westside Tavern, a clubby joint in the Westside Pavilion shopping mall, settled in a cushy booth under dim mood lighting.

"To thank you for all your help the other night," Kandi said, holding out a lump of misshapen red wool.

"How lovely," I lied. "My cell phone cover!"

"It's not a cell phone cover. It's a tea cozy."

"Right."

"That hole over there is where the spout goes."

There were several gaping holes in the lumpy mass, but I nodded as if I knew which hole she was talking about.

Our actress/waitress, a willowy blonde with shampoo-commercial hair, came over then to take our order.

"What'll it be, ladies?" she asked, flashing us a

blinding smile, just in case one of us was a casting director.

Kandi ordered the chicken Cobb salad, and I got what I always get at the Westside Tavern: cheeseburger with homemade potato chips.

"So," I said once our actress/waitress had skipped off, "what's your exciting news?"

I just hoped it was that she'd decided to give up knitting.

"I went to my money management class last night and met the most fabulous man!" she grinned. "A Russian violinist. His name is Alexi and he has the biggest, brownest eyes to come down the pike since Bambi."

Her own eyes were shining with the kind of fervor mine get when I see Ben & Jerry's on sale.

"And to think I almost didn't go! My car was in the shop, and I was planning to stay home, but at the last minute I took an Uber and was so glad I did. I took one look at Alexi, and I knew it was meant to be. Sure enough, the feeling was mutual. He asked me out to dinner tonight. Wait till I show you the adorable sweater I bought to wear on our date."

With that, she reached down under the table and pulled out a Nordstrom shopping bag.

"Whoa. I thought you'd given up shopping."

"I did. Back when I was shopping out of frustration over my crummy love life. But now that I've found Alexi, I'm shopping out of happiness. So it doesn't count."

Talk about world-class rationalization.

"How did you get your credit cards back so fast?"

"Actually," she said, blushing just a tad, "I never did cut them up. I put them in my safe deposit box. Needless to say, I was at the bank first thing this morning, and they got quite a workout. Look!" She held up a powder puff of a white cashmere sweater. "Isn't it gorge? And wait'll you see the lace bra and panties I bought. Not for tonight, of course. I want to save those for the honeymoon."

I gave it three weeks, tops.

Oh, well. At least she'd be happy for three weeks. And with any luck, she'd be too busy dating Alexi to do any more knitting.

"So tell me all about Bambi Eyes," I said, knowing I was about to unleash the floodgates. "Why was he taking the money management class?"

"Alexi wasn't at the class. He was my Uber driver. He works as a driver to pay the bills in between symphony gigs."

I should've known. Instead of a class full of men eager to learn about stable financial practices, Kandi had fallen for a violin-playing Uber driver.

"Honestly, Jaine," she gushed. "I think I've finally met Mr. Right."

I could practically see the bubble of hope dancing above her head, just waiting to be burst.

"But, Kandi," I said, unable to restrain myself any longer. "That's what you say about every guy you meet."

"Can I help it if I'm a positive person?" she said, a tad miffed at me for raining on her parade. "Look, I know sometimes I may fool myself, but this time it's different. I could tell by the way Alexi offered me a complimentary mint when I got in his car that there was something special about him."

Remember that, class.

Complimentary Mints = True Love.

But I didn't have the energy to launch into a lecture on unrealistic expectations, so I just sat back and listened as she babbled on, murmuring my approval at appropriate intervals.

Eventually our lunch showed up, and I dug into my cheeseburger with gusto.

Kandi was so busy yakking about Alexi, she barely touched her chicken Cobb salad.

But that's okay. It made a tasty dip for my homemade potato chips.

Frankly, I was appalled at Kandi's lack of willpower. The woman simply could not resist the lure of a shopping bag. Thank heavens we Austens are made of sterner stuff. Here, I was about to head off to Hawaii, but you didn't catch me running around shopping obsessively for flirty sundresses, cute capris, and strappy sandals. True, I'd been thinking about splurging on some sandals, but the more I thought about it, the more I realized what an unnecessary expense it would be—especially when my budget was so tight, it was practically in a tourniquet.

Yes, I, Jaine Austen, am a woman who walks on the sensible side of life, who trods on the path of industry, frugality, and—

Good heavens! What was I doing here at Nordstrom's semiannual shoe sale? With a strappy sandal in my hand?

Clearly some shopaholic demon had invaded my body and marched me over without my even realizing it.

I looked around at the racks and racks of shoes. All on sale!

No doubt about it. I'd died and gone to shoe heaven.

And before I knew what I was doing, I'd kicked off my Nikes and begun trying on sandals to take with me on vacation.

I tried on flat sandals, wedgie sandals, gladiator sandals, cork-soled sandals; sandals with flowers, sandals with butterflies, and fancy flip-flops.

Isn't shoe shopping the most marvelous fun? Where else can you try on something without having to look in the mirror at unsightly love handles or ghastly patches of cellulite? No hip bulges or tummy bumps. Just twinkly little toes popping out from some straps, your ankle looking practically as skinny as Gwyneth Paltrow's.

No wonder poor Kandi couldn't stay away from her credit cards. Why would anyone want to deprive herself of the pleasure of shoe shopping at Nordstrom?

I was standing there, admiring my tootsies in a pair of lace-up espadrilles—on sale for just thirty-nine dollars—when suddenly I realized I'd lost track of my hundred-dollar Nikes. (Yes, I'd paid full price for them, under the influence of a particularly hunkalicious shoe salesman.)

I raced back to the rack where I'd first kicked them off, but they weren't there.

Could I possibly be at the wrong rack? Frantically, I started weaving up and down the shoe racks, looking for my abandoned running shoes. But they were nowhere to be found.

Desperate, I grabbed a passing sales clerk, a harried guy whose arms were piled high with shoe boxes.

"You've got to help me!" I wailed. "I'm looking for a pair of white Nikes. Size seven and a half, with a small ketchup stain on the front right toe."

The sales guy blinked, boggled.

"Sorry, ma'am. We don't sell stained shoes."

"No, no. I don't want to buy them. I already own them. I put them down to try on some sandals, and now I can't find them."

A look of disbelief crossed his face.

"What're you, nuts? You think I'm going to run around looking for a pair of shoes you already own?"

Okay, so what he really said was: "I'll keep an eye out for them, ma'am."

And he was off like a shot to wait on his paying customers.

Just when I was getting panicky, wondering how I was going to walk back to my car barefoot, I looked over at a nearby clearance bin and spotted a familiar white running shoe poking out from the pile.

I raced over, and sure enough, it was my Nike with the ketchup stain on the toe. Practically swooning with relief, I grabbed it eagerly, then started rifling through the bin, searching for its mate.

Alas, I searched in vain.

But then I happened to glance over at the woman next to me—a hefty bruiser who bore an uncanny resemblance to the late, great Ernest Borgnine—

only to see her jamming her foot into my size seven and a half Nike.

"I'm sorry," I said, "but these Nikes aren't for sale. They're mine."

"Like hell they are," she growled. (And a most unpleasant growl it was, too.) "I saw them first."

With that, she started tugging at the shoe in my hand. Her biceps, I noticed, were the size of rump roasts.

I had to do something to stop her. In a tug-of-war, she was bound to win.

"Honest," I cried. "These shoes are mine. Look! There's a ketchup stain on the toe from a Quarter Pounder I ate the other week."

Eyes scrunched, she peered at the stain.

"I don't care," she proclaimed. "It's a small stain. And the price is right."

I saw now that a stray $19.99 sticker had attached itself to the shoe. No wonder she wanted my Nikes so badly.

"Okay," I said. "But I should warn you. I've got a terrible case of toe fungus. Highly contagious."

"What?" Quickly, she kicked off the shoe she'd been wearing. "Why didn't you say so?"

"Don't worry," I assured her. "It's hardly ever fatal."

Her eyes wide with fear, she slipped on her own shoes and hurried off into the crowd.

Yes, I know it was a dirty trick, making her worry like that. But she'd been such a pill, I thought she sort of deserved it, don't you?

Thrilled at last to be reunited with my Nikes, I headed over to a nearby chair to put them on.

Slinging the espadrilles I'd been wearing over

my wrist, I put on the shoe Ms. Borgnine had worn, and I was quite annoyed to realize that she'd stretched it out a tad. Then I picked up the other shoe, the one that was in the bin. But when I tried to slip it on, I felt something blocking my toes. I reached in and pulled out a piece of paper. It was a page torn from a magazine, folded up to fit in the shoe. I unfolded it to see an ad for Raid. The headline read RAID KILLS BUGS. But whoever had shoved the ad in my shoe had crossed out the word "bugs." So now it read simply:

RAID KILLS

A chill ran down my spine when I saw that the words "You're Next" had been cut out from a newspaper and pasted underneath.

Oh, hell. Clearly I'd just received a billet-doux from the murderer.

I whirled around, looking to see who could have left it. But everyone looked so ordinary, so innocent. Just a mom with a toddler in a stroller, an old lady with a cane, and some teenyboppers giggling over something on their cell phones.

But then, over by cosmetics, I saw a large woman in a caftan, her arms loaded with bangles, hurrying out of the store.

Deedee! Emmy must have told her I'd been checking up on her. And now she'd come to scare me off.

By the time I'd finished tying my laces, she was gone. I raced out of Nordstrom and spotted her down at the other end of the mall.

For one of the few times in my life, I actually ran in my running shoes.

Deedee was walking fast, but not fast enough.

Pushing my way past surprised shoppers, I finally caught up with her, grabbing her by the elbow.

"I know you're the killer!" I shouted.

By now a small crowd had formed around us. Which made it all the more embarrassing when the woman in the caftan turned around to face me.

Of course, as all you "A" students have probably already guessed, it wasn't Deedee, but some innocent shopper with a penchant for loose fitting apparel.

I would have offered her my profuse apologies, but I never got the chance.

Because just then a security goon showed up and hauled me off to mall jail.

Not for assaulting an innocent shopper.

But for shoplifting a pair of lace-up espadrilles— which, I now realized, I still had dangling from my wrist.

Chapter 23

"I swear I wasn't trying to steal the espadrilles!"

I was sitting in a windowless cubbyhole in the bowels of the mall, across from my arresting officer—a stocky mall cop, with sweat stains the size of Staten Island under his arms.

"I was just trying to catch the killer," I continued, pleading my case.

"What killer?"

"The person who poisoned the Skinny Kitty."

He shook his head, confused.

"You're looking for someone who killed a skinny cat?"

"No, no. Skinny Kitty is a cat food, and the guy who invented it got murdered. And now I'm trying to track down his killer."

"You some sort of detective?" the mall cop asked, giving his armpits an energetic scratch.

"Part-time semiprofessional," I nodded.

"Semiprofessional?" He shot me a skeptical

look. "From what I've seen, I'd say barely professional."

Ouch. That hurt.

At which point there was a timid knock on the door, and the shoe salesman I'd flagged down at Nordstrom poked his head in.

"You wanted to see me?" he asked the cop, whose name, according the tag on his shirt, was J. Schulte.

"You recognize this woman?" asked J. Schulte (or, as I liked to think of him, The Sweater).

"Yes, she was trying to find a pair of seven-and-a-half Nikes with a ketchup stain on the toe."

The Sweater blinked, puzzled.

"Nordstrom sells stained shoes?"

"No," I piped up. "They were my shoes. I took them off to try on the espadrilles, and then I couldn't find them and when I finally did this lady who looked like Ernest Borgnine was trying them on, and I had to pretend I had toe fungus so she'd give them back to me, and then I saw Deedee, at least I thought it was Deedee, and I'm pretty certain she's the killer since her husband didn't die of a heart attack like she said, but food poisoning just like Dean, so naturally I ran after her, only it turned out not to be Deedee after all and I didn't realize I still had the espadrilles until you showed up and arrested me."

I tend to babble when I'm nervous.

But fortunately, my stream of chatter was cut off by the phone ringing.

The Sweater answered it and motioned me out of the room.

I spent the next few minutes sitting in a tiny waiting area, under the watchful eye of a female security officer who in a former life had no doubt been an NFL quarterback.

After what seemed like a small eternity, I was summoned back to the august presence of The Sweater.

"I tried to pass on your story as best I could to the security executive at Nordstrom," he said. "You'll be happy to know they're not pressing charges."

Thank heavens for those wonderful people at that fabulous store!

"In fact," he said, "they feel so bad that you've had such a stressful experience, they want you to have this."

With that, he handed me a business card.

How nice. Feeling guilty for having me falsely arrested, I bet they were offering me the services of a personal shopper!

But then I looked down at the card, which read:

DR. ALICE RUDNICK
PSYCHIATRIST

"They suggest you seek counseling ASAP," The Sweater said. "Preferably with meds. I personally would recommend heavy doses."

Well! Of all the nerve! Implying that I was a raving loony.

I was so angry, I stomped right out of the security offices straight to my Corolla, fuming all the way.

Okay, so I stopped off for a Mrs. Fields cookie.

And the espadrilles.

And a flirty sundress.

Oh, hell. I was as bad as Kandi.

I don't know what possessed me to go on that crazy shopping spree.

I guess Dr. Alice Rudnick would say it was some sort of escape mechanism, that I shopped to forget the death threat I'd just received and the snake pit of danger my life had become.

But as I hauled my goodies back to my Corolla, whatever temporary respite I'd gotten from my shopping spree vanished, and a fresh wave of fear flooded over me.

I remembered all too well my Raid death threat, which lay like a burning ember in my pants pocket, and made a mental note to bring it to the cops the first thing in the morning.

Right then, though, all I wanted was to go home and soak in a nice relaxing tub, preferably with a glass of chardonnay at my side.

Back at my apartment, I found Prozac draped across my armchair.

"Oh, Pro!" I wailed, kicking off my Nikes. "I've had the most ghastly afternoon. I got a death threat from the killer, and I almost got arrested for shoplifting."

Through slitted eyes, she lobbed me a world-weary look.

Yeah, right. Whatever. At least one of us can get arrested in this town.

I headed to the kitchen for a rendezvous with my good buddy Mr. Chardonnay and had just pulled the bottle from the fridge when I heard the unmistakable sound of Lance banging at my door.

"Jaine, it's me. Open up!"

Clutching my bottle of chardonnay, I hurried to the door and opened it to find Lance looking utterly dejected, Mamie at his side.

He staggered in, still in the same outfit he'd worn that morning, his blond curls limp, his polka dot tie askew.

Mamie, trotting in behind him, made a beeline for Prozac's tush, which she began sniffing amiably.

"Horrible news," Lance groaned. "Mamie didn't get the part."

"Oh, no!" I tsked in sympathy. "Want some chardonnay to ease the pain?"

"Thanks," he said, grabbing the wine and glugging it straight from the bottle.

So much for my rendezvous with Mr. C. Why the heck hadn't I poured myself a glass before I answered the door?

"What a nightmare!" Lance said, plopping down on the sofa, cradling the wine in his lap.

"Mamie didn't fetch her newspaper on cue?"

"We didn't even get that far. Remember the trick I taught her to impress everybody? Picking up her toy Hermès bag and trotting around with it?"

"Vividly," I nodded.

"Well, it turns out the ad agency producer is a dedicated fashionista. She had a bag just like Mamie's. Only hers was the twelve-thousand-dollar original. When I told Mamie to go get the Hermès purse, instead of picking up her prop bag like we'd rehearsed, she went straight for the producer's twelve-thousand-dollar jobbie, snatched it up in her jaws, and got dog spit all over it."

"Oh, gaak, no!"

"The producer went ballistic, and Mamie got so discombobulated, she wound up taking a tinkle on the director's leg." He paused to take another slug from my wine bottle. "Needless to say, she didn't get the gig."

"I'm so sorry, Lance."

"Not only that, Deedee dropped her as a client. Poor Mamie," Lance said, shaking his head. "She's positively brokenhearted."

I looked over at Mamie, still sniffing Prozac's rear.

Trust me, the only brokenhearted one in that duo was Lance.

"I suppose I've only got myself to blame. I've taught Mamie to be so discerning, it's no wonder she went for the real bag."

At that moment, the discerning dog in question had abandoned Prozac's tush and was now industriously licking my big toe.

Prozac gazed down at her with pitying eyes.

Welcome to my world, fluffball.

"What a day from hell," Lance moaned. "I can't possibly think of a more horrible afternoon."

"I can. You could have gotten a death threat from a killer and almost been arrested for shoplifting."

"You poor thing," he said, swimming up from the depths of his own misery to wallow in mine. "Tell Uncle Lance all about it."

And I did. I told him about losing my shoes and

finding the death threat in my Nike and running after the ersatz killer with a pair of Nordstrom espadrilles and winding up in mall jail.

When I was through he shook his head, tsking.

"Espadrilles? Really? Jaine, honey. They're so last year."

"Lance, will you please focus? I just got a death threat from a killer."

"You know what you need, hon?" he said.

"A bottle of chardonnay without your drool all over it?"

"A fun night out. We both need one."

Which is why an hour later we were sitting on the patio of the swellegant Coast Café on the beach in Santa Monica, sipping martinis and looking out over the glorious Pacific Ocean.

How wonderful it was to loll among the rich and pampered, watching the sun go down and sucking the pimentos out of our olives.

Soon our martinis were doing their job, and our cares of the day were fading away.

"I suppose it's all for the best," Lance said, waxing philosophical. "I'm not sure Mamie and I are cut out to be stars, anyway. You know, life in a fishbowl, constantly fighting off the paparazzi. I'm definitely the kind of guy who needs his privacy— Oops. Hold on a sec while I take a selfie of me and my martini to post on Instagram."

We ordered the cheapest thing on the menu for dinner—hot dogs with fries.

I proceeded to swan dive into mine with gusto, while Lance flirted shamelessly with our gorgeous young waiter.

Lance was right. It was good to get out, especially on such a lovely night at the beach, the sun setting in a glorious ball of orange, the ocean breezes soft as velvet against my cheek. So what if my hair was now the consistency of a Brillo pad, and the carbs from my fries were frolicking gaily on my hips?

That ghastly death threat seemed like a distant memory—Dean's murder a million miles away.

I was sitting there, nestled in my bubble of contentment, when I saw a couple being seated at a secluded table in a corner next to a potted palm. Something about the woman's cap of shiny blond hair looked familiar. And then I realized it was Nikki, the food stylist. She reached across the table to hold hands with her date. This must be the boyfriend she mentioned, the guy she hooked up with after Dean dumped her, the one she was so in love with.

I glanced over to check him out and almost choked on a fry to see that it was Artie Lembeck, Dean's former business partner—the redhead in the baseball cap who'd brought champagne and cheese puffs to the funeral to celebrate Dean's passing. The guy who claimed Dean had cheated him out of his rightful fortune.

So Nikki was dating Dean's arch-rival.

I'd sort of written her off as a suspect, but now I wondered if Nikki was the killer, after all.

Had she blasted Dean's Skinny Kitty with Raid as payback for swindling her beloved?

Or had she merely phoned Artie and had him come over to do the job himself?

Suddenly I felt chilled.

And it wasn't from the cool ocean breezes—but from the realization that I'd not escaped the murder. Not one bit. I was still very much in the thick of it.

For all I knew, at that very moment I was sitting just a potted palm away from the killer.

Chapter 24

I spent a good half hour on the phone the next morning tracking down the detective who'd come to question me after the murder, the barrel-chested guy with the scar on his cheek. His name turned out to be Ken Carbone, and he agreed to see me at 9:00 a.m. that morning.

After a diet breakfast (cinnamon raisin bagel with butter, no jam), I headed over to his precinct in Hollywood, where I gave my name to a cop at the front desk and was instructed to wait.

I then proceeded to cool my heels for what seemed like a small eternity, sharing a bench with a stunning man in high heels and short shorts who was there to report a stolen wig.

"My Joan Collins *Dynasty* model!" he moaned in dismay. "They snatched it right off my head. I tell you, it's just not safe to walk the streets anymore!" Then, with a sly wink, he added, "Right, hon?"

Of all the nerve! He thought I was a hooker!

"I'd lose that COUNT CHOCULA T-shirt if I were

you, doll. You're not gonna score any johns in that getup."

Before I had a chance to defend my virtue, our tête-à-tête was interrupted by Detective Carbone, who came striding over in drill sergeant mode.

"Ms. Austen!" he barked. "Follow me!"

I leapt to my feet and hurried after him as he led the way to his desk in a large open bull pen of a room.

His desk was littered with piles of paper, but thanks to my keen powers of observation, I was able to zero in immediately on the most important item there: a box of goodies from Krispy Kreme.

One of them—a jelly doughnut—had been removed from the box and sat on a napkin next to a mug of coffee.

I must admit that doughnut looked mighty tasty, dusted with sugar and oozing jam, the very jam I'd denied myself on my morning CRB.

Carbone plopped down on an unlucky swivel chair that squeaked in protest under his weight.

"What can I do for you?" he then asked, motioning me to take a seat across from him.

"For starters, you can offer me a doughnut."

Of course I didn't say that. But you know I was thinking it.

And he certainly could have. He had a whole boxful. Surely, he could spare just one.

But putting all thoughts of doughnuts out of my mind, I turned to the business at hand.

"Someone left this in my shoe," I said, handing him my Raid death threat, which I'd carefully wrapped in a Baggie.

"Someone left a note in your shoe?" he asked, puzzled.

"It's a long story," I said, unwilling to relive the harrowing experience of yesterday's shoe-shopping expedition. "Just read the note, okay? I'm pretty sure it's from Dean's killer."

He reached into his desk for a pair of tweezers, which he used to pull the paper from the Baggie. Then he quickly perused the doctored Raid ad.

"The way I see it," I said, "that's a death threat."

"Sure looks like it," he agreed. "But why would the killer be threatening you?"

I was a tad reluctant to tell him I'd been investigating the case, especially since I was working without a PI license. The cops tend to get persnickety about stuff like that.

"I have no idea," I said, all wide-eyed innocence. "All I know is I'm being threatened."

"All right," he said, nodding solemnly. "We'll have this paper checked out in the lab. If anything shows up, we'll be in touch."

Thank heavens he was taking me seriously!

"In the meanwhile," he added, "I'd advise you to refrain from accosting large women in caftans in the mall."

Holy Moses. Busted. The mall cop must've checked out what I'd told him about Dean's murder and wasted no time ratting me out to the cops. Quel tattletale.

"Will do," I said, blushing I don't know how many shades of red.

I got up, eager to make my exit.

"Just one more thing before you go," Detective Carbone said.

Oh, foo. Now what?

"Care for a doughnut?" he asked.

How nice. The guy had manners, after all.

"I couldn't help but notice you've been staring at them since the minute you sat down."

"Was I?" I replied coolly, more than a bit miffed at his zinger.

He held out the box, and I eyed a sugar-dusted jelly doughnut longingly.

"The jelly doughnuts are great," he said, following my gaze.

But you'll be proud to know I didn't take any of his stupid doughnuts. I wouldn't give him the satisfaction.

No, sir.

I hung tough, and took an apple fritter instead.

Next stop, Artie Lembeck.

As Nikki's boyfriend, he certainly would have known about the Skinny Kitty shoot and could have easily zipped over to poison Dean's cat food.

Maybe that champagne at Dean's funeral had been a gift to himself for a murder well executed.

Back in my Corolla, I fished around in my purse till I dredged up the business card he'd given me at the funeral. Then I made my way over to the International Headquarters of Lembeck Enterprises, which turned out to be Artie's apartment in West Hollywood.

After parking in front of Artie's building, a shabby stucco affair with a row of dusty azaleas out front, I made my way up the front path, careful not to stumble over the deep cracks in the cement.

Pressing the button for "Lembeck" on a rusted intercom, I soon heard Artie's voice come on the line amid a blast of static.

"Who is it?"

"It's Jaine Austen. We sat next to each other at Dean Oliver's funeral."

"I remember you! The cheese puff lady. So nice you could stop by. Come on up!"

What an enthusiastic welcome. I must have made quite an impression on him. Evidently, I'd been able to convey empathy for his plight as a victim of Dean's cheating ways while scarfing down my cheese puffs.

He buzzed me into the lobby, where I boarded a creaky elevator to his apartment on the second floor.

Artie was waiting for me at his front door, grinning broadly, clad in a white apron. With his wiry red curls sponging out in all directions, he had the slightly crazed look of a mad scientist.

For a minute, I wondered if he'd recognize me from the Coast Café, but apparently he'd had eyes only for Nikki last night. He gave no indication whatsoever that he'd seen me staring at him at the restaurant.

"Come in!" he said, ushering me into a tiny living room crammed with cartons. "Excuse the mess. I'm afraid my apartment doubles as a warehouse for my inventions. I'm so glad you decided to stop by and check them out."

No wonder he seemed so happy I'd shown up. He thought I was there to buy something.

"It's a good thing you came when you did. I was

just about to start brewing a fresh batch of Bilk, and once I get started, I can't break for anything."

"Bilk?" I asked, puzzled.

"Beer, made from milk!" he said, beaming. "Let me show you."

He led me into his galley kitchen, every square inch of which seemed to be taken up with pots, barrels, hoses, burlap bags of malt and hops, and gallons of milk.

"Bilk is the alcoholic beverage of the future!" Artie was gushing. "It's a fantastic source of calcium. The only beer that gives you a buzz while it builds strong bones!"

"How very interesting," I said, forcing a smile.

"C'mon," he said, leading me back out to the living room. "Let me show you my other inventions. All available to order in bulk at low, low wholesale prices."

Oh, gaak! I'd just walked into an infomercial.

"Here's my latest," he said, grabbing something from one of the cartons. "My motorized ice cream cone." He held up a squat-bottomed plastic cone. "It's got a motor inside that spins the cup so you don't have to waste energy licking around the cone. Genius, huh?"

A plastic cone? Was he crazy? Half the fun of an ice cream cone is eating the cone when it's all soft and mushy with melted ice cream.

"Only nineteen dollars and ninety-nine cents! Twelve ninety-nine if you buy two hundred or more."

Twenty bucks for an ice cream cone? Over my dead fudge ripple.

"And here's my combination lipstick holder and

dog whistle," he said, holding up what looked like a tube of lipstick with a tiny whistle welded to it.

"Lipstick holder and *what*?" I asked.

"Dog whistle," he said with a proud nod. "No woman should be without one. Say you're alone in the dark, walking to your car, and a strange man approaches. You whip out your lipstick. Your potential attacker thinks you're merely applying makeup. But then you blow the handy-dandy dog whistle, and every stray dog in the vicinity comes running to your rescue, instantly scaring off your would-be assailant."

Clearly I'd stumbled into a Twilight Zone where bad ideas came to die.

"And look," he said, whipping out yet another item from one of his goody cartons. "My two-way toothpaste! With a cap at both ends. No more squeezing the end of the toothpaste tube! Only two dollars and ninety-nine cents. One ninety-nine for orders of five hundred or more."

Just what I needed. Five hundred tubes of two-way toothpaste.

"So what's it going to be?" he asked, rummaging around his coffee table for an order pad.

No way did I want to plunk down my hard earned cash for any of this nonsense, but I needed to stay on his good side.

"I'll take the motorized ice cream cone," I said, hoping the high ticket item would earn me extra brownie points.

"How many?"

"Just one. But I'll be sure and tell all my friends about it."

"Great!" he said, handing me a lime-green cone.

"And what the heck? I'll throw in a lipstick holder dog whistle. I just happen to have a few thousand extra in my closet. Not one of my better sellers."

No surprise there, I thought as I shoved it into my pants pocket.

Reluctantly I handed him a twenty-dollar bill, which he snatched away with record-breaking speed.

Why did I get the feeling this was the first sale he'd made in many a moon?

"Well, thanks so much for stopping by," he said, his hand on my back, propelling me toward the door. "I really should be getting started on my Bilk."

I couldn't leave. Not yet. Not without questioning him.

"Now that I think of it," I said, stalling for time, "I could use a tube of two-way toothpaste."

"Dandy!" he said, springing back for his order pad.

As he started to write out the order, I asked, as casually as possible, "So was Dean involved in any of these inventions?"

Artie barked out a bitter laugh.

"Are you kidding? The only thing Dean ever invented was his résumé."

"Everyone agrees he was a terrible guy," I said. "But still, it's hard to believe someone hated him enough to kill him."

"Clearly you didn't know him very well."

"I was there when it happened. My cat was in the commercial. It was pretty horrible, watching him die like that."

"Some people would've paid top dollar for front row seats."

"I don't suppose you saw anyone sneaking into the studio kitchen that day, did you?"

He looked up from his order pad, suddenly on guard.

"What makes you think I was at the studio?"

Time for an itsy bitsy fib.

"Nikki told me you two were dating, and I thought maybe you dropped by to say hello."

"I was nowhere near the studio. I was here in my apartment, brewing up a batch of Bilk."

He looked me straight in the eye, and it seemed to me like he was telling the truth. Then again, I believed the Bloomie's saleslady who sold me a vat of cellulite vanishing cream, so what did I know?

"I'm surprised Nikki told you about our relationship. We tried to keep it a secret from Dean and Linda. We were afraid Nikki wouldn't get the job if Dean knew she was dating me."

"Nikki and I got sort of close on the shoot, and I guess she figured she could trust me not to blab."

If I told one more lie, I'd turn into Deedee.

But thank heavens, Artie seemed to buy my story.

"Yeah, we had to keep everything hush-hush. Even though he dumped Nikki, Dean was the kind of guy who didn't want anyone else to have her. What a selfish bastard," he said, shaking his head in disgust. "Always cheating somebody. Not long before Dean died, I heard rumors that he and Linda signed a multimillion-dollar deal for some new cat toy Dean claimed to have invented."

I remembered the toy Linda had given Prozac to play with on the shoot, the catnip yarn. I bet that was the toy they sold.

"Lord knows who he stole that idea from," Artie was saying. "But I wouldn't be at all surprised if Dean had been planning to cheat Linda out of her half of the profits. Linda was a full-fledged partner in the business, you know. But that wouldn't have mattered to Dean. He'd rip off his own wife without a second thought. He was already cheating on her with the Pink Panther. Why not rob her blind in the business, too? That's how he operated. A born con man."

His rant was cut off just then by his cell phone ringing.

He picked it up and smiled when he heard the voice at the other end of the line.

"Nikki, honey. Guess who's here? Your friend Jaine Austen. I didn't know you told her we were dating. . . . You didn't tell her . . . ?"

Oh, dear. My cue to skedaddle.

And with that, I grabbed my purchases and ran—faster than a speeding motorized ice cream cone.

Driving home, I kept thinking about that multi-million-dollar cat toy deal.

Artie believed Dean was trying to cheat Linda out of her half of the profits. But if that were the case, and Dean wanted to get his hands on Linda's share of the money, Linda would have been the one murdered, not Dean.

And suddenly I wondered: What if it was the

other way around, and it was Linda who'd been trying to cheat Dean?

I flashed on the image of Zeke sitting side by side with Linda at the funeral. At the time, I assumed Zeke was the one madly in love. But who's to say Linda wasn't head over heels in love, too?

What if all the while Dean had been cheating on her with the Pink Panther, Linda had been burning some mattresses with Zeke?

Was it possible that her tears for Dean had been a highly perfected act, that she'd killed her husband to ace him out of a lucrative business deal? With Dean dead, Linda would be getting every one of those multimillion dollars. Not to mention avoiding a messy divorce.

Two perfect motives for murder.

I swerved over to the curb, inciting several angry honks—and a colorful assortment of four-letter words—from my fellow motorists. When the curses died down, I took out my cell phone and called Artie. After apologizing profusely for lying about my friendship with Nikki, I begged him to answer one final question.

"That multimillion-dollar toy deal Dean and Linda signed. Do you know for a fact if the deal ever went through?"

"No," Artie said. "It was just a rumor."

Damn. If only I knew for sure.

I hung up with a sigh, and left Artie to brew a fresh batch of Bilk.

Chapter 25

Two bombshells were waiting for me on my voice mail when I got home from Artie's. The first from my schizo Romeo, Jim Angelides:

Hey, Jaine. Hope you haven't forgotten about the Toilet-masters Fiesta Bowl tonight. Pick you up at seven. Arnold says Hi, and to wear something sexy.

What with all the hoo-ha of the murder, I *had* forgotten about the Fiesta Bowl. I'd been planning to call Phil with an excuse to get out of it, but I'd long passed the expiration date for excuses. No way could I cancel at the last minute and offend Phil. Who, by the way, was the voice behind message number two.

Jaine, sweetheart. Looking forward to catching up with you tonight at the Fiesta Bowl. Jim's so excited. He can't wait to see you again. And by the way, I still haven't gotten the copy for the Touch-Me-Not brochure. Think you can e-mail it to me by the end of the day?

Ouch. Once again, I'd been so caught up in

Dean's murder (see hoo-ha excuse above), I was woefully behind on the Touch-Me-Not brochure.

I absolutely had to hunker down at my computer and get cracking.

Which I did.

And after several sweat-filled, Oreo-fueled hours, I finally managed to send off my magnum opus (*Touch-Me-Not: The Hands-Free Flush of the Future*) to Phil.

My brochure winging its way through cyberspace, I sat back with that feeling of exhilaration that comes with a job well done. Or, in my case, a job done thirty seconds under deadline.

But my glow of accomplishment quickly faded when I checked my watch and saw that it was 6:45. Jim said he'd pick me up at seven. Which left me all of fifteen minutes to get ready.

Oh, well. No big deal. So what if I looked crappy? The last thing I wanted to do was encourage the guy.

Off I shuffled to my bedroom where I threw on skinny jeans, white silk blouse, silver hoop earrings, and my trusty Manolos. I didn't even bother to corral my curls into a ponytail. Instead, I left them loose and wild in what I hoped the Toiletmasters gang would think was a Boho Botticelli look.

As a concession to Phil, I slapped on some lipstick. But that's as far as I was willing to gussy up.

Just as I was blotting my lipstick, I heard the dreaded knock on my front door.

It was Jim, of course.

If I hadn't known about his precarious mental

state, I would have thought he looked pretty darn terrific in khakis and a sport jacket, his blue eyes sparkling, his surfer blond hair spiked with gel.

The guy was like a human Snickers bar—smooth and yummy on the surface, totally nuts inside.

I blinked in surprise to see Arnold in the crook of his arm, dressed in a teddy bear tux.

"Hello, Jaine," Jim said. Then, in Arnold's high-pitched voice, he added, "Hubba hubba, baby cakes!"

"You're bringing Arnold to the party?"

Jim nodded wearily. "He refused to stay home."

Then, catching sight of Prozac sprawled on the sofa, Jim asked, "How's your kitty? Still depressed?"

"I'm afraid so."

"Maybe Arnold can cheer her up. He's good with cats."

With that, he went over to Prozac and waved Arnold in her face, making kitchy-koo noises as Arnold.

Prozac lobbed him a look of utter disdain.

Somewhere out there, buddy, there's a padded cell with your name on it.

"Let me get my purse," I said.

"You're not going like that, are you?" came Arnold's falsetto whine.

"What do you mean?" I asked, turning around to face him.

(Can you believe I was actually having a conversation with a stuffed animal?)

"You're not wearing any makeup. Sorry, babe. But you can't get away with it. You need blush, and you need it bad."

"I've got a fabulous combination foundation/

blush/concealer out in my glove compartment!"
Jim cried, back in his own voice. "I'll go get it!"

And before I knew it, he'd tossed Arnold on the
coffee table and was dashing out the door.

I didn't even want to think about what Jim
was doing with a combination foundation/blush/
concealer in his glove compartment. Instead, I
headed for the kitchen for the weensiest sip of
chardonnay to help me face the hours ahead.

My, that sip felt good going down. So I had another. And another.

After a few soul-restoring seconds, I reluctantly
tore myself away from the bottle and returned to
the living room, only to get the shock of my life.

Remember how Emmy the Reiki healer promised
that any day now Prozac would get better and be
back to her old self? Well, she was right. I stared in
disbelief at Prozac, who was now prancing around
the room, full of pep and vinegar.

Yes, indeed. The Old Prozac was back.

Only one problem:

My peppy, vinegary furball had Arnold clutched
firmly in her mouth, dragging him around by his
tummy!

"Prozac! What do you think you're doing?"

She gazed up at me in ecstasy.

Playing touch football! Arnold's the football!

I quickly ran over and snatched Arnold from
her jaws.

She meowed in protest.

Hey, no fair! I was winning!

Then, abandoning her triumphs on the football
field, she jumped up on the sofa.

Time to resume my never-ending battle against the evil forces from the planet Chenille!

And with that she began mercilessly clawing my throw pillow.

Yes, my little angel was back in action.

But at what price?

Poor Arnold. I lifted his tux, and to my horror, I saw that his tummy seam was ripped open. Stuffing was already beginning to pop out. Jim was going to kill me when he saw this.

I raced to the kitchen and patched the seam shut with masking tape. Somehow before the evening was over, I was going to have to sew Arnold back together again. In the meanwhile, I hurried to my bedroom to blow-dry Prozac's cat spit from Arnold's tux. I'd just about finished when Jim came walking in the front door.

"Sorry it took me so long," he said when I dashed out to greet him. "I couldn't find the right size makeup brush."

Good heavens. He had makeup brushes in his glove compartment, too?

Was it possible Jim's former roommate had been Cover Girl Barbie?

He whipped out his magical cosmetic and began expertly applying it to my face.

"Voilà!" he said when he was through, admiring his handiwork.

"What do you think, Arnold?" he asked his roomie, whom I had clutched in my arms, far from Prozac's devil jaws.

Jim grabbed him from me and mimed the bear looking me over.

"Yowser!" was Arnold's appreciative reply.

"Well, time to go!" Jim said, packing up his cosmetics.

But I couldn't leave without my sewing kit.

"Wait!" I said. "I think my earring's coming loose. I'd better go put on a new pair. Be right back."

Grabbing my purse, I hurried to my bedroom and, after some frantic searching in my lingerie drawer, finally retrieved a sewing kit from some long-ago hotel visit. Quickly I slipped it into my purse and headed back out to the living room.

"I thought you were going to change your earrings," Jim said.

"Oh, right. Changed my mind. They don't feel loose, after all."

"She may be cute, Jim," I heard Arnold stage-whisper as we headed out to Jim's Porsche, "but I think she's a bit eccentric."

Look who's talking! I felt like shouting.

But instead, I kept my mouth firmly shut, praying Jim wouldn't feel the masking tape under Arnold's tux.

And off we went to the Toiletmasters Fiesta Bowl. Or, as I would soon come to think of it, Arnoldgate.

It was a long drive to Phil's house in Tarzana, a leafy suburban community deep in the wilds of the San Fernando Valley.

I spent the entire time crammed in the back seat of Jim's Porsche, my knees jammed in my chest, while Arnold luxuriated up front in the passenger seat.

By the time we got there, I was ready for back surgery.

As on our first date at the restaurant, Jim handed Arnold to me, instructing me to hide him in my purse.

"I don't wanna hide in her purse!" Arnold whined.

"You can either hide in her purse and come to the party," Jim said, "or you can sit out here in the car all night."

"Oh, all right," Arnold snapped.

Frankly, I was glad to have Arnold in my purse. The less Jim could touch him, the less likely he was to discover the hole in his seam.

Phil greeted us at the door to his sprawling ranch house, which, according to a plaque on his front door, had been dubbed "Flushing Acres."

He beamed in pleasure at the sight of us.

"Hey, you two crazy kids!"

Well, he got one of us right.

"Follow me," he said, ushering us inside. "The party's out back."

We followed Phil through his country-style living room and ginormous kitchen out to a backyard the size of a small theme park.

The yard had been transformed into a party venue, with floodlights and heat lamps and a buffet table on the patio. A deejay was off in a corner spinning records as a few hardy couples shook their booties on a makeshift dance floor.

Round tables had been set up on the lawn, with tiny vases shaped like commodes holding centerpieces of fresh-cut flowers.

An antique claw-foot bathtub, filled with ice, held bottles of beer and wine.

"So what do you think?" Phil asked, gesturing to the bathroom-themed splendor.

"Everything's so . . . festive," I managed to reply.

"It looks super, Uncle Phil," Jim grinned, looking deceptively sane.

"What a cute couple you two make," Phil said, beaming at us.

Any minute now, he'd be announcing our engagement.

"Help yourself to the buffet," he said. "And have fun!" he added, with a most unsettling wink.

We made our way through the crowd of plumbers, mostly burly guys guzzling beer and discussing their stock portfolios.

At last we reached the buffet table, the one bright spot on my otherwise dismal horizon. Phil's wife had set out an amazing spread: Swedish meatballs, chicken satay, baby lamb chops, cold pasta salad, and mountains of yummy sourdough rolls.

I piled food on my plate with gusto, making sure not to let my pasta salad spread out and take up too much space. With the precision of a civil engineer, I managed to load a sample of pretty much everything on one eight-inch plate.

"Hungry much?" I heard Arnold's voice snipe as I piled on a baby lamb chop. "Any more food on that plate, and you're gonna need a forklift."

Of all the nerve! I was getting sick and tired of Jim's acerbic alter ego.

And I wasn't the only one.

Across the buffet table a rather large woman in an I ❤ MY PLUMBER T-shirt looked up from where she was ladling Swedish meatballs on her plate and shot me a filthy look.

"I wouldn't talk if I were you, honey. You've got enough food there to feed a USO troop."

Oh, hell. She thought I'd just dissed her. Damn that Arnold and his high-pitched voice.

"I'm so sorry," I stammered. "It wasn't me. I didn't say anything."

"If you didn't," she said, oozing skepticism, "who did?"

What could I tell her? That it was my schizo date's teddy bear?

And then the most infuriating thing happened.

Jim smiled apologetically and said, "You'll have to forgive my girlfriend."

His girlfriend? On what planet?

"I'm afraid she's had a bit too much to drink."

The woman melted under his dazzling smile.

"What's a nice young man like you doing with her anyway?" she cooed, practically batting her eyelashes at him.

"She's not so bad when she's sober."

It was all I could do not to shove a baby lamb chop up his nose.

I stalked off in high dudgeon—Jim hot on my heels—and headed over to one of the dinner tables at the outskirts of the crowd, carefully choosing one without any partygoers, unwilling to risk another outburst from Arnold.

"I can't believe you let me take the fall for Arnold's wisecrack," I said, plopping down into a chair.

"I'm sorry, Jaine." Jim shot me a sheepish look. "I didn't want to get in trouble with Uncle Phil."

"But it's okay if *I* get in trouble with him? He's my boss, too, you know."

"I guess I just wasn't thinking."

"Forget it," I snapped.

By now I was so aggravated, I'd totally lost my appetite. Well, not totally. Somehow I managed to force down a lamb chop. And just the teensiest mouthful of pasta salad. And maybe a weensy dab of Swedish meatball—okay. So I ate everything. Are you happy now?

As soon as we'd sat down, Jim had me open my purse so Arnold could poke his head out and check the scene.

"Wow, what a palace!" Arnold said. "Why can't we live in a joint like this, instead of that crappy retirement home?"

"We will someday," Jim said in his own voice, "just as soon as I get myself established with Uncle Jim."

"Way to go, bro! It'll be like the Playboy Mansion! With a grotto and plenty of hot chicks!"

Yeah, right. The only hot chicks showing up at Jim's grotto would be from the UCLA Psychiatric Nursing Department.

"Let's dance!" Arnold piped up as the deejay started playing a slow tune.

For a frightening instant I thought Jim was going to start dancing with the bear.

But, no. He pushed Arnold back down in my purse—with outraged squawks from Arnold—and held out his hand to me.

"Shall we?"

Oh, groan. The last thing I wanted to do was dance with the guy.

"I'm not really in the mood."

"Please, Jaine," he pleaded. "Just one?"

He looked at me with those gorgeous blue eyes of his, eyes that would, under normal circumstances, have me melted in a puddle on the grass, but tonight just gave me the heebie-jeebies.

"Okay," I said, reluctantly getting up to join him.

"Don't forget your purse, Jaine. Arnold wants to dance, too."

Of course he did.

We made our way to the dance floor, where Jim insisted on keeping my purse unzipped so Arnold could "hear the music." Then he took me in his arms—arms that IMHO should have been tied up cozily in a straitjacket.

I tried to follow as he shuffled awkwardly, out of step with the music, but it wasn't easy, and I was constantly shooting nervous glances at my purse, hoping nearby dancers wouldn't notice Arnold inside.

I absolutely had to think of a way to get Arnold alone so I could sew him up.

"I think Arnold needs a potty break," I said. "I'd be happy to take him."

"Potty break?" Jim looked at me like I was the crazy one. "Arnold doesn't take potty breaks. He goes to the bathroom, and he doesn't need any help doing it."

So much for Plan A.

We continued dancing, me trying desperately to come up with Plan B and avoid Jim's two left feet, when I heard a familiar high-pitched voice.

"Whoa, Jimbo. What a klutz! Who taught you how to dance—Larry? Moe? Or Curly?"

"Shut up, Arnold!" Jim hissed.

But Arnold wasn't about to shut up.

"Next dance, Jaine dances with me. And I'll show her how it's really done."

I glanced around to see if anyone had heard Jim talking in Arnold's crazy voice, but thank heavens the music had drowned him out.

"If you step on her feet one more time," Arnold continued, on a roll, "she's gonna lose a toe."

"That's it!" Jim snapped, dragging me off the dance floor.

"This is why I never take you anywhere," he said, hissing into my purse. "You always sabotage my dates."

For a minute, I wondered if this was one of Jim and Arnold's phony fights, like the one they'd staged at the restaurant. But it couldn't be. For one thing, there was no bill to weasel out of. And for another, Jim looked really steamed.

"I'm sick of that selfish little brat always ruining things for me. And I'm sick of you, too!" he added, glaring at me. "Don't think I haven't noticed those come-hither looks you've been slipping Arnold, looking down at your purse every few seconds. You've got a thing for him, and don't deny it! Well, you can have him. I can do much better than you! In fact, there's a blonde over there who's a lot hotter than you!"

With that, he marched back onto the dance floor and asked a cute blonde to dance.

At last! I was alone with Arnold. My chance to sew him up.

Leaving Jim stomping on the poor blonde's feet, I quickly slipped into the house.

My plan was to sneak into an empty room, whip

out my sewing kit, and do some emergency surgery on Arnold. But I hadn't got past the kitchen when I bumped smack-dab into Phil. And he wasn't looking happy.

"Hey, Jaine. I was just talking to Maria Sanchez. She said you insulted her at the buffet table, that you made some crack about her taking too much food."

Damn that Arnold and his big mouth.

"I swear, Phil. I didn't say a word to her."

"Then who did?"

Jim may have been a raging nutcase, but I wasn't about to throw him under the bus.

"I don't know, Phil. I just know it wasn't me."

He thought this over for a bit and must have decided I was telling the truth.

"If you say so, hon." Then, breaking out into a smile, he added, "By the way, I took a look at the Touch-Me-Not brochure. Nice job!"

"Thanks, Phil!"

At least something was going my way this god-awful night.

"If you'll excuse me," I said, "I was just heading to the powder room."

"Around the corner," Phil instructed. "First door to your left. The toilet used to belong to W. C. Fields. I call it W. C.'s WC."

I proceeded to trot around the corner.

I did not, however, pop in to admire Phil's celebrity toilet. I couldn't risk someone with an overactive bladder banging on the door in the middle of teddy bear surgery.

Instead I slipped into the next room, which

looked like a guest bedroom, with a daybed and chest of drawers and fake ivy sprouting from a miniature bidet.

Taking a seat on the daybed, I fished Arnold out from my purse, along with my sewing kit.

As Arnold lay there in my lap, staring up at me with brown button eyes, I almost expected him to start yakking at me, demanding that I give him a local anesthetic and asking to see my medical degree. But, of course, without Jim at his side, he said nothing, the model patient.

Perusing the selection of threads in my sewing kit, I picked out a tan that was relatively close to the color of Arnold's fur, and—after undressing the patient and carefully removing his masking tape—I threaded my needle and began sewing.

All I can say is thank heavens for my mother, who'd taught me how to sew when I was a kid. My mom had been going through one of her "crafting" phases at the time and had sucked me up in her vortex of needlework, cross-stitching, and Simplicity Patterns.

(So, seeing as we're such good friends, if you ever need anything hemmed at the last minute, don't hesitate to ask my mom.)

In spite of my rigorous training, beads of sweat popped up on my brow as I sewed my first tiny stitches along Arnold's tummy seam. I soon began to relax, though, when I realized that because of Arnold's fuzzy nap, the patch job was practically invisible.

After that, my needle practically flew through the job.

I was feeling quite proud of myself and was just about to sew the final stitch when suddenly the door burst open and Jim came whooshing in.

"I've been looking all over for you—" Then, spotting the needle in my hand: "What are you doing to Arnold?"

"Um. Emergency appendectomy?"

"What???"

His face was now a dangerous red. Holy Moses. Something told me I was the one who'd soon be needing stitches.

But before Jim could do anything, Phil came hurrying in.

"Jim, I was just talking to Carole Sapin, one of my top plumbers, and she said you got fresh with her out on the dance floor."

Jim blushed and dug his foot into the carpet.

"Gosh, Uncle Phil, all I did was ask if she was wearing panties."

"Jim, Jim! What am I going to do with you?"

For the first time, Phil noticed me with Arnold on my lap.

"What are you doing with that teddy bear, Jaine?"

"She claims she's giving it an emergency appendectomy," Jim sneered. "She's nuts! Arnold had his appendix out years ago!"

"Wait a minute," Phil said with an aggrieved sigh. "Did you stop taking your meds?"

"I had to, Uncle Phil. They make my toes itch."

"Your mom told me you gave up your fixation with your teddy bear."

"I did. Charlie and I broke up last year. This is my new roommate, Arnold."

Phil turned to me with an apologetic shrug.

"I'm so sorry, Jaine. I thought he was taking his meds."

By now, I'd stitched my last stitch and snipped off the remaining thread.

"Here you go," I said, handing Arnold over to Jim. "Good as new. It's been swell dating both of you. Now if you don't mind, I'll call myself a cab and get going."

And without any further ado, I grabbed my purse and scooted out of there.

The last thing I heard as I headed down the hall was Arnold calling out to me: "You busy tomorrow night, babe? What do you say we give it a whirl? I'm much more fun than Jim!"

Clearly the patient had recovered from surgery and was doing just fine.

YOU'VE GOT MAIL!

To: Jausten
From: Shoptillyoudrop
Subject: Crazy Morning!

What a crazy morning it's been, sweetheart.
Today's the day of the Scrabble awards luncheon,
and as bad luck would have it, Alex Trebek's driver
never picked him up at the airport. So Lydia just
dashed over to get him. Which means I've got to
go to the clubhouse to take care of the floral
arrangements. I was supposed to pick up the
championship ring from the jewelers, where it's
being sized for Lydia. But I'll never have time to do
that now, so I've asked Daddy to go there for me. I
felt awful asking him to do it after he came so
close to winning the ring himself, but he's
graciously agreed to go.

XOXO,
Mom

To: Jausten
From: DaddyO
Subject: Daddy to the Rescue!

Apparently there's been some snafu at the airport
with Alex Trebek, and I've been assigned to pick
up the championship Scrabble ring from the
jewelers. Although by all rights the ring should be

mine, I've resigned myself to the fact that Lydia Pinkus, the cheating gasbag, will be wearing it on her pudgy little finger.

All I can say is it's a lucky thing for your mom that I can be counted on in times of crisis.

Love 'n' stuff from
Your can-do
DaddyO

TAMPA TRIBUNE

Alex Trebek Attacked by Local Tampa Vistas Man

The annual Tampa Vistas Scrabble Championship Awards Luncheon was disrupted today when internationally famed game show host Alex Trebek was tackled by local Tampa Vistas resident, Hank Austen.

"I was just about to eat my beef bourguignon," Trebek said, "when this crazy man came out of nowhere and grabbed me by the chest."

Mr. Austen claimed he was giving Mr. Trebek the Heimlich maneuver to dislodge a fourteen-karat gold ring he thought the game show host had ingested.

When asked to comment about the incident, Lydia Pinkus, Tampa Vistas Homeowners' Association president and incumbent Scrabble champion, said of Mr. Austen, "The man is certifiable. Why, just last week, he was caught looting my garbage can in his underwear."

To: Jausten
From: Shoptillyoudrop
Subject: I'm So Mad, I Could Spit!

I sent your father off on a simple errand to pick up a ring, and he wound up attacking Alex Trebek!

And PS! He had the gall to show up at the luncheon in those hideous Bermuda shorts!

XOXO,
Mom

To: Jausten
From: DaddyO
Subject: I Can Explain Everything!

Dearest Lambchop—

I suppose your mom sent you that clipping from the Tampa Tribune. I know it doesn't look good, but I can explain everything.

Just as instructed, I went to the jewelers and picked up the ring. At first I wasn't even going to look at it, a cruel reminder of how close I'd come to winning the tournament. But once I got out in the parking lot, I couldn't resist. I opened the jewelry box, and there it was, winking up at me in all its fourteen-karat gold glory.

I kept thinking that if Lydia hadn't pulled that stunt and hid my Lucky Thinking Cap, the ring might very well have been mine. And before I knew what I was doing, I'd slipped the ring out of the box and on my pinkie finger. A perfect fit! I drove home, admiring it all the way.

But when I got home and tried to take it off, things started going haywire. I guess my pinkie must have swelled on the ride home, because I couldn't get the darn thing off!

I raced in the house (luckily your mom had already left for the clubhouse) and ran my pinkie under cold water. The ring still wouldn't budge. I tried loosening it with butter, olive oil, and finally WD-40. Still nothing!

A lesser man would have panicked. But not your daddy. Cool and collected. I did the only sensible thing and called 911. Would you believe they actually giggled and told me they had better things to do than remove championship Scrabble rings from pinkies? Really, as soon as this whole ruckus dies down, I intend to write a letter to the mayor about those 911 people.

Anyhow, by the time I got to the clubhouse, I was forty-five minutes late. Most people had already served themselves from the buffet and were tucking into their chow.

Needless to say, your mom was a tad peeved when she saw me, wondering what had taken me so long. Hiding my "ring" hand in my pocket, I mumbled something about traffic being a bear and handed her the jewelry box, which I'd cleverly tied with a bow so she wouldn't open it. Luckily she didn't seem to notice how light it was and, after shooting me one final dirty look, scurried off to put it on the awards dais.

I was standing there with my hand jammed in my pocket, pinkie hidden, wondering how the heck I was going to get the ring off my finger, when I looked over at the buffet table and saw a vat of creamy white ranch dressing near the salads. Hoping the oil in the dressing might do the trick, I casually sauntered over and—after checking to make sure no one was watching—plunged my pinkie into the goo and began rubbing it into my finger.

Eureka! The dressing was working its magic, and at long last the ring was coming loose! But my hands were so darn slick from the dressing, I lost my grip on the ring and watched in disbelief as it flew across the buffet table and landed plop in the beef bourguignon!

And it was at that very moment that Alex Trebek came back for seconds on the beef bourguignon. I gasped as he picked up the ladle and scooped up some stew from the exact same spot where the ring had landed!

I couldn't possibly let him eat it! So I started racing to his side. But just then a busboy showed up with refills for the scalloped potatoes and blocked my path. Before I could stop him, Trebek had scooped up the beef bourguignon and was headed for his table.

I tore after him but was unfortunately intercepted by your mom who'd peeked inside the jewelry box and discovered that the ring was missing. With no time for explanations, I hurried to Trebek, who by now was digging into his beef bourguignon. He took one bite and started coughing.

Oh, no! He'd swallowed the ring! So what else could I do but yank him up from his seat and give him the Heimlich maneuver? (Which I'd fortunately learned from a *Simpsons* episode where Homer almost chokes on a pork rind.)

But just as I was squeezing Alex's ribs and mentioning my prowess in the categories of Geography, Fifties Music, and People in the News, I heard somebody on the other side of the room shout out, "What's this ring doing in my beef bourguignon?"

Obviously, I'd made a mistake. Alex hadn't swallowed the ring, after all. Someone else had dished it out instead. In no time, I retrieved it, and after your mom washed it off in the ladies' room, the ring was as good as new.

A win-win situation as far as I'm concerned.

I don't see why everyone is making such a big fuss.

Love 'n' snuggles from
DaddyO

P.S. Alex was so understanding. After I explained to him what happened, he promised to send me tickets to watch a studio taping. Too bad he can't get me into his own show. But I'm sure *Wheel of Fortune* will be lots of fun.

To: Jausten
From: Shoptillyoudrop
Subject: Monumental Gall!

Can you believe the nerve of your daddy? After practically cracking poor Alex Trebek's ribs, he actually had the monumental gall to ask him for tickets to his show! I may never speak to him again.

XOXO,
Mom

To: Jausten
From: DaddyO
Subject: In the Doghouse

Looks like I'm in the doghouse with your mom, Lambchop. She's giving me the silent treatment. There's only one way to worm my way back into her good graces. It's the ultimate sacrifice, but I guess I'm going to have to make it.

To: Jausten
From: Shoptillyoudrop
Subject: Can't Stay Mad Forever

Wonderful news, sweetheart! Daddy just threw away those hideous Bermuda shorts. I guess I can't stay mad at him forever, can I? Well, must run and shower. Daddy's taking me to Le Chateaubriand for dinner tonight.

See you soon in L.A.! Can't wait for a lovely, drama-free vacation.

XOXO,
Mom

To: Jausten
From: DaddyO
Subject: Don't Tell Mom

It was painful, but I had to do it. With heavy heart, I threw those fabulous Bermuda shorts in the garbage. But it was worth it to have your mom speak to me again.

On a happier note, guess what I just sent away for? A Make-It-Yourself Ukulele Kit! It'll be perfect for our trip to Hawaii. I can't wait to put it together and wow the gang at the luau!

Don't tell Mom, though. I want to surprise her!

Love 'n' snuggles from
DaddyO

Chapter 26

Prozac was at the top of her game the next morning, clawing me awake for her breakfast with her usual gusto, yowling at the top of her lungs.

Minced mackerel guts, please! With extra guts! And make it snappy!

Music to my ears.

I watched her inhale her mackerel guts, thrilled to have my feline chowhound back in action. Then, still in a rosy glow, I settled down on my sofa with my coffee and CRB and checked my cell phone messages.

Acck! I gulped in dismay to see five texts from Arnold, begging me to go out with him, each signed with a throbbing emoticon heart.

And if that wasn't enough to put a dent in my morning, there were the e-mails from my parents. Can you believe Daddy tackling Alex Trebek and giving him the Heimlich maneuver?

Rest assured he would not be playing Final Jeopardy any time soon.

But I couldn't worry about Daddy (or his plans to serenade the people of Maui with his hand-made ukulele), not when I still had a murder to solve.

I thought about that multimillion-dollar cat toy deal Artie told me about, and once again I wondered if Linda bumped off Dean to ace him out of the profits.

But had the deal really taken place?

I couldn't very well ask Linda. Not without admitting I suspected her of killing her hubby.

Then I thought of someone I could ask: the Pink Panther. She and Dean had been more than just business associates. Way more. Surely he would have told her about any deal in the works.

"Ms. Austen!" she cried when I called to make an appointment to see her. "I've been waiting to hear from you. So what did your editor say? Did she like the pictures of Desiree?"

Foo. Another lie come back to bite me in the fanny. Those of you "A" students out there will no doubt remember my whopper about *Cat Fancy* magazine wanting Desiree for their first ever center-fold. I really had to nip this fairy tale in the bud and tell her that my fictitious editor had decided not to go with a centerfold, after all.

"Desiree and I have been so excited!" the Panther gushed. "This centerfold has been such a ray of sunshine in our lives after the trauma of Dean's death."

Cripes. I couldn't very well stomp on her ray of sunshine, could I?

"My editor loved the pictures," I said, plowing ahead with my lie.

"That's marvelous. I've been going through Desiree's photo albums and found some adorable snapshots you may want to use in addition to the centerfold. Why don't you stop by, and I'll show them to you?"

And so later that morning I found myself being ushered into the Panther's palatial bedroom by her maid, Sofia.

The Panther, clad in white capris and a slouchy pink cashmere tunic, was gazing fondly at a bunch of photos spread out on her satin duvet. Lounging alongside the pictures were her German shepherds, Tristan and Isolde, and of course, the would-be centerfold, Desiree.

"How lovely to see you," the Panther said, offering me a perfectly manicured hand and almost blinding me with a honker pink sapphire ring. "And thank you again for making this centerfold possible. It's given me something positive to focus on, and I'm very grateful."

From beneath their Botoxed brows, her eyes did indeed shine with gratitude.

By now I was feeling so guilty, I was actually considering writing *Cat Fancy* and pitching Desiree for a story.

I oohed and aahed as the Panther showed me pictures of her beloved furball—frolicking with a Cartier necklace, sleeping on a pink satin pillow, and curled around a bottle of Dom Pérignon.

Finally, when I'd oohed my last ooh and aahed my last aah, she swept the photos up in a manila envelope for me to show to my "editor."

"I don't suppose you've heard anything new

about Dean's murder," she said, handing me the envelope.

Just the opening I'd been looking for!

"Actually, I heard a rumor that shortly before Dean died, he and Linda had signed a multimillion-dollar cat toy deal. And I was wondering if Linda might have killed Dean to keep all the money for herself."

"Linda?" She blinked in surprise. "I doubt she'd have the nerve. She seems too weak to be a killer."

"Appearances are deceptive," I said.

"I guess they can be," she agreed.

"So do you know anything about the cat toy deal? Was it true? Or just a rumor?"

"Dean had been bragging about it to me. But that doesn't mean it was true. Dean was a wonderful man," she said, her eyes growing soft at his memory. "So charming, so charismatic. But he often exaggerated things to build himself up. Maybe he had a deal. Maybe he didn't. With Dean," she shrugged, "you never knew."

"Sorry I can't be more help," she said when she saw the disappointed look on my face.

Then her eyes lit up. "But I know who'd have an answer for you. Dean's attorney. I've got his phone number in my office downstairs. Wait here while I get it. You can play with Tristan and Isolde while I'm gone."

At the mention of their names, the two hulking dogs woke up from where they'd been snoozing on the duvet and began growling.

"Tristan! Isolde! Be nice to Ms. Austen. No biting," she added, wagging a stern finger at them.

And off she skipped, leaving me alone with her

canine mafiosi. Who continued growling most men-
acingly, throwing in some fang-baring for good measure. I spent a terrified second or two before they
finally decided I wasn't worth noshing on and resumed their snooze.

Glancing around the room, my eyes were immediately drawn to the Panther's huge walk-in closet.
Unable to resist the urge to snoop, I tiptoed inside.

Unlike my closet at home, with clothing jum-
bled together like remnants at a yard sale, the Panther's closet had been organized to within an inch
of its life.

Dresses, skirts, slacks, blouses were in separate sec-
tions, all standing at attention on couture wooden
hangers, not one item of clothing touching another.
There were shelves for shoes, cubbyholes for hand-
bags, and everywhere I looked, I saw different
shades of pink. A locked door in the corner led to
what I assumed was either a panic room or a small
bank vault.

And in the center of it all was a ginormous jewelry case, stocked with such fabulous doodads, I
felt like I'd wandered into a branch of Tiffany's.
Hundreds of thousands of dollars' worth of gold
and diamonds and pink sapphires sat under lock
and key. On top of the glass case were the Panther's costume jewelry pieces, stuff she felt safe
leaving out on display.

I was gazing down at the Panther's honker rings
when I noticed a ring on top of the case that
looked familiar. An eye-catching piece of bling
with pink stones set in the shape of a flower.

Yikes. It was the pink hibiscus ring Nikki was

wearing the day of the shoot! The one that went missing when she left it to get a snack at the buffet table. I picked it up and examined it. No doubt about it. It was the exact same ring. What on earth was it doing here in the Panther's closet?

There could be only one explanation. The Panther must have stolen it the day of the murder, when Nikki left the cat food unattended.

Was the Pink Panther the one who sprayed the Skinny Kitty with Raid? But why? She was one of the few people who actually liked Dean. Why on earth would she want to kill him?

And then I looked up and understood everything.

There, in the doorway, was the Pink Panther. And she wasn't alone. Standing at her side was Linda, a gun in her hand. A gun aimed most distressingly at my heart.

I'd been so engrossed in my snooping, I hadn't heard them coming.

Now I looked at the two of them standing side by side and realized I'd been right about Linda. She'd grown tired of Dean's cheating ways and found a new partner. But it wasn't Zeke she'd fallen for. It was the Panther.

All along the two of them pretended to be enemies while they plotted to kill Dean and cash in on his multimillion-dollar cat toy deal.

"I had a feeling you'd be trouble," Linda said, eyes like steel behind her harlequin glasses. "You really should have minded your own business. I tried to warn you with that Raid ad. But did you listen? Noooo."

Now she was aiming the gun at my gut.

"And it wasn't very smart fibbing to me about *Cat Fancy*," the Panther piped up. "I called them the minute you left the house the other day. They'd never heard of you."

Here I thought I was putting one over on her, and she was the one setting a trap for me. She'd undoubtedly lured me over to her house today to find out how much dirt I'd dug up about Dean's murder.

"Oh, well," Linda said. "No harm, no foul. You won't be around to poke your nose in things anymore. Not after today."

That sure didn't sound good. I had to keep them talking while I thought of a way to worm my way out of this mess.

"So my theory was right," I said. "You killed Dean for the money. Now you won't have to split the profits from your cat toy deal."

"We killed him," Linda said, "because he was a cheating, lying bastard, and he deserved to die." Then, with a sly wink, she added, "And for the money. I gotta admit, it was quite an incentive."

"You were the one who sprayed the cat food," I said to the Panther.

"It was all very serendipitous. We'd been planning to kill Dean by putting cyanide in his martini. But that day at the shoot, I took a break from my 'work session' with Dean to go to the ladies' room and saw that Nikki had left the Skinny Kitty out on the counter. With the can of Raid right there on the shelf. So I just nipped right in and gave it a spray! Easy as pie!"

She smiled with pride.

"How did you manage to be . . . intimate with him?" I asked. "That can't have been easy."

"Honey, I just closed my eyes and thought of all the millions of dollars at the end of the rainbow. How do you think I got all this?" she said, pointing to her mammoth jewelry case.

"We had so much fun fooling everyone, didn't we, hon?" Linda said, flinging her free arm around the Panther's shoulder. "Remember that scene at the funeral reception?"

Reprising the role she'd played that day, that of the grieving widow, Linda drew herself up with outraged dignity and huffed, "Please leave. You're not welcome here."

They both broke out giggling like teenagers.

"Dean never suspected a thing," the Panther said. "Not for a minute. I used to go over to their house to be with Linda in the middle of the night, and he never knew."

So it wasn't Dean the Panther had been visiting that night when Zeke spotted her outside his cottage. It was Linda.

"From the moment we met at the charity ball, Linda and I clicked. Dean, egomaniac that he was, assumed that he was the one I was interested in. What a fool."

"At first we figured I'd just get a divorce," Linda chimed in. "But a divorce from Dean would have been ugly. And so expensive. And why pass up all those millions from the cat toy deal? It seemed silly to let him have half the money. He didn't deserve it, anyway. The catnip yarn wasn't even his idea. He bought it from some poor soul out in West

Covina for five hundred dollars. Swindled the guy, just like he swindled Artie Lembeck."

"But enough chitchat," the Panther said with a bright smile on her pink lips. "Time to kill you, hon!"

"Just one more question," I said, still trying to keep them talking. "With all your jewels, why did you steal Nikki's ten-dollar ring?"

"As a memento of my very first murder!" The Panther grinned.

"No more stalling," Linda said, waving her gun. "Time to check out, hon."

"But you can't shoot me. What if Sofia hears?"

"We're not going to shoot you," the Panther said. "We're going to lock you in my fur closet."

The Panther opened the door I'd seen earlier, the one I'd thought led to a panic room. It was a tiny hole of a room lined with a few empty shelves. Not a fur coat in sight.

"Where are the furs?" I asked.

"Furs are so yesterday," the Panther said, with a wave of her fuchsia nails. "I sold them years ago. Had the closet converted into a freezer so I wouldn't have to run downstairs for ice cream."

"Where's the ice cream?" I asked, looking at the empty shelves.

"Sorry, hon. I'm on a diet. If I knew we were going to kill you today, I would've laid in a farewell pint for you."

"Please," Linda sniffed. "The last thing she needs is a pint of ice cream. Not with those thighs."

Of all the nerve! If she hadn't had that gun pointed at my innards, I would've stung her with a bitter retort. As it was, I just mumbled something about not being very hungry anyway.

"Just as well," Linda said. "Once you're locked inside, we're going to set the thermostat to freezing. So I doubt you'd appreciate any ice cream."

"If the cold doesn't kill you," the Panther chirped, "the lack of oxygen will. And don't even think of calling for help," she added. "Sofia will never hear you in the kitchen."

"Let's drive out to Malibu for a nice leisurely lunch, sweetie," Linda said. "By the time we get back, she should be dead."

"Wait!" I cried in a last-ditch effort to save my life. "I told my neighbor where I was going, and that I suspected Linda of killing Dean. So if anything happens to me, the police will know it's you two."

All lies, of course, but I was gambling it would work.

A gamble, alas, that didn't pay off.

"We'll take our chances," said Linda, calling my bluff.

With that, they shoved me in the closet and slammed the door shut.

Instantly, the tiny room went black. Not a sliver of light crept in from under the door. I was sealed in tight.

And suddenly, from a vent above me, I felt a blast of cold air. Very cold air.

Oh, Lord. I really was going to freeze to death!

I began screaming at the top of my lungs. But just as the Panther had predicted, nobody came to my rescue.

I started doing jumping jacks, trying to keep

warm. But then I realized the more I exercised, the more oxygen I was using up.

If only I had something to eat, some calories to stoke my body heat.

I reached into my jeans pocket, hoping to find an abandoned sour ball, when I felt something cold and metallic. What the heck was it? I couldn't see a thing in this black hole. Fingering it, I finally realized it was the lipstick holder Artie had given me yesterday.

Great. Just what I needed. Lipstick, so I could look good in my freshly dug grave. But then I remembered it was a combination lipstick holder and *dog whistle*!

Maybe if I blew the whistle, Tristan and Isolde would start barking, summoning Sofia from downstairs.

I felt around for the whistle part of the contraption and was just about to put it to my lips when I hesitated. What if Linda and the Panther were still in the house? What if they heard the whistle and came running in to pistol-whip me into silence?

I wanted to wait a few more minutes to make sure they were gone. But by now, the freezing air was blasting through the vents like snow in the Artic. I was so damn cold, my fingers were beginning to feel numb. I couldn't afford to waste any more time.

I had to risk it. Gathering my courage, I put the whistle to my lips and blew.

Dead silence.

I slumped down to the floor, defeated.

The darn thing didn't work.

Then, just as I was resigning myself to a frosty

death, Tristan and Isolde erupted, barking wildly.
I blew the whistle again. More frantic barking.
Omigosh. It must have been one of those whistles
that emit noise at a frequency only dogs can hear.

I continued to toot the crazy contraption until
at last I heard footsteps.

I just prayed it wasn't Linda and the Panther.

My heart pounding wildly in my chest, I waited
for whoever it was to speak.

And then, at last, I heard a frightened voice ask,
"Qué pasa?"

Thank God! It was Sofia!

"Help me!" I cried. "I'm locked inside! Call *la
policía! La policía!*"

There was silence on the other side of the door.
Oh, hell. What if Sofia was in the country illegally
and was afraid of the police? What if she called the
Panther instead and was instructed to let me die?

For several minutes I heard nothing. My heart
sank. This was it.

There I sat, teeth chattering, skin crawling with
goose bumps, Artic air blasting at me from all sides.

Damn it all. Why was I always getting myself into
these scrapes? Why couldn't I have left everything
to the police? So what if I missed my Hawaiian vacation? At least I'd be alive, and not a human Pop-
sicle.

And suddenly I thought of Prozac. Poor, dear
Prozac. Who'd take care of her when I was gone?
Who'd feed her minced mackerel guts? Who'd
give her belly rubs and pick her hair balls out of
the freshly washed laundry?

A big fat tear rolled down my cheek and froze
halfway down.

Then, just as I was ready to give up all hope, I heard it—a faint wail. I couldn't be sure, but it sounded like a police siren. Soon I heard pounding on the front door. Then footsteps clomping on the stairway, growing closer and closer.

And then, finally, the sweetest words I'd ever heard (aside from "Would you like whipped cream with that?"):

"Hang in there, ma'am. We'll get you out."

And indeed, five minutes later, a police locksmith had opened the lock, and I walked out of my prison, icy cold, teeth chattering—but alive!

I flung my arms around Sofia, thanking her profusely.

She soon had me bundled in a pink cashmere blanket while I gave my statement to the police.

Eventually, Detective Carbone showed up with jelly doughnuts, bless his soul, and told me that Linda and the Pink Panther had been arrested out in Malibu, in the middle of their Cobb salads, and charged with attempted murder (mine).

When I'd answered my last question and scarfed down my last doughnut, I headed outside, reveling in the warmth of the sun on my face and vowing never again to complain about heat waves.

Later that night, when I was curled up in bed under my down comforter, watching the news with Prozac, I saw footage of the two killers being hauled off in handcuffs to a police van.

And as I watched the hot pink soles of her Louboutins disappear into the van, I couldn't help but wonder how the Pink Panther was going to look in a bright orange jumpsuit.

* * *

I'd barely had time to recuperate from my near brush with death when Lance came bounding into my apartment the next morning.

"You'll never guess who's a star on the Internet!" he cried, grabbing half of my cinnamon raisin bagel.

"You're right," I said wearily. "I'll never guess. So tell me."

"Prozac! Someone posted a video of her on YouTube. Look!" he said, pointing to his cell phone. "It's called *Where's the Beef?*"

And there was Prozac on the screen, perched on the buffet table at the Skinny Kitty shoot, scarfing down roast beef as only she can eat it, sucking it up like a kitty tornado.

Someone at the shoot must have been watching her all along.

"It's gotten over two hundred thousand hits!" Lance squealed.

"Did you hear that, Prozac?" he said, turning to my princess, who was busy battling aliens from the planet Chenille.

He shoved the phone under her nose, and she stared at it, fascinated.

"You're an Internet sensation!"

I swear, she understood exactly what he was saying.

Because suddenly she sat up, preening, batting her big green eyes, head tilted ever so coyly.

I'm ready for my close-up, Mr. DeMille.

There'd be no living with her now.

And to think. She still had eight more lives to go.

Epilogue

The minute they were taken into custody, Linda and the Panther began ratting each other out. Their sworn statements damning one another—along with a chilling e-mail correspondence between the two of them plotting to kill Dean—should be enough to keep them behind bars for years.

And as you probably know if you've seen her picture on the cover of th*e Enquirer*, the Panther looks quite fetching in orange. Last I heard, she was voted Best Dressed in her cell block. Meanwhile, Linda has quickly risen in the ranks of the incarcerated and is now known to her homies as "The Enforcer."

All you animal lovers will be happy to learn that Tristan, Isolde, and Desiree were adopted by my rescuing angel, Sofia, who is now working for one of the Real Housewives of Beverly Hills.

You're not going to believe this, but Deedee wound up paying me every cent she owed me, including the two hundred and six bucks from our lunch at the Peninsula. She recently rescued an amazingly talented cat from a shelter and has just signed the little cutie to star in a national cat food commercial. To be directed by none other than Ian Kendrick.

As for Ian, he finally faced up to the fact that he was a raging alcoholic and sought help from, of all people, Emmy, the Reiki healer. Today Ian is celebrating six gin-free months of sobriety and is dating one of his Mighty Maids.

And remember that poison search on Zeke's computer? It happens he was merely doing research for his novel. Which has yet to be published. But on the plus side, he sold his tell-all story about Linda (*Black Widow: My Life with a Cold-Blooded Killer*), which will soon be a Lifetime Movie-of-the-Week.

As I suspected, Kandi's romance with Alexi didn't last. She finally dumped her violin-playing Uber driver when, after two months of dating, he was still charging her to ride in his car.

And good news for the House of Wonton. They got a four-star review in the *L.A. Times*, and now the place is packed. You can't get in without a reservation. The hostess now greets her guests in Escada and Jimmy Choos.

Here on the home front, Lance is head over heels in love, dating the photographer who took Mamie's publicity photos. As for Mamie, she's thrilled to be an anonymous doggie, chasing her tail and sniffing stray tushes.

After the first flush of excitement from her YouTube stardom died down, Prozac went back to her old ways, battling evil aliens from the planet

Chenille. Which reminds me, I've absolutely got to go to Bed Bath & Beyond to buy some new throw pillows.

I'm happy to report that my trip to Hawaii with my parents was fantabulous. Daddy was unable to assemble his Make-It-Yourself Ukulele. (Mainly because Mom tossed some key pieces in the garbage when he wasn't looking.) So we jetted off to Maui, strings free, for seven glorious days in the Hawaiian sun. True, I had to spend those days in an Outrageous Orange tankini, but it was wonderful to be with my parents, who, as predicted, showered me with love and banana daiquiris.

Aside from that one incident at the luau with Daddy and a rubber chicken (don't ask!), it was a most delightful time.

Well, gotta run. Her Royal Highness is yowling for a belly rub.

Catch you next time!

P.S. Remember Artie Lembeck? The hapless inventor? Well, it turns out that Bilk, his milk-based beer, is all the rage in Japan. Artie's raking in a fortune. He and Nikki got married in a beautiful beachside ceremony in Malibu. Nikki wore her pink hibiscus ring, and every guest got a complimentary tube of two-way toothpaste.

Freelance writer Jaine Austen thought working for a knock-off reality show in the tropics would be paradise. But when she and her kitty 'Prozac' find themselves trapped between a dimwitted leading man, catty contestants, and a cold-blooded murderer, the splashy gig becomes one deadly nightmare . . .

Jaine's life has been a royal pain since she started penning dialogue for *Some Day My Prince Will Come*—a cheesy dating show that features bachelorettes competing for the heart of Spencer Dalworth VII, a *very* distant heir to the British throne. As if fending off golf-ball–sized bugs on a sweltering island wasn't tough enough, Jaine must test her patience against an irritable production crew and fierce contestants who will do anything to get their prince . . .

But Jaine never expected murder to enter the script. When one of the finalists dies in a freak accident, it's clear someone wanted the woman out of the race for good—and the police won't allow a soul off the island until they seize the culprit. Terrified of existing another day without air conditioning and eager to return home, Jaine is throwing herself into the investigation. And she better pounce on clues quickly—or there won't be any survivors left . . .

Please turn the page for an exciting sneak peek of
Laura Levine's next Jaine Austen mystery
DEATH OF A BACHELORETTE
coming soon wherever print and e-books are sold!

Chapter One

I swear, it was a miracle. Okay, maybe not as big as the parting of the Red Sea. Or Daniel surviving that lion's den. Or how M&M's melt in your mouth, not in your hand.

But a miracle nonetheless.

I watched in disbelief as my cat, Prozac, lay snoozing on my bed in her spiffy new cat carrier. Yes, Prozac, the cat whose longest record for staying silent in her carrier was about thirteen and a half seconds, had been napping for a whole twenty minutes without a peep.

And I owed it all to my good buddies at Wiki-How, who'd given me some much-needed tips on how to prepare my kitty for an overseas airplane flight.

I'd been feeding her in her carrier for the last several days, getting her used to her plush new accommodations, throwing in one of my old cashmere sweaters for good measure. Now the place was like a second home to her, a kitty pied-à-terre.

And Prozac's exemplary behavior was only one of the many miracles that seemed to be floating my way.

Just last week, after answering an ad in *Variety*, I'd been hired as a writer on a TV show shooting on a Pacific island off the coast of Tahiti.

The show in question, called *Some Day My Prince Will Come*, was a *Bachelor* type rip-off, where a gaggle of gorgeous young bachelorettes gathered together to vie for the hand of a handsome European noble-man.

Wait. Did you actually think people on reality shows just say what comes out of their mouths without any help? That enemy housewives just happen to be seated across from each other at par-ties in the Hamptons? That drunken catfights erupt out of sheer chance? I hate to be the one to dis-illusion you, but the shows' producers are the ones plotting all these lively stories, and, at least on *Some Day My Prince Will Come*, there was a writer on hand churning out bon mots for the characters to say other than, "Eat dirt, you bitch/skank/ho!"

And I, Jaine Austen—ordinarily a writer of ads and brochures for small businesses like Toiletmasters Plumbers (*In a Rush to Flush? Call Toiletmasters!*)—had been hired to write said bon mots.

Can you believe it? I was getting paid real money to jet off to be a TV writer in a tropical par-adise!

And not only was the show's producer letting me bring Prozac; for once in her feisty life, my fe-line significant other was cooperating with me, hanging out in her new cat carrier without the slightest yip of protest.

How lucky could one gal get?

Of course, there's always a fly in the ointment, and the fly at that particular moment was my neighbor Lance Venable, who lives next door to me in a duplex on the very outskirts of Beverly Hills, about as far from Rodeo Drive as Outer Mongolia is from the Champs-Élysée.

That day, Lance was sitting on my bed, helping me pack. And by helping me, I mean driving me crazy.

With each item I tossed into my suitcase, he wailed stuff like:

My God! Elastic-waist pants? Are you insane?

Who was the last person to wear that bathing suit? Ma Kettle?

Yuck!! Where'd you get that dowdy top? Forever 71?

Lance, who fondles the feet of the rich and famous at Neiman Marcus's shoe department, fancies himself a fashion guru and is forever bombarding me with unwanted advice.

"How do you expect to meet the handsome show biz exec of your dreams if you show up in these ghastly outfits? Don't you have anything more sexy? A flirty little sundress?"

Somehow I resisted the urge to strangle him with my Ma Kettle bathing suit.

"The closest I've got to flirty is this," I said, holding up my prized I'M OUT OF ESTROGEN AND I'VE GOT A GUN T-shirt.

"Whatever you do," he said, blathering on, "promise me you won't wear any of your pathetic elastic-waist capris."

"Yeah, right," I said, shoving in another pair when he wasn't looking.

"I'm so sorry I can't keep Prozac while you're gone," he said, making a tsking noise at Pro's carrier. "But you know how it is when she and Mamie get together. Like Thelma and Louise on steroids."

Only too true. Prozac has been known to lead Lance's adorable pooch Mamie on all sorts of daring escapades, including but not limited to chewing on electrical wiring, gnawing at baseboards, and a little game they've invented called Bowling with Houseplants.

"Not a problem," I assured him. "The show's producer has pulled some strings with the locals in Tahiti so Prozac won't have to be quarantined."

"Isn't bribery wonderful?" Lance gushed. "If you ask me, it's the bulwark of a civilized society."

"And besides," I said, "I don't think it's a good idea for Prozac and me to be apart. Too much separation anxiety. All that yowling and screaming and crying."

"True," Lance nodded. "And Prozac gets sort of upset, too."

At which point, my pampered princess awoke from her slumber and sauntered out onto the bedspread, yawning a yawn the size of a sinkhole.

My, that nap was refreshing!

And with that, she promptly curled up into a ball and began another one.

"This is so darn exciting!" Lance said, scratching Pro behind her ears as she dozed. "Just think what this job could mean!"

"I know. Maybe I can make the transition from small-time ad copywriter to big time TV writer! Maybe I'll never have to write another ad for Toiletmasters ever again."

"There's that, of course, and your chance to meet that European nobleman. The prince of *Some Day My Prince Will Come.* Promise me you'll find out if he has a cute available brother. I've always wanted to date nobility."

"Got it, Lance. My top priority will be finding you a noble boyfriend. I'll get to work on it as soon as my plane lands."

"Aren't you an angel," he said, my sarcasm whizzing past him undetected.

"I hope you haven't forgotten," I said. "When I'm gone, I need you to take in my mail and mist my Boston fern."

"No problemo, honey. It's as good as done. Which one's the Boston fern?"

"The green thing with leaves."

I led him into the living room and pointed out a delicate fern I'd recently bought and had been nursing tenderly.

"Got it," he said. "Mist Boston fern."

"Every day."

"Every day. Just call me Mr. Greenthumbs."

"Thanks so much, Lance. I really appreciate it."

"Don't be silly, hon. That's what friends are for. Well, must run and feed Mamie. I'll pick you up bright and early tomorrow to take you to the airport. Just remember—"

"I know. I know. No elastic-waist pants."

And off he zoomed to his apartment.

I ordered Chinese food for dinner that night and ate it in bed, Prozac chowing down on bits of shrimp from my shrimp with lobster sauce, a cool breeze wafting in from my bedroom window. I didn't know it then, but I was to think of that breeze longingly in the days to come.

Hours later, I settled down to go to sleep, thrilled about my exciting new job, certain I was jetting off to paradise.

Little did I realize I was heading straight for the jaws of hell.